# "Well, there you go. Longest eight-minute ride of your life," Jacob said.

Heather unbuckled her seat belt and faced him. "Aren't you going to stay to help decorate the tree and see the lighting?"

He really had nowhere else to be. Technically, he was on duty. And technically, *this* was his important assignment today. "I guess I could stay for a bit." He shut off the car and reached for his gloves in the backseat, just as she went to grab hers.

Their heads butted and she jumped back. "Ow."

He laughed. "Sorry. You stay there. I'll get the gloves."

Instead of handing hers over, he held one open for her.

She sent him a funny look as she slid her hand into the soft cashmere, then she held her other hand up for the second. "I'll pretend that wasn't totally awkward," she said as she opened the door.

He touched her arm, stopping her.

She turned back in surprise. "What's wrong?"

"Nothing. I just want to say thank you...for making the effort." He wasn't exactly making it easy for people in town to get to know him, and she could have continued ignoring him like everyone else.

"No problem...but I'm going to be gone soon, so you'll have to step up if you want people around here to accept you."

And what if he only wanted acceptance from the one person who was leaving soon? Then what?

Dear Reader,

By now, it's probably obvious just how much I love writing holiday-themed romances. The first book in this small-town series is about finding love during the Christmas season, and I thought it was fitting to end the series on the same note. Heather and Jacob's story is the final book in the Brookhollow series, and it was definitely bittersweet to write the final sentence. I have spent two years in this small town that has come to life on the page, with characters who feel like friends and story lines that I've always wanted to write.

I hope you will enjoy this slightly suspenseful conclusion to the series and fall in love with Heather and Jacob as we say goodbye to Brookhollow.

All the very best this holiday season from my family to yours. I hope love, peace and happiness find you wherever you are—small town or big city.

xo

*Jennifer*

# HEARTWARMING

## *Love, Lies & Mistletoe*

——

*Jennifer Snow*

**HARLEQUIN® HEARTWARMING™**

Recycling programs
for this product may
not exist in your area.

ISBN-13: 978-0-373-36747-4

Love, Lies & Mistletoe

Copyright © 2015 by Jennifer Snow

All rights reserved. Except for use in any review, the reproduction or utilization of this work in whole or in part in any form by any electronic, mechanical or other means, now known or hereinafter invented, including xerography, photocopying and recording, or in any information storage or retrieval system, is forbidden without the written permission of the publisher, Harlequin Enterprises Limited, 225 Duncan Mill Road, Don Mills, Ontario M3B 3K9, Canada.

This is a work of fiction. Names, characters, places and incidents are either the product of the author's imagination or are used fictitiously, and any resemblance to actual persons, living or dead, business establishments, events or locales is entirely coincidental.

This edition published by arrangement with Harlequin Books S.A.

For questions and comments about the quality of this book, please contact us at CustomerService@Harlequin.com.

® and TM are trademarks of Harlequin Enterprises Limited or its corporate affiliates. Trademarks indicated with ® are registered in the United States Patent and Trademark Office, the Canadian Intellectual Property Office and in other countries.

Printed in U.S.A.

**Jennifer Snow** lives in Edmonton, Alberta, with her husband and five-year-old son. She is a member of the Writers Guild of Alberta, the Romance Writers of America, the Canadian Author Association and shewrites.org. She is also a regular blogger on the Harlequin Heartwarming Authors site and is a contributing author to *Mslexia*, *WestWord* magazine and *RWR*. Her 2013 holiday romance, *The Trouble with Mistletoe*, was a finalist in the 2014 Golden Quill contest and the Heart of Denver Aspen Gold contest. More information can be found on her website, jennifersnowauthor.com.

### Books by Jennifer Snow

### Harlequin Heartwarming

*The Trouble with Mistletoe*
*What a Girl Wants*
*Falling for Leigh*
*The Mistletoe Melody*
*Fighting for Keeps*

For all of the Brookhollow fans who have followed the series—laughed and cried along with me and who continue to show a level of love and support that I could only have dreamed of—thank you!

## Acknowledgments

I can never say it often enough—thank you to my wonderful agent, Stephany Evans, who was the first one to believe in this series. And a special thank-you to editor Claire Caldwell, who offered valuable feedback on this story, along with my editor Victoria Curran. As always, this book is stronger because of you.

# CHAPTER ONE

"IS THAT THE one that got away?"

Jacob Marx placed his cell phone facedown onto the bar and glanced over his shoulder where Heather, the pool hall's bartender, was so close, strands of her long, dark brown hair rested on his shoulder. The scent of peppermint filled his nose. Huh, must be a holiday thing—last month she'd smelled like pumpkin spice. Not that he paid much attention; he just remembered how it had left him craving a Starbucks pumpkin spiced latte.

"No," he said, turning his attention back to the rum and Coke he'd been nursing for an hour. He wasn't much of a drinker, but sitting at the bar beat being alone every evening, thinking about the life passing him by in New York. He'd done that enough in his first few weeks in tiny Brookhollow, New Jersey, located right between Nowhere Land and Boringsville.

Heather went around the bar and set down a tray of empty beer glasses. "Are you sure? 'Cause it would explain a lot," she said, stacking the dirty dishes in the dishwasher.

Jacob picked up the phone, and closing the photo of his sister and eight-year-old nephew, he tucked it into his pocket. "Yeah, like what?" He leaned forward on the bar. This wasn't a conversation he wanted to have, but the talkative brunette was likely to tell him what she thought anyway.

"Like why you're such a—"

"Heather, we need another round on lane four." Candace, the waitress working the bowling alley side of the local hot spot, passed them carrying a food order from the kitchen.

The smell of the hot wings on the tray tempted Jacob to place an order of his own, but checking his glucose monitor, he decided not to mess with his currently stable blood sugars.

"I'll be right back," Heather said, filling a tray with beers from the mini-fridge behind the bar.

"Take your time," Jacob mumbled. He'd rather not spend his evenings at the pool hall when he wasn't on duty, but, unfortunately, in a town as small as this one, there were few options. Other than this pool hall/bowling alley/movie theater complex, the only other bar in town was the Green Gator, a karaoke joint. And he'd rather have his eyes poked out than go there.

He watched Heather carry the drinks to the bowling lane and collect the cash from the under-forty league members. The teams were practicing for their annual holiday bowling tournament, which had been so well-advertised and talked about all over town that anyone would think it was the Super Bowl.

A holiday bowling tournament was creating an excited buzz. Man, this town couldn't possibly be more boring.

But boring, quiet, uneventful was what he'd wanted, right?

Jacob drained the contents of his glass and threw several bills onto the bar as he stood.

"Hey, where are you going? We haven't finished our discussion yet," Heather said, returning. The holiday music had stopped playing, and she reached for another CD. More Christmas tunes. Same playlist every night that week. They'd already had the argument that it was too early to be playing that crap, but he'd lost and she'd only turned the music up louder.

"We weren't having a discussion. You were just insulting me, so I think I'll head out."

"Look, I didn't mean any offense," she said, as the first few notes of "I'll Be Home with Bells On" started to play.

"Could have fooled me," he grumbled, sliding into his leather jacket.

"All I'm saying is people around here are curious about you. You've been here for four months, and no one really knows your deal." She slid the other CD back into its case and turned to lean her hip against the bar.

"My deal?" he asked, his gaze returning to hers.

"Why you're here."

"Because it's such a quaint, idyllic town isn't enough reason?"

Heather shrugged. "Fine. But just so you know, when people around here get curious about someone, they start speculating on their own. Believe me, I've heard a dozen rumors already." She turned away from him and resumed hanging a set of colored Christmas lights behind the bar.

Again, too early, but at least she hadn't

asked for his help. Christmas wasn't exactly his thing. Or at least it hadn't been for the last few years.

Jacob hesitated. He didn't give a rat's behind what these local people were saying about him, but his gut tightened at being the topic of conversation. Had someone actually figured out why he was there? Small-town gossip made him nervous, and while he had confidence in Sheriff Bishop's discretion, he could never be too sure. Thirteen years on the job had made it impossible to trust anyone. Probably why he'd never gotten married. Actually, *precisely* why he hadn't gotten married.

Sighing, he sat back down. "Okay, let's hear them."

Heather continued singing as the song reached its chorus, ignoring him now.

"Hey, Talks-a-lot!"

She turned with a wide smile that caught him off guard, and he felt the tips of his ears grow hot.

He hadn't meant to blurt out his secret name for her. The truth was he had one for almost everyone in town. Four months in sleepy, low-crime Brookhollow was driving him mad. He had to do something to entertain himself. And he didn't want to get attached to anyone or anything. Nicknames helped.

"Talks-a-lot, huh?"

He shrugged.

So did she. "I'm good with that. Been called worse. Okay, so here's what I've heard." She lowered her voice. "Blink once if it's true, twice if it's not."

"No."

She huffed. "Fine. Well, one story is that you shot a fellow cop in New York and you felt so guilty about it, you needed to get away."

"I have shot a fellow cop before. Don't feel the least bit guilty." The rookie officer had caught a bullet in his left butt cheek in a liquor store robbery shoot-out, after ignoring protocol and advancing on the perpetrator. He'd been lucky it was only his butt; if Jacob hadn't fired when he had, the guy may not have walked away at all. "What else you got?"

Her eyes widened for a quick moment, then she said, "Another theory is that you were fired, and no other big-city department would hire you."

That was a little closer. "Fired for what?"

"The thoughts on that are varied. Some people say it was for withholding narcotics, others for killing an innocent bystander in a shoot-out. One person was kinder and said it was because you'd gotten strung out and went a little crazy."

That was kinder? "That all you got?"

"Pretty much...the others are too ridiculous to be true."

Right.

These people knew nothing. Reassured and relieved, he stood again and reached for his gloves. "Well, sorry to say they are all wrong. I'm just here for a change of scenery."

"No one's buying that story, Jake—I mean, Sheriff Matthews," she said.

Jake. Sheriff Matthews. Man, the worst part about this whole thing was not even being allowed to keep his own name. He hated when people called him Jake, but at least he answered to it. Better than getting used to something totally different, and he wasn't about to argue any of the conditions of his placement. Originally, they'd wanted to send him with his sister and nephew to some remote location, indefinitely, under the federal witness protection program. He'd been lucky to convince the department to let him stay close to New York and take on this mundane sheriff position instead. He'd claimed he wanted to stay nearby for when and if the drug case went to court and they needed him to testify, but the truth was he was still on the undercover case…just not officially.

"I'm not asking anyone to buy it," he said, heading toward the door. He just needed them to mind their own business. "Have a good night."

HEATHER CRADLED HER cell phone against her shoulder as she carried the heavy garbage bag through the back door of the pool hall. She set the trash down on the icy ground next to the already heaping bin, making a mental note to call the disposal company in the morning to come empty it. When she'd taken over running the bar from Melody Myers eleven months ago she a) hadn't expected it to be so hard and b) hadn't expected to be running it longer than six months.

"You still there?" her older sister said on the other end of the line.

"Barely," she mumbled, glancing at the seconds ticking away on her phone. Cameron had left her on hold for almost nine minutes.

"Sorry… I'm working, you know," she said distractedly.

Heather shivered in the late November air as she made her way back inside. "So am I."

"Yeah, at some crappy pool hall in the middle of nowhere. Heather, you have an MBA."

"I know," she said, tugging the heavy metal door closed behind her and locking it. She hadn't forgotten how hard she'd worked for the life and career she'd once had in New York; she was just struggling to figure out how to get back there, to all of that. "That's why I'm asking you for this favor."

"Heather, this is Highstone Acquisitions in Manhattan. Not some rinky-dink firm."

She sighed, suppressing the urge to remind her sister that she had worked at Clarke and Johnston for over ten years. They weren't a rinky-dink firm, either. "That's why I want to apply for a job there."

"Heather, you know I love you and I want nothing more than to have you back here in the city, but this is Rob's employer. Asking him to stick his neck on the line for you is…"

Heather gaped. Sticking his neck on the line? Seriously? "Thanks for the vote of confidence, Cam," she said. "You know what?

Never mind." She'd look up the firm herself and apply for the acquisitions agent position without Rob's help. It would be the fourth one she'd applied for in a year. She'd yet to even be called for an interview. And it baffled her. Her résumé was solid. She had the MBA Cameron had just mentioned. It was as though her previous employer had blackballed her somehow, she thought bitterly.

Calling in the favor to her sister's husband had meant swallowing her pride, but she was getting desperate. She had exactly five hundred and seventy-two dollars left in her bank account, after depleting her savings for the past year while she searched for a job.

"I'm sorry," Cameron said, sounding sincere. "That's not what I meant." She sighed. "Okay, Rob's direct boss is Mike Ainsley. He owns the company. His phone number…"

Going to the register behind the bar, Heather ripped off a piece of receipt paper. "Can't I just email him?"

"He'll probably want you to email a résumé, but Rob always says he likes to have a chat with potential candidates first."

That made sense, and she wasn't opposed to calling him, she was just hoping for more time to prepare for a discussion with the man. She wanted to make sure she got a shot at this position. "How old is he?"

"Old. Anyway, it doesn't matter. You're looking for a new employer this time, not a potential boyfriend, remember?"

Heather cringed. Her sister would throw *that* in her face again. "Believe me, I've learned my lesson about that," she mumbled. Three years in a relationship with her boss at Clarke and Johnston, only to lose him as both employer and boyfriend, had taught her to diversify.

Workplace relationships were not an option anymore.

"Good. So, just put away your sarcasm and resist every urge to be funny, and get through a short telephone call. We really do want you back here in the city."

She wanted to get back to her old life, too. She'd been away and out of the game long enough. Her career as an acquisitions agent, buying out smaller companies on behalf of million-dollar clients—usually box stores and hotel chains—had come to a halt after she'd been fired and dumped in the same week. She'd hightailed it to Brookhollow for her friend Victoria's wedding and a mini-vacation. She hadn't planned to stay for two years. The reminder of her friend momentarily gave her pause. "Look, Cam, I'll be there as soon as I can, but Victoria is depending on me now, too." Victoria ran a B and B in town. Her business partner and best friend had died months before in a car accident, and Heather had stepped in to help as much as possible. Days at the Brookhollow Inn's front desk and evenings at the pool hall were starting to take their toll, but leaving both her friend and the bar shorthanded made her feel guilty.

Yet every time she checked her bank account, she was reminded of how much she needed to get a job and get back to the city. She was volunteering her time at the B and B in exchange for a room, and the bar paid minimum wage and was never busy enough for her to make much in tips. "Victoria never expected you stay, and she's a good friend—she'll understand your decision. Just like you supported hers to move back to Brookview."

"Brookhollow."

"Sure, whatever. Call Mike Ainsley and secure this position before Christmas. We really want you to spend the holidays with us this year. Last year wasn't the same without you."

Guilt washed over her. Without their parents, she and her sister had always spent the holidays together, but the year before she'd decided to stay in Brookhollow, knowing that Christmas in the city—her first one single and alone—might be too depressing. But the holiday hadn't been the same for her, either. And the truth was, she wasn't happy in the small town anymore. It was time to move on. "I'll call him in the morning."

JACOB UNLOCKED THE back door of the three-story house on Pine Street where he was renting the attic-turned-bachelor-suite from Mrs. Kelly, a retired schoolteacher. Despite the late hour, all of the lights were on. He suspected she waited up for him every evening, and he sighed when he heard the sound of her slippers shuffling down the hallway.

"Jake, that you?" she called.

So much for sneaking upstairs unnoticed. "Yeah, Mrs. Kelly, it's just me."

"Hi, dear," she said as she entered the back porch off of the kitchen. "I was hoping you'd be home sooner."

Home? Hardly. Home was a two-bedroom apartment in the city that he hadn't seen in three years, first living undercover in a dive motel in Brooklyn, where he slept with his clothes on and his gun under his pillow, and then hiding out here in Brookhollow, where the only danger—for now—was this woman's nosiness.

Home was such a distant memory, he wasn't sure he'd recognize it even if he ever did see it again.

He sighed. "Why? What did you need help with?" In addition to paying three hundred dollars in rent for the twenty by twenty, six-foot high space that had given him a permanent neck cramp from stooping, he'd also become her jar opener, her sidewalk clearer and, most recently, her plumber.

"Well, I wanted to start my holiday decorating…"

"Isn't it a little soon?" Heather could argue that businesses needed to get an early push on the season, but individuals? Was that really necessary?

Mrs. Kelly's expression revealed that she thought he was crazy for even making the suggestion. "Of course not."

"Right. Okay, so what do you need?" Because he knew that's where this was headed.

"Well, my nephew used to come and help me get my things out of the storage space...but he's away at the police academy in Boston."

That's right, her nephew was Cody Kelly, the young man who'd been counting on the sheriff's position here in Brookhollow once he graduated in a few weeks. Well, the kid could have it...as soon as Jacob didn't need it anymore.

"He'll be here during the holidays of course, so don't worry, you'll get a chance to meet him."

He wasn't worrying, and he seriously doubted he'd be attending the family's holiday festivities. The young man probably wasn't thrilled that Jacob had taken his position and wouldn't be excited about meeting him, either.

"But in the meantime..."

"You'd like me to get your decorations out for you."

She smiled. "You are such a sweet boy."

"First thing in the morning, I'll get everything out before I go to work," he said, turning the corner and starting to climb the stairs.

She hurried after him. "I was kinda hoping to get started tonight."

Jacob poked his head around the corner, checking the time on the microwave. "It's eleven-thirty. You want to start decorating now?"

She nodded. "I'm a bit of a night owl."

He stifled a yawn. "Mrs. Kelly…" How did he tell the woman that, just because he was renting space in her home, she couldn't expect him to be there to help her with every project? That he preferred his privacy and space. He should never have ignored his gut, which had told him moving into her attic apartment would be a mistake. The price had been right, and at the time, he'd hoped he wouldn't need the place for more than a few weeks, a month at most. But a few weeks had quickly turned into four months and counting.

Four long months hiding who he really was, avoiding meaningful contact with people in town, trying to get used to once again being a beat cop—handing out tickets and issuing fines—and desperately trying to convince Mrs. Kelly that he could do his own laundry and that she didn't need to go into his apartment for any reason, especially not to put away his clothes. He'd learned quickly to keep anything personal in his locker at the station, away from curious old eyes.

The only thing he kept close by was his gun…and he hoped his landlady wouldn't be nosy enough to check inside the toilet tank in his bathroom.

But just in case, better to stay in her good books… "Where is the storage space?"

Her eyes lit up. "Well, since I turned the attic into an apartment, I've been storing everything in the crawl space," she said, leading the way.

He hesitated. Crawl space?

"Come on, I'll show you."

He followed. "Mrs. Kelly, do you mean like underneath your house? That kind of crawl space?"

"That's right," she said, opening a half-size door beneath the staircase at the end of the hall. She reached inside and pulled a string attached to the lightbulb in the low ceiling. "Everything is in here."

Yeah, everything like spiders, mice, enough dust to induce an asthma attack in the healthiest of lungs…

"I can no longer bend enough to get in there," she said.

Jacob glanced at her. Mrs. Kelly was barely five feet tall; if she couldn't bend low enough, how could he? "Huh, Mrs. Kelly... I'm not sure I'm the guy for this job. Why don't you hire a junior high kid to come over after school and help you? Pay them twenty bucks, and I'm sure they'll be eager to help any way they can."

"Pay someone?" She looked at him as though he'd suggested burning it all. She shook her head. "No need. You're here. There's only four or five boxes." She peered inside the space and waved him closer.

Sighing, he got down on his knees and crawled beneath the stairs. The cold draft coming from the large, uninsulated space made him shiver. He hoped she didn't have any snow globes among her decorations; they were probably frozen solid.

"They are all over in that far corner."

Of course they were.

"Most of them are labeled."

Most?

"If you're not sure, open the top flaps. It should be easy to tell what's Christmas stuff and what's not." She moved past him and straightened. "Thanks, dear. I'll leave you to it."

He closed his eyes and shook his head, not for the first time wondering if maybe staying in the city and putting his life at risk was such a bad option after all.

Of course the department hadn't left him much choice. It was either get out of town while the gun smoke settled on the bust that had gone wrong or be permanently removed from the force.

Heading farther into the space, he grabbed several nearby boxes and propped open the door.

"Oh, Jake, please close that while you're in there. That draft is really cold."

Right. "Okay, Mrs. Kelly," he mumbled, moving the boxes aside and letting the door close behind him.

He was grateful for his jacket and gloves as he moved toward the corner where she said the boxes would be. Dishes… Clothing… Christmas decorations—in a far back corner behind dozens of other boxes. He sighed. It had been a long time since he'd needed to dig out holiday decorations…and he'd been hoping to avoid any reminder of better, happier times. He reached for the boxes and tried to simply focus on the task ahead of him. He just needed to get through the season.

HEATHER DESCENDED THE refinished hardwood staircase at the Brookhollow Inn the next morning, skipping the third from the bottom step that always creaked, despite Victoria's husband's many attempts to fix it.

The inn had been Heather's home for a year and a half, but when she'd moved in, she'd had nowhere else to be. Visiting the quiet, laid-back small town had seemed like a great break from her stressful life in the city, but the desire to move on was increasing each day, especially as her bank account balance dipped lower.

She scanned the dining room, but it was empty. The B and B's occupancy rate had dwindled in recent months, since the weather turned colder and the roads were less than ideal to travel on. And they wouldn't be filling up again until the week before Christmas, when the inn would be full with guests visiting local family for the holidays.

She turned the daily calendar at the check-in desk. Almost another year wasted, without figuring out a plan for her future.

Well, it was time.

She reached into her jeans pocket and retrieved the piece of register tape from the bar. Mike Ainsley and the position at Highstone Acquisitions might be the answer to that. Tucking it in her hand, she poked her head into the kitchen.

Empty.

She headed toward the back of the house, listening carefully for Victoria's voice. Her friend habitually sat in the back sunroom, feeding her baby girl, Harper, around this time every day. Usually, her off-key singing voice could be heard torturing a lullaby, but today it was quiet. Maybe she hadn't arrived yet.

One glance through the glass walls of the sunroom revealed that it was snowing heavily, big fluffy white flakes collecting quickly on the already-covered ground.

The grandfather clock in the front sitting room chimed. Nine o'clock. Cameron had texted to say Rob had reluctantly agreed to give his boss a heads-up that she would be calling and that Mike Ainsley was expecting her call at nine. Heading back to the front desk, Heather pulled her cell phone from her purse.

Crap! She had to start remembering to plug in her phone at night. The dead battery light flickered a second longer, then the phone shut off completely. Wonderful. She'd have to make the long distance call at the desk. Luckily, she'd recently taken over paying the B and B's invoices, so she would know how much to reimburse Victoria for the call.

She wondered if her friend would accept a payment plan schedule.

But what if her friend noticed the acquisition firm's number on the bill? She bit her lip.

Two minutes past nine.

Picking up the receiver, she heard nothing. No dial tone. The line was dead.

What the…?

Glancing at the display screen on the phone revealed the connection with the server was down. Fantastic. She jiggled the mouse for the computer and waited for the reservation screen to appear. Great, the internet was down, too.

She wanted to scream. Stupid weather caused this to happen often around here. How many times had she told Victoria's husband, Luke, that the internet phone system may be cheap, but it wasn't reliable? And now was not the day to have her point proven. 9:04. What had her sister said about Mike Ainsley? He was old-school and didn't appreciate lateness.

This wasn't exactly her fault, but unless the other man had ever lived in a middle-of-nowhere town, he was probably not going to accept her excuses. Sitting in the chair, she noticed the old rotary phone on the corner of the desk. The phone lines should still work, just not the computerized system. Diving for it, she held her breath as she picked up the receiver.

Dial tone. Success. Thank God they'd kept the landline as a backup.

Man, this thing was heavy, she thought, retrieving the number and slowly dialing it. Good thing this wasn't a real emergency. Finally, when the phone started ringing, she sat straighter, mentally rehearsing her pitch.

"Happy holidays. Thank you for calling Highstone Acquisitions, how may I help you?" a chirpy receptionist's voice said.

"Hi, this is Heather Corbett. I'm calling for Mr. Ainsley."

"Mr. Ainsley, Junior or Senior?" she asked.

Great, there were two of them. Thanks for the heads up, Cam. "Senior, I believe. Mike."

"Mike is Junior. Michael is Senior. Which is it?"

Oh, come on. "The one in charge of hiring?"

"I'll put you through to HR," the young woman said in a tone that made it possible to imagine her rolling her eyes.

"Oh, no, actually Mr. Ainsley, Senior, I think, was expecting my call at nine," Heather said.

"It's ten after."

*It is now!* "I know, I apologize. I was having technical difficulties this morning." With a phone. Wow—could she sound any less competent?

"Hold the line," the receptionist said.

A second later, the sound of voices outside the B and B caught her attention, followed by the scrape of a metal shovel clearing the steps. Victoria and her husband, Luke, were there. Heather's eyes widened.

"This is Michael Ainsley," a deep voice said on the other end of the line.

She swallowed hard, watching the front door, hoping her friends would remain outside long enough to get this man to agree to review her résumé. "Hi, Mr. Ainsley, this is Heather Corbett, Rob Ashley's sister-in-law."

"Yes, he said to expect your call."

"Right, yes, so I'm interested in the opening for an acquisition agent that you have for the new year," she said quickly.

Outside, slamming of the car door and more scraping.

"Well, we are hoping to fill the position in the next few weeks, preferably before the office shuts down for the holidays. We are closed from…hmm, let me find my calendar…"

Oh, my God! "Right, for the holidays, I understand. Anyway, I'd love to send you my résumé."

"Well, before we get to that, I have a couple of questions."

"Okay."

"The most obvious one, of course, is why should we consider you for the position?" he asked, before erupting in a terrible fit of coughing.

"Um…" Still coughing.

"Sorry…give me…just a sec…" he said between coughs, and she could hear him set the phone down.

She closed her eyes and rested her head against her hand. Come on.

"Sorry about that. Terrible cold…it seems to have migrated to my lungs."

"Terrible…just awful. To answer your question, though, I think I would be a great candidate for the position based on my years of experience in a similar role with Clarke and Johnston Acquisitions in New York City…"

"We do things a little differently around here, I'll warn you."

"That's okay. I'm a quick learner, and I'm loyal," she said and cringed. Sure she was; that's why she was desperate to get this job and bail on one of her best friends.

The outside porch door opened, and her heart raced.

"We do appreciate long-term employees. Your brother-in-law has been with us probably the least amount of time and he's been here…"

"Ten years, I know," she said quickly, hearing the stomping of boots in the entryway. "Anyway, sir, I really would love to send you my résumé, and I'm available for a face-to-face interview anytime." Not exactly true, but she would make time.

Any second now, Vic would enter, and she really wasn't ready to tell her friend that she hoped to move back to the city. She'd rather wait to tell her once she knew for sure about the job…maybe by phone. She shook her head. Victoria deserved better after all their years of friendship. She would tell her…soon.

The door opened, and Victoria came in, carrying a wailing Harper in her car seat. Weighed down with the baby, a diaper bag and several grocery bags, she struggled to close the door.

"Do you have children?" Mike asked.

"Some help, please?" Victoria said at the same time.

"No!" Heather answered Mike's question.

"Seriously?" Victoria shot her a look before noticing she was on the phone. "Oh, sorry," she said, setting the crying baby girl on the floor and shutting the door against the cold breeze.

"Okay…because we expect our employees to travel quite a bit," Mike said.

Heather plugged her other ear against the

earth-shattering wails. "I understand. That's not a problem."

Victoria unharnessed Harper from her car seat, and the crying stopped immediately.

Finally.

"Who are you talking to?" she mouthed.

Nosy much? Heather shook her head, hoping Vic would move on.

She didn't. Instead, she bounced Harper on her shoulder as she paced in front of the desk.

"Okay, send me your résumé, and I'll have a look," Mike said.

"Great. Where should I send it?" she mumbled into the phone, turning her back to Victoria.

Please, let the email address be an easy one that she wouldn't have to write down.

"Michael…underscore  Ainsley…underscore nineteen…not the numerals, actually spelled out…at Highstone…no, wait… Did I say the nineteen?"

Heather sighed. "Yes." Forget it, she'd ask her brother-in-law for the email later.

"Great. So, Michael…underscore…" The man's voice broke into another fit of loud, throat-ripping coughs.

Victoria moved to stand in front of her,

her eyes wide. "They sound terrible—who is that?" she asked. "And why are you on the rotary?"

"Hey, anyone notice that the connection for the network is down?" Luke asked, entering a second later.

Heather nodded and gestured at the receiver in her hand.

"I'll try to fix it," Luke said, coming around the desk.

*Sure, why don't they all hang out there?*

He glanced at her with a frown. "Who's dying on the phone?"

*She* was.

"Sorry, Heather. Did you get that email?"

"Yes, sir," she lied. "Thank you. I'll send it right away," she said quickly, hanging up the phone.

*Oh, my God.*

Victoria was staring at her.

"What?"

"You're leaving, aren't you?" she asked, still bouncing Harper on her shoulder.

"No, of course—" She stopped. She couldn't lie to her friend. "Yes…as fast as my little legs can go." She stood and hugged her. "I'm so sorry, Vic."

Victoria waved a hand. "Don't be. I knew this wasn't a permanent situation. It's fine," she choked out, as tears formed in her eyes.

"Oh, Vic—don't do that!"

"They're happy tears, see?" She faked a weird, grimace-type smile.

Luke laughed behind the desk. "Yep, those are happy tears."

Heather shot him a look. "Nothing is definite yet. I haven't even sent my résumé."

"What company is it?"

"Highstone Acquisitions."

Victoria's eyes widened. "That's wonderful! I applied there three times when I worked for Clarke and Johnston."

Heather frowned. "I never knew that. Why didn't you tell me? My brother-in-law works there—I probably could have gotten you an interview."

"You were dating our boss, remember? Not exactly a trustworthy vault back then," she said, looking envious. "So if Rob works there, you're sure to get the position." She didn't sound thrilled.

"Not necessarily," Heather said, but she prayed Victoria was right.

"Well, if you need a reference or anything…"

"No offense, Vic, but I don't think I'll be adding front desk clerk to my résumé."

"I meant a coworker reference from when we worked together at Clarke and Johnston," she said, playfully slapping her arm.

Heather smiled at her friend. Nearly all traces of the high-powered, New York City woman had disappeared from her over the past few years, except for the tiniest spark in her eyes when she talked about her former life in the city. "Thanks," she said.

"I'm going to go feed the baby now," Victoria said, choking up again as she left the room.

"No crying!" Heather called after her.

Luke checked the phone and then pointed at her. "*You're* going to be crying if you remind Victoria again about how much she loved her life in New York."

## CHAPTER TWO

"WHAT ON EARTH is that old lady doing?" Jacob mumbled, leaning low in the driver's seat of his squad car to peer through the windshield. The people around here made no sense to him.

Rolling down the passenger-side window as he slowed the car and pulled to the side of the road in front of Ginger Snaps, the bakery he avoided on Main Street, he called out, careful not to startle the woman and extra careful not to use the nickname he'd assigned to her. "Ginger! Mrs. Norris—what are you doing?"

The woman was standing on a plastic step stool on the icy ground outside her bakery, holding on to the side of the building for support and using the end of a broomstick to swipe at the large icicles hanging from the awning.

She stopped and turned to look at him. "I'm clearing the awning of icicles. You threatened me with a fine if I didn't do it, remember?" she snapped.

"You're eighty years old. You shouldn't be doing that. I meant ask someone to do it for you." He'd noticed her granddaughter, Leigh, and her husband going inside the bakery at least once a week. And he was sure the guy was renting the space above the bakery for an office. Some bestselling author or something. Jacob may not care about the goings-on in town, but little escaped his notice.

"I'm seventy-seven," she said, resuming her attempt to knock them loose, swinging the broom haphazardly.

He swallowed a curse and climbed out, sliding his hands into his gloves. "Get down, please," he said, taking her elbow to assist her.

"Don't get fresh with me, young man."

Wow. "Just making sure you don't break your neck on all of this packed snow that I'm pretty sure I asked you to have cleared weeks ago," he said, taking the broom.

"I'll do that next," she mumbled.

He shook his head as he opened her bakery door and waved her inside, trying not to breathe in the delicious smell of gingerbread and cinnamon.

She muttered something under her breath as she passed him, and he couldn't be sure that it was an insult aimed at him, but it certainly wasn't "thank you."

"Hey, Sheriff Matthews, when you're done over there, could you maybe come do mine, as well?" Tina Miller, or Nosy Nelly, as he liked to think of her, called to him as she wrote on the specials board outside Joey's Diner.

He gave a mock salute and continued working. The day before, he'd issued twenty-four-hour warnings to the business owners along Main Street to clear their awnings of these dangerous icicles. By the look of things, everyone had ignored him. Except Ginger. Well, they wouldn't be laughing when an icicle fell on a passerby, and they were suddenly smacked with a lawsuit.

Oh, what was he thinking—no one sued anyone around here. A New York City boy from the time he could walk, he was so far out of his comfort zone in Brookhollow, he couldn't even remember what his comfort zone felt like. But it certainly wasn't this sense of being watched from afar and speculated about on a regular basis. He'd told himself that he was being paranoid, and that was natural given the extreme circumstances. But after his conversation with Heather the night before, he knew that wasn't the case. People were watching and speculating and judging.

After clearing the awning, he went inside the bakery and immediately wished he hadn't. The tempting aromas were almost too much to resist. But diabetic from the age of eight, he rarely consumed sweets or refined carbs. Keeping his blood sugars under control was his first priority. "Here are your broom and your step stool," he said, leaving them inside the door.

"Did you want a muffin or something?" Ginger offered begrudgingly.

"No. What I want is for you to ask your granddaughter or her husband to come clear the walkway…or at least put salt or sand on it or something." He was wasting his breath. No one around here listened to him. He was just the big-city, hotshot cop who didn't understand about small-town life. Well, they were right about that. And unfortunately, uncleared walkways and awnings just didn't compare to drug deals and dangerous criminals on his scale of what mattered. But unfortunately, this

was what he was reduced to dealing with…
and he was still a cop, for better or worse.

"Will do," she said, rushing to the kitchen
at the sound of the oven timer.

"No, you won't," he mumbled, heading back
outside.

As he returned to the squad car, his glucose
monitor beeped. Great, he was low. He could
have had a muffin. He sighed as he checked
the numbers. Three point four and dropping.
This stupid disease was responsible for all of
this, he thought, the memory of his last day
undercover never too far from his mind.

His blood glucose monitor had been beeping that day, too, revealing that his sugar levels were dropping steadily for almost an hour.
He'd searched his vehicle for a juice box or a
granola bar…an old doughnut or candy…

But found nothing.

He hadn't expected to be waiting that long
for Leo Gonzales to emerge from the warehouse. Most exchanges happened quickly, so
as not to draw attention. All Jacob had needed
was visual confirmation that Gonzales was
dealing with Mario Lorenzo, the drug lord
they'd been chasing, and he'd have everything
necessary to put the man away for a long time.

His two-year undercover stint would be over and he could resume some semblance of a life after debriefing and resocialization.

The longer he'd been under, the harder it had been to remember who he really was. He tried to visit his family—his sister and nephew—a weekend every month or a few stolen days over the holidays, but it had been getting tougher to leave the cartel unnoticed. Tougher to leave the persona behind and become Uncle Jacob again. Then to go back to being a drug-pushing thug.

Deciding to work undercover hadn't been easy for him, knowing he'd have to leave his family for long periods of time, but he'd gone into policing to make a difference, and despite the extreme living conditions and having to pretend to be something he despised, he was so close…he *was* making a difference…

The door to the warehouse opened, and he sat straighter, but Gonzales exited alone, scanned the area, then went back inside. It wasn't enough. He needed to see Gonzales and Lorenzo together.

The monitor had beeped.

Crap. He needed to eat. But he'd waited two years for this opportunity; he couldn't leave now. Three SWAT team vehicles were parked two blocks away, awaiting his signal. He couldn't sacrifice two years of weight gain, drug use and hurting people when they were so close.

Searching his duffel bag in the backseat, he found half a chocolate bar. Who knew how long it had been in there, but he didn't care—he needed to get his sugars up.

He scarfed it down, but twenty minutes later, his blood sugar continued to drop again.

Two point one. Stress often had this effect on his body.

Sweat collected on his back beneath the bulletproof vest he wore and ran down his forehead. His mouth was dry and his hands unsteady.

*Come on. Come out.*

Fifteen minutes passed. The monitor continued to beep relentlessly, and his vision started to blur. He glanced at the reading. Under one. Even if they did come out, there was nothing he could do now except signal. He would be completely useless in helping to arrest these guys.

He prayed he wouldn't lose consciousness before he could at least do that much.

His head swayed, and he fought to focus as the warehouse lights went off.

What? That wasn't right. Where were they? Was there another entrance into the building? He'd scoped the place out the night before. He reached for his radio, but it fell to the floor on the passenger side of the car.

When he reached for it, his vest pressed against the steering wheel and sounded the horn.

Oh, no.

The warehouse door opened, and Gonzales and Lorenzo exited, Gonzales's gaze landing directly on Jacob, as if he knew he'd be there. Jacob grabbed the radio and hit the button for the signal as gunfire rang out and his world went black.

That day, four months ago, would have put an end to Mario Lorenzo and his cartel if the drug lord hadn't escaped before the SWAT teams arrived. Now all that would put the man behind bars was Jacob's statement, which was still under evaluation because he'd lost consciousness immediately after the visual confirmation, making his observations questionable. While Gonzales had been caught with enough evidence to put him away, the head of the operation was still a free man until a court case could be scheduled, and Jacob had his day on the witness stand.

Shutting off the vehicle, Jacob jogged across the street to Joey's. The diner's fifties-style décor, complete with red leather bar stools and a jukebox in the corner, was seriously something out of the movie *Grease*, but he had to admit the food was better than anything he'd ever tasted.

The place was packed. Every table and booth was occupied, and even the stools at the counter were all taken. The plates piled with eggs, pancakes, sausages and toast passing by him, as Tina and her daughter, April, delivered the meals, made his stomach growl and his mouth water. His monitor beeped again. He could get something to go. Sit in the car and eat until his blood sugar returned to normal.

Going to the register, he waited. He knew what he wanted. Eggs Benedict and a side order of bacon. Two side orders of bacon.

Tina moved past him and rang in an order.

"Hi, can I place an order to go?" he asked.

She didn't glance up as she said, "You'll

have to give me like ten minutes, we're backed up in the kitchen."

Once his blood sugar level started to drop, it went down quickly. He didn't want to pass out in the busy diner. So far, he'd been successful in keeping his diabetes to himself…except for Mrs. Kelly who'd found one of his needles in his bathroom when she'd been cleaning. He cringed at the memory. She had accused him of being a drug addict and had refused to give him back his insulin until he'd explained everything to her and then reassured her, he could clean his own apartment. "Can I at least order now?"

"I told you, you're going to have to wait. Tables get priority over takeout," Tina said.

He sighed and turned to lean against the counter. He'd leave and go someplace else, but the fact was there was nowhere else. No pizza places within a ten-mile radius, no sub sandwich chain stores, no familiar coffee shops… just Joey's Diner. God, he missed the city.

He spotted Heather sitting alone at the corner booth near the window, hesitated for a fraction of a second, then headed toward her.

She had a laptop open on the table and was typing furiously with one hand, while eating—eggs Benedict, of course—with the other.

"That's quite the talent," he said.

"Lucky for me, I'm ambidextrous," she said with a quick glance in his direction.

"Well, I can see that you're busy, but if I promise to be quiet, can I share your table?"

She looked surprised when she finally gave him her attention. "You always eat alone."

"And I would today, but all the tables are full, including the bar stools."

"So you only want to eat with me because there's nowhere else to sit?"

"Exactly."

"Charming."

"Honest."

She laughed and gestured for him to be her guest. "Go ahead."

He slid into the booth. "Look, if it makes you feel better—if I have to sit with someone, I'm glad it's you."

Heather's expression was one of amusement as she said, "Am I supposed to be flattered?"

"Yes. You're probably the only person in Brookhollow that I can actually tolerate." He shrugged out of his jacket and tucked it next to him on the seat.

"Tolerate? Wow. Anyway, you promised not to talk, so shhh, I have five minutes to finish this," she said, resuming her typing.

Jacob silently nodded and leaned back against the cushioned booth. He attempted to flag Tina for coffee as she passed, but she ignored him. "If only the food wasn't so good around here," he mumbled.

"You're talking."

"Sorry." He stared out the window for a long moment, then he said, "What are you doing, anyway?"

She cocked her head as she glanced over the top of the computer. "You barely talk to anyone around here, unless it's to yell at them about a hazardous front step or something, and now you can't shut up?"

"I don't yell. I ask. They ignore. So, what are you working on?"

"A résumé," she said, lowering her voice.

"Don't you already have two jobs in town?"

"It's for a job in New York."

"What kind of job?"

"One I won't get if I don't send this. Hold on," she said, typing a few more things.

He watched her lips move as she scanned the screen in front of her.

Cute.

In fact, if he allowed himself the opportunity to look, *she* was cute. Long, dark hair that once again smelled like peppermint and waved around her shoulders beneath the purple hat she wore. Her hazel eyes had flecks of gold around the center that resembled a starburst, and her long, thin neck was exposed beneath her slightly open scarf.

"What's with the hat and scarf inside?" It was like eighty degrees inside the crowded diner.

"I'm always cold," she said, closing her laptop.

"Done?" he asked.

"Yes." She gathered her things and stood, sliding her arms into her jacket.

"You're leaving?"

Reaching for her coffee cup, she drained the contents. "Yes. You already said you just wanted my table."

"But you were going to tell me about the job in New York." Any opportunity to talk about the city made him feel better. Being around a fellow New York native somehow made him feel better, too. Probably why he found himself at the pool hall bar far too often.

"No, I wasn't." She tapped his shoulder as she passed him on her way to the door. "You're not the only one around here who can be mysterious. Bye, Sheriff Matthews."

Jacob turned in the booth to watch her leave, fighting an odd sense of disappointment. He had a table; what did he care if she wasn't sticking around to eat with him? Eating alone hadn't bothered him before. Doing *everything* alone in Brookhollow hadn't bothered him before. But lately...

As the holiday season drew closer, he felt the void of family and friends much more than usual. For the two years he'd spent undercover, he'd been unable to slip away to see Amber and Kyle on Christmas Day. He swallowed hard. This year was supposed to have been different, their first Christmas together as a family. Some of their family, anyway.

Heather passed Sheriff Bishop on his way into the diner. She said something to him before leaving, and the man laughed, his gaze immediately landing on Jacob.

Great. He turned back in the booth and caught April's arm. "Can I please order?" he asked, his glucose monitor beeping again.

"Sure." She glanced toward the kitchen,

then leaned closer to fill his coffee cup. "And I saw you helping Ginger just now," she whispered, "so I'll try to make sure they don't do anything to your food this time."

This time? He'd been eating at Joey's almost every day for weeks. How often were his meals tampered with? "Why are they messing with my food?" And they claimed people in small towns were nice.

"Because you keep messing with them," she said.

"How?"

"The fine for the parking out back."

"It's a fire lane," he argued.

"And then the expired liquor license thing."

"They need a valid license." *Give me a break*. They were angry at him for holding them responsible for breaking the law? Besides, those warnings had come from Sheriff Bishop—Jacob had just been the messenger.

"All I'm saying is, I know you're probably bored out of your mind—"

Understatement.

"—with the lack of real crimes around here, but maybe don't focus so heavily on the place that feeds you," she said with a wink. "Now—eggs Benedict?"

"Yes, preferably without spit," he mumbled.

"I'll see what I can do," she said as Sheriff Bishop joined them. "How's my favorite sheriff today?"

Subtle.

Jacob took a sip of his coffee. Lukewarm.

"I'm great, April. Just coffee, please," Sheriff Bishop said.

"You got it. I'll go grab a fresh pot."

Jacob sighed.

"Eating alone?" the older man asked.

"Have a seat, please," he said, staring out the window. Across the street, he saw Ginger chipping away at the block of ice outside her front door. Unbelievable.

"How's it going?" Sheriff Bishop asked.

"Fantastic," Jacob grumbled.

"It'll get easier. Once they get to know you a bit, they'll warm up."

He didn't want them to warm up; he wanted to get back to his life in the city. Besides, how was anyone supposed to get to know him when he couldn't be honest about who he was and why he was there? And while everyone thought he was a major annoyance? So for that much, he couldn't blame them. "Well, having to issue all of these warnings aren't helping."

The man smiled. "Ah, they'll get over it. We've been down a sheriff since the last guy retired, and I've been too soft on them. Give them time."

He didn't want to give them time. He wanted to leave Brookhollow. "Have you heard anything?" Jacob asked quietly. He'd asked the same question every day for four months. The answer was never promising.

April returned with fresh coffee and poured a cup for Sheriff Bishop and graciously topped his up with the hot liquid, checking to make sure Tina wasn't watching.

"Thanks."

When she left, Sheriff Bishop shook his head. "Nothing."

Jacob sighed. He knew the NYPD had guys on the case, and that they were doing everything they could to bring Lorenzo in, so Jacob could testify against him and then return to his life, but he also knew the department was being careful. They weren't about to get aggressive, risking the lives of several other officers, just to bring him back. That was assuming he even had a job to go back to. Blacking out and compromising his position had raised flags about Jacob's ability to do his job effectively.

Heck, even *he* was questioning his ability.

Which was exactly why he was here. He had an informant working on the docks at the Port of Newark Terminal, and Jacob was expecting the guy to give him a "wrong number" call when he knew Lorenzo would be there. And that would be Jacob's cue to move in. Disobeying orders and getting involved with a case that he'd been removed from was wrong, but it was his only opportunity to prove that he could still be a valuable member of the force.

And if it was just his life to consider, he might be able to show more patience and resolve, waiting for either the department to catch Lorenzo or the call from Emilio in Newark.

"Anything from Amber or Kyle?" he asked.

"There may be something in your locker at the station," Sheriff Bishop said quietly.

Jacob almost smiled at that. "Amber?" he asked, hopefully.

Sheriff Bishop shook his head.

Of course not. His sister was still far too angry at him for making her uproot her entire life and move into the federal witness protection four months ago. But he'd had no choice. Jacob couldn't protect them anymore, and when Kyle had been approached outside of school by a stranger with a note for his uncle, meant as a warning, their only choice had been the program. Amber had been furious that Jacob expected her to leave her art gallery and take Kyle out of school to move to the middle of nowhere. They'd all had a life in the city—one that had changed abruptly.

Because of him.

He didn't even know where they were, for *their* safety. Letters back and forth were the only form of communication allowed, and they were filtered through the US Marshals and Sheriff Bishop, who also read the correspondence.

April brought over his breakfast, and he shot a look behind the counter at Tina. "Is it safe?" he asked April.

She nodded.

He picked up his fork and dove in. At that point, he wasn't even sure if he cared if they'd done anything to it. He was starving, and he knew he'd be helping Ginger Norris with her sidewalk in a few minutes. He needed his blood sugars up for the job.

# CHAPTER THREE

JACOB ENTERED THE locker room at the station a few hours later. All afternoon he'd been dying to read the letter from his nephew, but a few emergencies had kept him busy. Pearl Howard, the woman who owned the flower shop on Main Street, had reported a lost cat, and it had taken nearly an hour to locate the tabby—locked accidentally in her coat closet when she'd come home from the supermarket. Unbelievable. In the city, he'd never have answered a missing cat call.

What constituted an emergency in Brookhollow was so different from in New York, and by now Jacob should have learned not to answer the more ridiculous calls. They were making him crazy. Unfortunately, he had to keep up the act.

"Hey, Jake," Ethan Bishop, Sheriff Bishop's son and head of the fire department, said as he entered the shared locker room, removing his jacket.

"Hi." Jacob sat on the bench and removed his boots.

"I heard Mrs. Howard found her cat," he said, hanging his gear on the hook and reaching for his jeans.

"She sure did."

Ethan laughed. "I swear she locks him away on purpose to have us stop by for company."

Pearl *had* looked slightly disappointed to see Jacob pull up in the squad car instead of the firemen. "I wouldn't doubt it." She had invited him to stay for tea and cookies afterward, which he'd refused, so instead she'd asked him to clear her walkway, which he'd done.

"Hey, man—do you ever wish there were real emergency calls around here? A burning shed, at least?" He couldn't understand how guys like Ethan—young, fit, ambitious and hardworking—could be satisfied with the snail's pace of life in Brookhollow.

But Ethan shook his head. "Nope. The last time there was a real fire here, it was in my wife's garage."

"Oh, man. I'm sorry."

"Nah, it worked out for the best. She wasn't there, and the garage got rebuilt to code, which

I'd been begging her to do for years. But it was still scary."

"I guess in a small town, a real emergency could mean your own family or friends are involved." Heck, even in New York, his job had affected the well-being of his family.

"Yeah, that's why we're totally fine being bored out of our minds," Ethan said, grabbing his winter coat from the locker. "Hey, I know some of the guys asked you before, but...here," he said, taking a folded piece of paper from his pocket and handing it to him.

Jacob opened it. The bowling league again.

"We need a couple extras for the tournament in a few weeks. If you know how to roll a straight ball even just by fluke, you're in, if you're interested," he said.

"Thanks. I'll...uh...think about it."

"Okay. See ya around," Ethan said as he left.

Alone, Jacob balled the paper and tossed it into the trash can in the corner. Bowling was something he and Kyle used to enjoy together. They'd even joined a family league before Jacob had taken the promotion to undercover agent. The disappointment on Kyle's face when he'd told him their weekly bowling nights would be suspended for a while had torn a hole through him, and participating in the sport now, without his nephew, would make him feel like crap.

Reaching into the back of the locker, he retrieved the already opened letter from Kyle. The return address had been cut from the corner of the envelope, and for the millionth time, Jacob wondered where they'd been sent. He hoped it was somewhere sunny and warm and fun, at least. He wished *he* was somewhere warm, sunny and fun. Hiding out on a beach in California surrounded by beautiful women and unlimited cocktails would be easier to swallow. An image of Heather behind the pool hall bar flashed in his mind. Okay, two out of three, but still no beach. And besides, she'd told him earlier she was applying for a job in New York. Pretty soon, the only thing making his time there bearable would be gone.

Unfolding the letter, he read.

Dear Uncle Jacob,
How are you? We are fine. Mom says hello, even though she said she is still mad at you. I'm not. The school here is

better than the one in New York, they even have snowboarding lessons.

Snowboarding lessons? Colorado?

Mom says you're probably lying around on a beach somewhere.

Ha! He wished he'd been able to be honest with his sister about his plan when he'd told her he wasn't going into the program with her and Kyle—it might have made her a little less angry with him. Maybe.

I've made some new friends and I'm ahead of everyone with math and English, so the teacher asked me to be her helper. Isn't that great?

Jacob breathed a sigh of relief. That *was* great. For a kid who struggled with Asperger's and being bullied, it was great to hear he was doing well in this new place. No doubt a small town, where their story wasn't being questioned as much as his own, and where people were accepting of them as a young single mom and son starting over in a new place.

I'm going to see Santa next week at the
mall. I'm going to ask him to make sure
the police catch the bad guys wanting to
hurt us, so we can all be together again in
time for Christmas. You ask for the same
thing, too, okay? Maybe if we both ask
for it, we'll get it.
Love you Stinker,
Kyle

Jacob sighed as he folded the letter. If only
he still believed in Christmas miracles…but
he'd stopped believing in holiday magic a long
time ago.

IT WAS GOING to take a Christmas miracle to
get her out of Brookhollow before the holidays, Heather thought as she stared at the
returned email notification. Invalid email address was the reason the résumé she'd sent to
Mike Ainsley hadn't been delivered. Almost
twelve hours later! Shutting down the email
on her phone, she dialed her sister's number.

"Hello?" Cam's sleepy voice said after the
fourth ring.

"Were you asleep?" She glanced at the beer-
can-shaped, neon-rimmed clock above the

bar. Her sister was a night owl, so she hadn't thought twice about calling after ten.

"No. I'm going over some testimonies for court tomorrow, what's up?"

Cam was a prosecuting attorney for the DA's office in New York and often brought her work home with her. Heather marveled over her sister's ability to juggle her important, high-powered career with being a wife and mom. Cameron had inherited their parents' work ethic and ambition, but had somehow gone above that and developed a work-life balance. Tonight she sounded stressed, though, and Heather almost hesitated before saying, "You gave me the wrong email address for Mike Ainsley."

"No, I didn't. You must have written it down wrong." This was exactly why her sister was so great at her job. She was never wrong and had a way of wording things that made people question their own arguments.

"Maybe," Heather mumbled. "Either way, the résumé I sent today bounced back."

"Come on, Heather. One sec…" She heard the sound of shuffling papers. "Okay, write this down…"

After Heather copied the insane email address for the second time, she tucked the paper into her apron pocket. "It's a wonder any of his emails actually reach him. What's with this crazy email address anyway? I doubt M Ainsley at Highstone Acquisitions was taken," she mumbled.

"I don't know," Cameron said distractedly. It sounded more like *I don't care.* "Send it again now."

"I can't. I'm at work. I just checked the email on my phone."

"Well, leave work and go send it. This is more important."

Her sister didn't get that she had responsibilities here that she couldn't just abandon. "Cam, I'll send it again in the morning. I have to get back to work. Talk soon," she said, disconnecting the call as the front door opened and Sheriff Matthews entered.

*If I was going to eat with someone, it would be you.* Not exactly a charmer, but his earlier words in the diner seemed to almost mean more, coming from him, than the most flowery compliment from anyone else. Niceness was obviously not his forte. "Hello again," she said as he took his usual seat at the bar.

"Can I ask you something?"

"Sure."

"Do you put stuff in my drinks?" He removed his leather jacket and pushed up the sleeves of his dark blue crew neck sweater as he sat, revealing several scars on his left forearm. They only enhanced his rugged, manly attractiveness.

He was a great-looking guy. If he could work on his game a little bit, he wouldn't have any trouble attracting women around town. "Like what—roofies?" She'd never had *that* much trouble securing a date, she mused.

"No, like spit."

She laughed so hard her sides hurt, and she bent at the waist. When she looked at him again, his unamused expression made her laugh even harder. "I'm sorry..." She struggled to catch her breath. "Tina and Joey are actually tampering with your food at the diner?" Wow, they must really not like this guy. She almost pitied him. Sure, he was rude, and arrogant, and condescending... Wait— where was she going with that thought?

"Can I get a beer, please?"

She nodded, suppressing another laugh. Reaching into the mini-fridge, she took out a bottle of the brand he usually ordered, twisted off the cap and handed it to him. "Want to start a tab?"

He usually paid cash, and it annoyed her, as she had to constantly ring in his drinks and cash him out each time. But still, she always asked, and that evening, he surprised her.

"Sure."

She smiled. "Great. ID, please."

"Really? I'm sitting right here. And I'm a police officer. I'm not going to skip out on the bill."

"Rules are rules. Aren't you always going around trying to enforce the rules?" she said, hands on her hips.

Jacob reached into his pocket and retrieved his wallet, then hesitated for a second before handing her his driver's license.

She took it and glanced at the photo. Then glanced at him. Then back at the photo.

"I was a little heavier then," he said, gulping his beer.

"A little?" she asked. "And what's with the bushman's beard?" The guy in the picture was hardly recognizable as the man sitting in front of her. His brown hair was longer, and his expression was dark, making him look more like a criminal than a cop.

"Do you always criticize people's ID photos?" he asked, as she tucked it away with the others behind the register.

"Usually not in front of them," she said with a grin.

She went to grab a food order from the kitchen, and when she returned to gather cutlery and condiments from the bar, she asked, "Is the station entering a float into the Christmas parade?"

"Christmas parade? Really? The only street long enough to accommodate a parade around here is Main Street, and how many floats could a parade here possibly have?" He shrugged before answering her question. "I have no idea."

"Doesn't matter," she said, adding glasses of beer to the tray. "Our float is going to win anyway. Melody Myers and Brad Monroe are back in town for the holidays, and I've convinced them to perform Christmas songs all along the parade route." She wasn't sure if Jake had ever heard of the country music stars, but whether he had or not, he nodded.

"What theme are you going with?"

Heather shook her head. "Uh-uh, you're not

getting any more information from me about our entry."

He sighed. "I was just trying to be polite. It seemed as though you wanted to talk...as usual."

"I was just wondering if you guys were competing. The float designs every year are a big deal and kept under wraps. We don't want people stealing each other's ideas." She reached for extra napkins and picked up the loaded tray.

"Seriously? It's a parade float."

She shot him a look. "Well, our team is not disclosing any information—we know we have a winning design."

"Team?"

"Yeah. Each float is only allowed to have four people working on it, and their names have to be submitted before construction starts."

"Wow, this thing is pretty regulated...more than anything else in town."

Heather laughed. "Christmas is a big deal around here, in case you haven't noticed," she said, coming around the side of the bar.

"The house across the street from me looks

like it was decorated by Santa's elves on crack—believe me, I've noticed."

Heather laughed again as she made her way to the bowling alley to deliver the order.

On her way back, she stopped at a corner booth where Lindsay Harper and Noah Parks sat cuddled together on the same side. They'd been together for four months, and it was rare to see one without the other. It was even rarer to see them without five children in tow—they'd recently adopted Lindsay's nieces and nephews. "Hey, guys. Date night?"

Lindsay nodded "The kids are with Ben and Lily."

The kids' godfather had moved to town recently to help Lindsay with the five children who'd been left in her care after the sudden, tragic death of her brother and his wife. And to everyone's surprise, he'd soon started dating Lindsay's friend Lily, who owned a clothing store on Main Street.

Families really did come in all shapes and sizes, Heather marveled.

"What can I get you guys?"

"A beer for me and…" Noah glanced at Lindsay.

"A Bloody Mary, please, with extra celery sticks and pickled veggies," she said.

Noah glanced at her. "Hungry?"

"Twelve-hour shift, remember—I'm starving," she said, removing her coat to reveal her nurse's uniform.

"Menus, too, please, Heather," Noah said, glancing toward the bar. "Oh, great. No one have fun—Sheriff Matthews is here."

Since Jake had arrived in town, he'd butted heads with no one more so than Noah, a former MMA fighter who ran the at-risk-youth program at the local community center. Both men had the town's best interest at heart, but they had different ways of dealing with things. Completely opposite ways, in fact.

"He's easing up a little, I think," Heather said, not sure why she felt the need to defend Jake, except that he was a nice guy.

Sort of…somewhere deep down…maybe?

"Tell that to my kids at the center. They're terrified of doing anything wrong. He keeps watching them, waiting for one of them to mess up," Noah said.

"Maybe that's not necessarily a bad thing. I mean, I haven't heard about any graffiti problems lately or any of the kids getting hurt," she reminded him.

"Sorry, Heather. It's going to take quite a bit of convincing for me to like that guy," Noah said, his gaze locked on the back of Jake's head.

Well, the two men could agree to disagree. It wasn't her problem. She wouldn't be in town much longer anyway, she hoped. "I'll go get your drinks," she said, going back behind the bar.

Opening the beer for Noah and mixing Lindsay's drink a moment later, she said, "Hey, I was just talking to Noah…"

Jake groaned, casting a glance over his shoulder toward their table.

Okay, so the feelings were mutual between the two men.

"And I was thinking maybe you should try easing up a little on the surveillance around the community center."

He laughed. "Has everyone in town voted you the person to 'deal' with me…talk me down a bit?"

She was starting to think so herself. "I'm just saying those kids are not that bad. Noah's on them like white on rice—you can ease up a little. Maybe even offer to help out at the center or something." Putting in a few hours with at-risk kids would be a better way to get involved in the community, instead of making enemies out of everyone.

"I don't think so. And trust me, this cute, quaint little town may not be as safe as everyone wants to believe. False sense of security is common in places like this, where you all feel as though you know one another. But just because nothing bad has ever happened here, doesn't mean nothing ever will." He reached for his coat and tossed several bills onto the bar.

Retrieving his ID, she handed it to him.

"Nighty-night, Talks-a-lot," he said with a wink as he headed toward the door.

"JAKE—PERFECT TIMING," Sheriff Bishop said as he entered the station the next morning.

Crap. That sentence was never followed by something good. "What's up?" he asked, removing his jacket and draping it over the back of his chair before wiping the snow from his dark hair.

"We just got a call from Darlene Dawson. She's in charge of town events…and she said they still need several more floats for the Christmas parade."

"Okay…"

"So we've decided to enter one this year," he said.

Why did he get the feeling that he would somehow get roped into helping? He sighed. "I still can't believe a town this small even has a parade," he mumbled, pouring a cup of weak coffee.

"It's for the kids," Sheriff Bishop said. "My daughter and her sons live in Nashville now, but they'll be home soon for the holidays, and I know my grandsons would just love to ride on the float."

Fantastic. Jacob still didn't know what any of it had to do with him. If he had his way, he would sleep away the holiday. He'd all but given up on the idea that he could be back in the city by Christmas, so he'd accepted the fact that it would be another lonely one for him.

"Anyway, I just thought you might want to take on the project."

What on earth would give the older man that idea? His holly, jolly demeanor? He shook his head. "No, thanks."

"Jake, I know you're hoping to get back…home…someday," he said, lowering his voice. "But you're here now—why not try to make the best of the situation, get involved with the community, get to know people better? You might actually like it here."

Doubtful. "Sorry, Sheriff Bishop—Christmas just isn't my favorite time of year, and I'd rather leave float-building and other holiday events to the people who enjoy them." They couldn't force him to participate, after all.

Sheriff Bishop frowned but then nodded. "Okay, I understand."

It didn't sound as if he did, but Jacob wasn't about to explain that he'd spent the past two Christmases alone in a dingy hotel room, and that the one before that he'd put his own father in jail. Prior to the Lorenzo case, he'd been investigating corporate fraud cases, and his father's company had been found guilty on several counts. Nope, this time of year wasn't exactly a good one for him.

"Well, I'll need you to stick around for a while this afternoon," Sheriff Bishop was saying. "I need to drive to Newark to pick up the flatbed trailer for the float."

Jacob's ears perked. "Newark?"

Sheriff Bishop nodded, printing off the information for the rental place.

He cleared his throat. "You know, I could go pick it up for you." The perfect opportunity to sneak off to Newark to meet Emilio at the dock without anyone questioning him.

He frowned. "But you just said you weren't interested."

Jacob sighed. Like it or not, he'd just agreed to help with the float. He shrugged. "It's for the kids, right?"

Sheriff Bishop grinned, handing him the printout and his truck keys. "Tell Ted at Xtra Lease to send the invoice to the station."

"He'll be okay with that? He'll know who I am?" he asked, reaching for his jacket. He wasn't thrilled about taking care of the rental, but he was eager to check in with Emilio. Make sure the man hadn't changed his mind about helping him.

"I told him to expect you," Sheriff Bishop said with a grin.

Of course he had.

WITH THE TRAILER attached to Sheriff Bishop's Ford F-350, Jacob drove to the Port Newark Container Terminal. Emilio worked as a container inspector, and the inside man had allowed more than ten containers of illegal drugs and contraband to pass through clearance in the two years that Jacob had been undercover. When the man had announced that he wanted to get out of the cartel business, his life had been in jeopardy, but Jacob had offered him another solution. Working for the good team, Emilio had agreed to let him know when the next shipment was arriving in the port. It had been the backup plan in case the original bust had gone wrong—which it had.

Of course, no one knew about plan B except the two men.

Turning onto the yard, Jacob parked the truck near the empty container stacks in the storage facility and jumped down. He raised the collar of his coat to shield his face against the blowing snow and made his way toward Emilio's office at the far end of the yard.

An eerie sense of déjà vu made him shiver as he recalled the last time he'd visited the man here. Gun loaded, his mind racing and his heart thundering, he'd been there to "take care" of the older man. With one of Lorenzo's goons at his side, he'd had no idea how he was going to get out of shooting the man without blowing his cover. Luckily, the other young man had had an even weaker stomach for murder, and he'd disappeared behind the containers, puking long enough for Jacob to make his pitch to Emilio, fire off his weapon and meet the guy as he was returning—looking more than a little relieved that Jacob had "taken care of things" without him.

Knocking on the office door, he scanned the area. Containers were being unloaded at the port terminal, and the place was full of people. He'd never been here during the day before, and he hoped no one questioned his presence. Though his sheriff's badge in his pocket gave him a much stronger sense of peace than the illegal gun he'd carried the last time he was there.

Emilio opened the door. "Can I help you?" he asked, his frown indicating that he didn't recognize the forty-pound-lighter, clean-shaven cop.

"Emilio, it's me," he said, lowering the collar. "Jake."

Still, the man hesitated, holding the door open just a fraction. "Jake who?"

Jacob held out his hand to reveal the knife-wound scar he'd suffered from the guy before he'd had a chance to explain that he was undercover and was trying to save his life. "The man you stabbed."

Emilio's eyes widened. "Jake?" He opened the door wider and ushered him inside. "You look so different."

"More handsome, I hope," he said, shaking the man's hand.

"Well, you're no Channing Tatum," Emilio said. "You're also not supposed to be here." He lowered his voice. "I heard your cover was blown, and the bust was…a bust."

Jacob nodded. He really shouldn't be there, but not hearing anything from the man was starting to make him feel nervous. He was placing his fate in the hands of a guy who'd been playing for the other side for a long time, and with Jacob gone, he might feel as if his only choice was to shift his loyalty back to the cartel. Being there was an opportunity to feel the guy out and reassure him that he was still on the case. "I just wanted to stop in and see if there was any word on the baby?" he asked loudly, glancing around the office trailer and taking inventory of the security cameras. Everything at the docks was monitored.

Emilio looked nervous as he caught the

code word. "Nothing yet. In fact, it's about a week overdue."

Jacob smiled, patting the man on the back. To anyone watching, he was just an old friend stopping by for a visit. One who expertly turned his face away from all camera angles. "Well, they always come when they're ready. Be sure to let me know as soon as he or she arrives," he said.

"Jake, are you sure about this?" Emilio sat behind his desk, and Jacob could see his hands shaking.

Reaching casually for the volume button on the stereo, the sound of "Jingle Bell Rock" drowning out his words, he leaned closer as he said, "Yes. I'm sure. And this is your way out once and for all, Emilio. Call the number I gave you immediately as soon as you know anything."

"He's coming here himself," the man mumbled.

Jacob forced his voice to sound worry-free as he said, "I know. And that's why I need to be here, too." As soon as he could arrest the man in action, accepting his cargo, the faster Emilio could be free of his involvement, the court case could be over, and his sister and nephew could go home...*he* could go home.

The man swallowed hard. "Okay."

Jacob touched his shoulder. "Emilio, we both need this." This shot at redemption was the only way either of them could move on with their lives.

"I know, Jake. I won't let you down."

He nodded. Unfortunately, it wasn't Emilio he was worried about.

# CHAPTER FOUR

"THE STATION DECIDED to enter a float after all?" Heather asked as Jacob entered the Millers' barn the next day. The old stalls had been transformed into a place where they could work privately on their floats and store them until the parade.

Heather was wearing yoga pants and a sweatshirt, with her dark hair pulled back, and he almost didn't recognize her as the same woman who tended bar every evening at the pool hall. This look was better, he decided. Though admittedly, he liked every look she had. There was just something about her that attracted him—her smart mouth, maybe.

For more reasons than one, he shook the thought away and cleared his throat. "Apparently they needed several more, so Sheriff Bishop signed us up."

She looked around him and frowned. "Where's the rest of your team?"

"Just me," he said, feeling slightly embarrassed that he'd been deemed so unlikable by the folks in Brookhollow that he couldn't even enlist the help of three people with his float.

Some of the guys at the fire hall had excuses for not wanting to help: Noah was already working on the community center's float for his Turnaround program, and Ethan was helping Bailey with the garage's float. Other guys just refused to acknowledge the email he'd sent out.

And Sheriff Bishop had simply tapped him on the shoulder and wished him luck, claiming one of them needed to be around the station in case of emergency.

Jacob was on his own, but it was worth it for the chance to check in with Emilio the day before. Besides, he'd throw a few things onto the trailer—a tree, an inflatable snowman and a cut-out Santa, maybe—and call it a day. It wasn't as if he actually cared about winning the competition. And he knew as long as Sheriff Bishop's nephews had something to ride on, the older man would be happy.

"The parade is in three weeks," Heather said. "Most of us have been working on our floats for over a week now." She glanced inside his stall and pointed to the empty flat-bed he'd rented. "You've got a lot of catching up to do."

"Yes, I know. So, I better get started," he said, moving around her and entering the stall where he'd placed all of his supplies the evening before. He still didn't have a truck to pull the float in the parade yet, but he'd figure that out later. Or, with any luck, it would be someone else's problem.

Heather followed him. "What's your theme?"

Theme? As if. "Thought everyone had to keep their ideas hush-hush?" He stood tall, widening his chest and shoulders to prevent her from seeing beyond him. Without her crazy heels, she was only five-four, maybe five-five. Still as high energy as ever, though.

"We don't have to," she said with a shrug, curiosity shining in her eyes.

"Ah, but *you* chose to," he said, winking at her. "Bye, Heather." He entered his section and closed the door on her pout.

WITH VICTORIA'S MOTHER babysitting Harper and answering phones at the B and B, Heather and Victoria headed out early the next morning. Mike Ainsley had confirmed receipt of her résumé when she'd resent it to him, and within an hour, he'd requested an interview with her the following day, so the two women had decided to go interview-clothes shopping.

"Thanks for coming with me," Heather said, as Victoria turned her truck onto Main Street, biting the curb. Heather bounced in the seat and laughed to herself. Her friend was the worst driver she knew.

Victoria didn't seem to notice that she'd narrowly missed hitting the mailbox on the corner. "Of course. This is exciting. I'm happy for you," she said, but her voice sounded forcibly chipper.

"I'm really sorry I'm leaving, Vic."

"It's totally fine. I knew you weren't planning to stay forever."

Even so, Heather couldn't help but feel guilty. Victoria had lost her best friend and business partner in an accident five months before…and now Heather, too, was leaving. Her friend had been there for her when she'd lost so much, and abandoning her now made her stomach knot. "If you need me to stay longer…" *Please, please, don't say you need me to stay longer.*

"No. You're taking this opportunity—you

deserve it. We really need to start thinking about a more permanent situation at the inn anyway." She paused. "Who knows? Maybe I'll go with you," she said, teasing, but there was definite longing in her voice.

"You love your life here, don't you?" Her friend had married her high school sweetheart, she was running a successful business, and now she was a mother to a beautiful baby girl. If she wasn't happy with her choices, she was a terrific actress.

"Yes! Of course…it's just some days, I miss it. I miss the city and the career…and feeling as though I was more than just mom and wife, you know?"

Actually, she didn't, so she just nodded. Like her career-minded parents in the early days of their marriage, she'd never really felt a longing to have a family. She wondered if, like them, she'd have that urge someday. She wasn't sure she would, and at thirty-five, her time to make the decision was growing short. Right now, she wanted to focus on putting the part of her life she knew she wanted back on track.

Main Street was anything but its usual calm as they approached. She frowned as Victoria parked, taking up two spaces outside Lily

Duke's clothing store. Daisies and Dukes was partitioned off with yellow police tape, and both sheriff cars were parked on the street in front of the building. The large storefront window was shattered, and the holiday display was destroyed.

"What on earth?" Victoria asked as she shut off the truck.

The two women climbed out and headed for the entrance.

"Sorry, ladies, this is a crime scene. We're not allowing anyone inside," Jake said, blocking their entrance to the store. Hands at his hips, a serious scowl on his handsome features, he looked…different. A good different.

Fantastic, her attraction to authority figures was turning her insides to mush. *This is* Jake, *not a hot police officer*, she reminded herself.

Well, actually…

She glanced around him. Lily was inside, her head in her hands, sitting at the counter. Lindsay and Noah were there with her. "They're inside." She pointed to the group.

"Yeah, they were here before us," he mumbled.

"Well, pretend we were, too," she said. She grabbed Victoria's arm and moved past him.

"Hi, guys," Lily said, glancing up as they entered, ignoring Jake's protests.

Sheriff Bishop waved as he assessed the damage in the window. "Good morning, ladies."

"What happened?" Victoria asked.

"Looks like someone threw a brick or something through the window last night. When I arrived this morning, it looked like this." Lily bit her lip and stared at the mess of her window display.

"If there'd been an alarm…" Jake said behind them.

"Shh," Heather told him. Lily was upset enough. No point making her feel worse.

"Just saying," Jake said, but he stopped his spiel.

"Was anything stolen?" Victoria asked.

"Not that we can tell," Lindsay said. "Noah said even the back safe wasn't tampered with."

"Well, that's a relief." Heather glanced around the store. All of the display racks were neatly arranged, and nothing seemed out of place except the glass in the front of the store. Looked like a case of minor vandalism. Brookhollow had had a graffiti problem for a few months before Jake arrived and scared all the teens stupid. This appeared to be a similar issue.

But Lily shook her head. "Not really. That means this was probably a warning." Her hands were shaking, and her voice was unsteady. She was terrified.

"Why would you think that? Were any other buildings hit?" Heather couldn't imagine why anyone would warn Lily about anything. She was one of the sweetest, nicest women she'd ever met.

Lindsay pulled them aside. "She's freaked-out because her ex-husband was released from jail in Newark yesterday," she whispered, casting a quick glance toward their friend.

Well, that explained why Lily was so distraught. She'd fled her abusive ex almost two years ago. "That's awful."

Victoria's eyes were wide. "There's no way he could know where she is, though, right?"

Lindsay shrugged. "We hope not."

Heather sighed, but then her gaze landed on Jake, and she narrowed her eyes. She marched over to him. "Did you do this?" she hissed.

"Are you insane? I'm a cop," he said.

"Yeah. One with something to prove."

"Excuse me?"

"You want us all to start taking security seriously…"

"Do you hear yourself?" he asked, crossing his arms across his chest.

For the first time, she noticed he wore a bulletproof vest over his jacket. "Expecting a shoot-out?" She raised an eyebrow, but again the sight of him in uniform was…uncomfortably intriguing.

He opened his mouth to answer, but a woman's voice in the doorway caught everyone's attention.

"Hello…"

"I'm sorry, we're closed this morning," Lily said.

"Did you not see police tape outside?" Jake asked. "Seriously—everyone out!" he barked. Clearly he was at the end of his rope with everyone disregarding his authority.

Lindsay and Noah started to protest, but Lily nodded. "It's okay, guys. I'm good. Listen to Sheriff Matthews."

"Um…sorry, we didn't mean to cross the tape, but my son has something to say," the woman in the doorway said, nudging a boy in a hoodie and baseball cap into the store.

The kid looked to be about fourteen; his head

was down and his shoulders were slumped forward. "I wanted to apologize. I broke your window last night," he told Lily.

"You did?" Relief, not anger, was evident in her voice.

"Yeah. It was an accident. A couple of guys and I were having a snowball fight after we left the diner…"

"A snowball did this?" Sheriff Bishop asked from inside the window display, where he was sweeping broken glass into a dustpan.

"Okay, it was more like an ice-ball fight," the kid said. Then, turning back to Lily, he added, "I'm really sorry. I'll pay to replace your window." He didn't sound happy about the offer.

Lily moved forward and hugged the kid.

He looked both surprised and embarrassed as he struggled to break free.

Lily smiled as she released him. "That's okay. Thank you for coming and telling me."

"So, I don't have to pay for the window?"

"No."

"Yes, you do," his mother interrupted sternly. "It will come out of your allowance."

"Yes, ma'am." The kid stuck his hands into the pocket of his sweatshirt.

"Sorry again, Lily. My husband will stop by later today with the money," the woman said, leading her son out of the store.

"Okay, thank you," Lily said, and a collective sigh of relief ran through the group. "Just a few reckless kids. I feel silly now for being so worried."

Heather felt Jake's breath against the back of her neck. "I'll take that apology now."

She scoffed. "No way. I'm still not convinced you didn't have something to do with it," she said, moving along the racks of clothing on the wall behind them. She picked up a charcoal suit jacket and pretended to study it, painfully aware of his shocked expression at her back.

"You're kidding, right? The kid confessed." He followed her. He took the charcoal jacket and handed her a light gray one instead. "Better."

She hid her surprise at the gesture and continued her drilling. "Well, you did leave the bar early last night…so you have no alibi. And after what you said about Brookhollow not being as safe as everyone thinks it is…" She shrugged, tossing the jacket over her arm. It actually was the better choice.

"That wasn't a threat, it was a caution."

"Well, you need to be careful what you say. People don't know you well—they could assume the worst. I mean, maybe if you actually interacted with people around here, let them get to know you a little bit…"

"Yeah, I'll take that into consideration," he said.

"You could start with the annual tree lighting tonight." It wasn't really her thing, either; it only served as a reminder of the tree lighting in Rockefeller Center that she probably wasn't going to attend again this year. But she'd promised Melody's boys she'd be there.

Jake sighed. "I'm escorting the tree from the Monroe farm to the park this afternoon." He sounded as thrilled about it as a root canal.

"That should be fun. You should act more excited."

"If you think so, why don't you ride along with me?" The words seemed to surprise him as much as her.

She glanced toward the counter. Lily, Victoria, Noah and Lindsay had all stopped talking and were watching the interaction between her and Jake. Heather's cheeks reddened, and she shot them all a look suggesting they resume their own conversation. Which they ignored, waiting for her answer to Jake's request.

So was he.

"Okay, fine. Sure…why not?" It wasn't as if there was any real danger of falling for the guy. She had one foot out of town already. And if she could introduce him to some people, and they started seeing him at local events, they might have an easier time accepting him. She knew what it was like to be the new one in town—and the different one. Maybe she could help Jake get better settled before she high-tailed it back to New York.

"Wow, THIS REALLY is boring," Heather said, staring through the windshield of the sheriff squad car later that day.

Jacob leaned one elbow against the window and rested his head in his hand. They were inching along behind the trailer carrying the thirty-foot evergreen that would be decorated and lit that evening in the town square.

"Told ya," he said. Not for the first time did he regret losing the rock-paper-scissors match to Sheriff Bishop to decide who would do this.

Heather tapped her candy-cane striped fingernails on the dash and then turned to him. "So, where are you from exactly?"

"Manhattan, born and raised."

"Really? Like in the city, not in a suburb somewhere?"

"In the city." He was so much a city boy, in fact, that he'd been born in the taxicab on the way to the hospital. His father was a workaholic, and living in a high-rise apartment in Manhattan made for an easier commute. His mother had stayed at home with him and his sister until her death when he was thirteen, and she'd always hated living in the city—especially when she'd had to deliver a baby in the back of a cab.

"Any siblings?"

"A sister."

"And your parents?"

"Pass."

"You don't want to talk about your parents?"

"You know, I'm not a big backstory kind of guy." His mother's death and his father's imprisonment were things he'd rather not discuss. Few people ever got close enough to hear those tales. "Why don't you talk, since you are so good at it?" he said, glancing at her.

She hit his arm but shrugged. "Sure. Unlike you, I've got nothing to hide. What do you want to know? Ask away."

"Tell me about this job you want so badly in New York," he said, relieved she was more than willing to turn the attention on herself. He really didn't want to lie to people here in Brookhollow, but giving too much of himself and his history away could be dangerous. The media attention on his father's criminal case three years ago had been extensive. He didn't expect the people in this small town to remember the events as vividly as he did, but he couldn't let his guard down. Hiding out this close to the city in the high-profile job of sheriff was already a risk.

Heather kicked her feet free of her heeled leather boots and tucked her legs under her on the seat. "It's an agent position with Highstone Acquisitions."

Highstone Acquisitions. Why did that sound familiar? He vaguely recalled seeing an office building in downtown Manhattan with the letters *H* and *A* on the side; that was probably it. "Acquisitions? Like buying out companies?"

She nodded. "Usually small mom-and-pop shops in locations where the company's cor-

porate clients would like to open a competing store or hotel..." She paused. "I know, it's
not exactly a save-the-world kind of job, like
yours, but the companies are well-compen-
sated and in most circumstances, the owners are ready to retire or sell." Sometimes the
deals were tougher with resistant store owners, but she made peace with her chosen career by knowing that all acquisitions were
done fairly and were usually appreciated by
the communities eventually. And besides—
her parents had started their own acquisitions
company, and they had been good people.

"I'm not judging." He caught her smile out
of the corner of his eye. "That's what you did
before moving here?"

She pointed at him. "Let's get one thing
straight—I didn't *move* here. I'm visiting."

He chuckled. The woman didn't want to
belong to this town any more than he did.
"My mistake. So, business acquisitions is your
background?" he asked again.

She nodded. "Yes. My parents started their
own acquisitions firm years ago, but they sold
the company a few years before they died,
hoping to start enjoying life and the money
they'd put away over the years. Unfortunately,

they'd waited a little too long. Anyway, I'd learned so much about the process from hearing them talk about different mergers and acquisitions over the years that, after graduating college with a business degree, I applied to the firm. It wasn't their company anymore, but it felt like the right thing to do…somehow…" Her voice trailed.

"Well, what made you take a break from it? To *visit* Brookhollow?"

She sighed. "I was fired."

"From a company your own parents started? Tough break."

"It gets worse. The guy who fired me was my boyfriend of three years," she finished.

"Wow, really tough break. Guess you learned your lesson about dating the boss, though, huh?" he teased.

She hit him again. "Hey! It had its perks… while it lasted," she said with a laugh. "Anyway, there's no fear of falling for the boss in this position—he's like eighty years old or something."

"Why Highstone?" he asked, still wondering why he knew the name.

"My brother-in-law works there. When I was with Clarke and Johnston, we sometimes

competed for the same corporate accounts—
made for some interesting family dinners."
She grinned. "Rob told me about the position
and put in a good word for me." She frowned
then, worry flickering across her features, but
he was too lost in his own thoughts to question it.

Rob. Highstone Acquisitions. This was
all sounding too familiar. His eyes widened
slightly. No way, her brother-in-law couldn't
be Rob Ashley, his attorney's husband. That
would mean his attorney, the woman in the
city trying everything she could to speed
up this court case, was Talks-a-lot's sister?
The world really was small—too small. He
gripped the steering wheel tighter. "So, your
brother-in-law is in acquisitions—what does
your sister do?" he asked as casually as possible.

"Cameron's a lawyer," she said.

His heart pounded in his ears. Fantastic.
Just great. His attorney was Heather's sister.
*Take a breath.* Cameron had no idea where he
was. Even if Heather had mentioned to her sister that Brookhollow had a new deputy sheriff, there was no way she would assume it was
him. And why on earth would Heather even

mention it? No, everything was fine. "And Cameron's your only sister?"

"Yeah. My parents started their family later in life. *Really* late in life. Mom was in her early forties and Dad was fifty when Cam was born, four years before me, and she finished raising me after our parents died a year apart eighteen years ago."

"That must have been hard."

"It was challenging for sure. I was finishing high school, and Cam had just enrolled in law school. Money wasn't a problem—our parents left us quite a nest egg and trust fund. The house in Brooklyn was paid off, but things weren't the same without them. Cameron had to take on a lot more than she should ever have had to." She paused. "She never complained."

"You two are close?"

"Really close. That's just another reason I'm dying to get back to the city. Last year I spent the holidays here in Brookhollow with Victoria and Luke, and while it was wonderful, I missed the city." Jacob sensed there was more she wasn't saying, but he wasn't exactly forthcoming with his own life story, so he didn't press her for more than she'd already shared.

"There is definitely something magical

about New York at Christmastime," he said, because it was a standard response. He didn't actually enjoy the festivities in the city. His family had never taken the time to celebrate most things, as his father had worked long hours and traveled a lot, but his mother had insisted they all stop everything on Christmas day to be together. That had changed after her death, but once Kyle was born, he and his sister had put more emphasis on Christmas, especially after their father had gone to jail for embezzlement and Kyle's father had left Amber to raise the boy alone. The three of them were all each other had. But then the past two years he hadn't been able to be with them…

And once again, this year, he had no one and no reason to celebrate.

But next to him, Heather nodded. "For as long as I can remember, on Christmas Eve, our family would go skating at Rockefeller Center and then make a holiday wish on the tree."

"What would you wish for?"

She shrugged. "Anything we wanted. The only rule was that it couldn't be something materialistic."

"Sounds nice."

She nodded. "It was…and I'm looking forward to doing it again this year. I never realized how important traditions were. Last year, it felt like there was something missing, you know?"

He knew exactly what she was talking about. "Yeah, I do."

She eyed him. "That sounded suspiciously like backstory."

"It wasn't. I was just trying to empathize to be polite," he said as he pulled into the park behind the trailer and came to a stop. "Well, there you go. Longest eight-minute ride of your life," he said, turning toward her. He kept the car running and his seat belt on.

She unbuckled hers and faced him as she slid her feet back into her boots. "Aren't you going to stay to help decorate the tree and see the lighting?"

He hadn't planned on it.

And he couldn't tell if she was asking because she wanted him to stay…or if it was simply a question. Not that it should matter, but it kinda did. "I'm not sure…"

She didn't say anything as she zipped her boots.

He really had nowhere else to be. If he went back to his apartment, Mrs. Kelly would only have more work for him. He'd seen her to-do list on her fridge that morning and had also noticed his name next to certain items. He shook his head. "I guess I could stay for a bit." Technically, he was on duty, but technically, *this* was his important assignment today. He shut off the car and reached for his gloves in the backseat, just as she went to grab hers.

Their heads butted, and she jumped back, holding her forehead. "Ow."

He laughed. "Sorry. You stay there. I'll get the gloves."

Instead of handing hers over, he held one open for her.

She hesitated, sending him a funny look as she slid her hand into the soft cashmere, then she held her other hand up for the second. "I'll pretend that wasn't totally awkward," she said with an odd-sounding laugh, as she opened the door.

He touched her arm, stopping her.

She turned back in surprise. "What's wrong?"

"Nothing. I just want to say thank you…for making the effort." He wasn't exactly making it easy for people to get to know him or like him, and she could have continued ignoring him like everyone else.

"No problem…but I'm going to be gone soon, so you'll have to step up and start making an effort on your own if you want people around here to accept you," she said.

And what if he only wanted acceptance from the one person who was leaving soon? Then what?

"MELODY, BRAD, THIS is Sheriff Matthews—Jake." Heather did the introductions beside the Christmas tree trailer moments later, her mind still a little rattled by Jake's gesture with the gloves. What *was* that? For months, the guy had barely spoken to anyone, and now he was warming up? To *her*, of all people? And why did it make her feel kind of flushed? She must be coming down with something.

"Brad and Mel are Nashville's hottest performing duo right now," she told Jake, trying to shake off whatever had happened inside the squad car and focus on her friends. But her gaze lingered slightly too long on Jake's handsome face, the five o'clock shadow at his jawline just a little too tempting.

Clearly, she'd been single too long. That was all.

"I wouldn't go that far," Melody said, shaking Jake's hand. "Great to finally meet you. Sheriff Bishop is my dad, so I've heard a lot about you."

Brad shook his hand next. "Yeah, we've heard you've been creating quite a stir around town."

Melody shot her partner a look. "Don't pay attention to him. Everyone creates a stir around here at one time or another."

"I don't mean to. Just doing my job," Jake said tightly.

Heather bit her lip as Jake stiffened. "Shall we decorate?" she asked, taking his arm and leading the group toward the large crowd gathered in the town square, watching as the work crews hoisted the tree from the bed of the truck and carefully positioned it in its stand. On the side street, the fire truck was ready to lift the mayor to the top so he could place the star, as was the annual tradition.

"Not exactly the Rockefeller Center tree, huh?" Jake whispered.

"Not exactly," she said, feeling embarrassed by her full disclosure in the car. Maybe she needed to take a page from his book and not say everything that popped into her mind.

Getting close to an attractive man weeks before she left wasn't the smartest idea. Especially not when the man in question was so guarded and unwilling to open up about himself. That would be a challenge in the best of circumstances. And not one she was willing to take on.

She'd let her heart dictate her life choices before, and ultimately things hadn't worked in her favor. She was determined not to let men or relationships jeopardize her plans anymore. Her career would be her number one priority. If she found someone while she wasn't looking, then great, but she was thirty-five years old; she had to get serious about her future.

And the man standing next to her couldn't be further from what she envisioned. Most of the men she'd dated were more like her—big city, career-minded. She'd never even considered dating any of the men in Brookhollow. One, she hadn't been ready for another relationship, and two, though they were sweet and nice, they were not her type. Jake was a step closer, but he'd said he was in Brookhollow to stay, and she certainly wasn't. Plus, long-distance relationships had never worked for her in the past. "Welcome, everyone, to the seventy-eighth annual tree lighting," Mayor Parsons said from the bucket at the end of the fire truck's ladder.

Applause erupted as he placed the star on top, then everyone rushed toward the decoration table.

Heather and Jake hung back.

"Every year my sister and nephew and I go to the annual lighting, and then we have hot chocolate and roasted chestnuts from that grumpy vendor who's always there…"

Heather turned to him in surprise. "Bah Humbug Frank!"

Jake's eyes lit up as he laughed. "Bah Humbug Frank?"

"My sister and I gave him that nickname when we were kids." Funny how the grumpy vendor was part of both of their holiday memories.

He nodded. "It's fitting."

She wasn't sure why he'd changed his mind and shared a piece of himself with her, but she decided to push for a little more. "Are you planning on spending Christmas with your family…in the city?"

He hesitated. "Um… I'm not sure yet." He stared at his feet.

Well, *that* offered her no information at all. If anything, it just made her more interested in what could be holding him back.

She shook off the curiosity that would ultimately land her in a position she didn't want to be in. At the decoration table, she picked up several oversize baubles and handed one to Jake. "Well, we're both here now," she whispered. "Let's get decorating."

As HE DROVE along Main Street later that evening, Jacob couldn't get his mind off of Heather. He couldn't believe she was his lawyer's sister. But come to think of it, she was a lot like Cameron. The two women shared many of the same features: the long dark brown hair, the hazel eyes and the same straight nose and high cheekbones. Both beautiful. Both sharp-tongued and quick-witted, with a no-nonsense, go-getter attitude. Both talkative. That could be a problem.

He shook off his apprehension. Cameron wouldn't assume it was him if Heather did mention something about a new sheriff in town…and even if she did, the lawyer knew not to voice any suspicion.

Cameron Ashley had been appointed the attorney on this case for good reason: the woman had the best track record of anyone working in the DA's office. She was focused, driven and understood everything that was at stake in this case. The one and only time he'd met her, she'd had an odd way of reassuring him while giving it to him straight: because of his mess-up, his testimony would be flawed in the eyes of the court. They had their work cut out for them. Or at least she did. All he had to do was sit and wait.

Which wasn't something he could do. He wasn't confident that his testimony would put Lorenzo away, but if he could catch the man in action again—on video—there would be enough evidence to convict him.

Despite discovering the connection between the women that afternoon, he felt comfortable around Heather. There was a sense of familiarity there. Bonding with a fellow New Yorker, that's all it was, he told himself before his thoughts could wander off unchaperoned.

Then why had he pulled that stunt with the gloves?

He stopped at the only streetlight in town, which blinked yellow as a four-way stop at this hour of night, and lingered far too long, reflecting on the afternoon. She'd opened up about herself, about the job in the city and her family, and he'd experienced a connection with her that he was forced to admit went deeper than their shared hometown. She'd looked so cute, rubbing her forehead after their heads had collided, and he'd allowed himself to let his guard down and share a moment with her.

But that was all it could be—one moment. His life was far too complicated to draw someone else into it. Not that he thought she wanted to be drawn in. She was leaving Brookhollow the first chance she got; she'd made that obvious enough.

He wondered if she'd consider staying...at least a little longer?

"Damn, Jacob, what are you doing?" he mumbled, running a hand through his hair and continuing on down the quiet, deserted Main Street. The woman was leaving Brookhollow, and he had to start putting some distance there, otherwise things could get complicated and messy. His life was already far too complicated and messy. If he got involved with Heather, it could compromise this case and put his family's lives at risk. Getting involved with him could potentially put her at risk, too. Keeping people at a distance was easy for him; he just needed to get his head on straight and stop letting this time of year get to him.

As he passed Daisies and Dukes, he noticed that the front window had been replaced and the holiday display was set up again. The broken glass had been cleared from the sidewalk and the police tape removed from the building. He also noticed the interior lights were still on. All of the stores on Main Street closed at six, and it was after eight-thirty.

Lily could be doing inventory or paperwork, he thought, slowing the vehicle in front of her shop. Or she might have just forgotten to turn off the lights. Leaving the vehicle running, he climbed out of the car. His boots left a trail in the freshly fallen snow as he walked toward the front door.

Wrapping his hands around his eyes, he leaned against the glass and peered inside. He didn't see her in there. Maybe she was in the back. He tried the door, but it was locked.

Good. Smart. People were finally listening. He knocked on the door and waited.

The cold wind howled, and a gust of snow blew across his feet. Since the sun had set, the weather had changed. A damp chill in the air now penetrated his jacket and made him shiver. He raised his collar up around his neck and shoved his bare hands into his pockets as he waited.

And waited.

A long moment later, he raised a hand to knock again, and this time he saw movement in the back office area. Didn't look like Lily... too big. A man?

He'd seen her around town a few times with Ben Walker, but he was taller than the person Jacob glimpsed now. Thirteen years as a cop had trained him to gather details about a possible perpetrator in an instant. His heart beat a little faster as adrenaline began pumping through him.

It was almost a relief to be feeling this way again. His instincts and reflexes hadn't been put to the test for months. The last time he'd been in a situation like this, he'd blacked out before he could react.

He knocked again. "This is Sheriff Matthews. Open up, please!" Maybe overkill if it turned out to be nothing, but better to be prepared. People around here thought he was overzealous anyway.

The light went off in the back room, but no one came to the front of the store. He narrowed his eyes to peer inside again. What was going on in there? He banged on the door, louder, harder. Nothing. Someone was in there, and they were obviously ignoring him.

He hit the button on his radio. "Sheriff Bishop, come in."

A second later, the sheriff's reply came through the static. "Yes, Jake?"

"I'm at 26 Main Street," he said, checking the number on the outside of the building.

"Lily's store, yes. What's the problem?"

"The interior lights are on, and I've seen movement inside—believed to be male, about six foot three, no more description currently…"

"Maybe she's working late."

"I haven't gotten a visual on Lily, just the male suspect."

"Suspect?" He sounded slightly annoyed. "Maybe a boyfriend?"

"Not able to confirm the identity of the

male inside," Jacob said, scanning the store again. The light in the back room was still off, and he couldn't detect any movement. "I'm going around back. Requesting backup."

"Jake, I'm in bed. I'm sure it's nothing… again," the older man said with a yawn.

That was the response to requesting backup? "Sir, I really think we should check this out," he said as he made his way toward the alley between the buildings.

It was darker back there, and he wished he'd brought his flashlight from the vehicle.

The older man sighed. "Fine. Be there in ten. Over."

*Ten?* The man lived a block away. Even in the city, backup would be there in less than that. "Okay. Over." As he rounded the back of the stores, he counted the unmarked doors. Twenty-four, twenty-five… Lily's was the third one in. The door was slightly ajar.

He contemplated waiting for Sheriff Bishop, but ten minutes was too long to just stand out there waiting. Besides, if the woman was in trouble, a lot could take place in that time. A shiver ran through him. He'd seen far too often what could happen in ten minutes. Cautiously moving closer to the door, his hand on the weapon at his hip, he surveyed the area.

There was no one around. No one. Not even a stray cat. In Brooklyn, even a back alley would be alive at eight-thirty at night—drug deals going down or people Dumpster diving. Never empty, never so eerily quiet. He couldn't decide which was worse.

Placing a hand inside the door, he slowly opened it and glanced inside. A long dark hallway led to the office. Several garbage bags sat near the door, and broken-down cardboard boxes were propped up against the wall.

Maybe Sheriff Bishop was right, and Lily was just working late and hadn't heard him… and now he was probably going to frighten her. He listened for a second and heard what sounded like crying.

He couldn't wait for backup. He entered the building, and keeping his right shoulder to the wall, he walked quietly, slowly toward the office. As he drew closer, he could make out muffled voices. A man and a woman's… he couldn't pick out the words, but the man's were angry…and the woman's were fearful. His blood ran cold.

He touched the button on the radio. "Sheriff Bishop, your ETA?" he whispered.

"Five minutes. What's happening, Jake?" the other man asked loudly. Jake winced, as the voices in the room quieted.

They'd heard him.

Turning down the volume on the radio, he moved to the other side of the door and took a deep breath as he reached for his weapon. Backup was still too far away; this was all on him. "I believe we have a situation. Unidentified male and female inside the office," he said quietly into the radio. "Going in. Over."

As he reached for the door handle, he heard another door opening. The one leading into the front of the store. Then Lily's scream.

He turned the handle, but it was locked. He took off in a sprint toward the back door, tripping over the boxes as they slid onto the floor. He righted himself and ran into the alley, heading for the street.

"Help!" Lily yelled. Her voice echoed, and the sound made him run even faster. Adrenaline soared through him, and for the first time in months, he recognized himself: he had a purpose, he had a real situation, he had to do what he was trained to do.

As he rounded the corner, he saw the stranger dragging Lily down Main Street.

"Hey! Stop! Police!" he called, but the guy broke into a run, stopping only long enough to toss a struggling Lily effortlessly over his shoulder.

A better look revealed the guy had to be closer to six foot five, and he was big...really big.

Lily kicked and beat her fists against his back, but the man kept moving.

Jacob struggled to catch up. What was the guy going to do? *Carry* her out of town? He didn't see a vehicle parked anywhere. But then he heard the beep-beep of a car unlocking in the next alley, two blocks away, and he quickened his pace. If they made it to the car, his chances of rescuing Lily would be a lot worse. He could lose them by the time he made it back to his squad car. And he couldn't count on Sheriff Bishop to appear in time.

Closing the gap by a few feet, Jacob saw Lily's face—her expression both terrified and relieved to see him. Her right eye was swollen, and her lip was bleeding. "Sheriff Matthews..." Her voice sounded so far away, even though she was almost within arm's reach.

The man picked up speed as he neared the last corner.

Damn. It had to be the ex-husband, the ex-con. A man who'd spent three years in jail for domestic abuse. A man who'd reportedly beaten his wife to an inch of her life before she'd been able to escape and flee to the safety of Brookhollow's medical clinic.

Jacob reached for his gun for the first time in almost a year, his heart racing. Lily, wiggling and flailing, blocked a clear shot, one he would normally feel comfortable taking, but if he didn't fire at the man, this could be a missing person case in a matter of minutes...

Jacob stopped running and took aim at the guy's left shoulder. The red dot appeared on the back of the man's jacket, but Jacob hesitated. If he shot and the guy dropped Lily, she could get knocked out by the ice on the cold ground below. She'd be falling headfirst from about six feet. He lowered his aim to the guy's left leg instead and fired.

The man's leg gave way, but he continued running, though slower now.

The man was a machine. Jacob picked up the pace again, careful on the slippery ground. How many times had he asked these store owners to clear the walks? He closed the distance between them and grabbed the man's shoulder. "Stop, you're under..."

The unexpected blow to his jaw staggered him, and he blinked, struggling to refocus as his grip tightened on the perp, and he pointed the gun. "Put her down," he said, feeling a trickle of blood near his lip. He tasted copper in his mouth, but he held steady, his gun pointed at the man's head.

"Sheriff, you're way out of your league here," the man snarled, still holding Lily's legs tightly as he flicked a blade in his other hand.

Fantastic. Jacob would prefer bullet wounds to stab wounds any day. "Drop the knife and put her down. You just got out of prison— stabbing a cop and attempted abduction will definitely break your parole conditions," he said.

"And shooting me will result in a guilty conscience for a man who's probably never drawn his weapon before now."

That might be true if he was just a small-town sheriff. "Last chance to drop the knife and put the woman down." Blood stained the front of the man's jeans and dripped to the snow on the ground.

"Please, just let me go, Carl," Lily pleaded.

The sound of her voice seemed to spur Carl to action, and he lashed out with the knife.

Jacob shot him in the arm, and the knife fell to the ground.

So did Lily.

Jacob kicked the knife away, out of reach, and lunged toward the man, but before he could reach him, Carl collapsed.

Unconscious.

Gun still pointed on him, Jacob approached cautiously. The man lay still, eyes closed, as Lily scrambled to her feet on the slippery sidewalk outside of Joey's diner. "What happened?" Jacob asked, reaching for her and pushing her behind him.

"An i-i-icicle," Lily said tearfully. She was shaking violently.

He quickly removed his jacket and wrapped it around her, noticing the broken four-inch-wide icicle lying on the sidewalk next to the guy's head. A pool of blood was collecting beneath him. Unbelievable. "I told everyone those things were dangerous," he muttered, for once relieved that no one had listened.

"HE WAS GOING to kill me," Lily told Lindsay at the medical clinic twenty minutes later. She was still shivering, despite the heated blanket and Lindsay's comforting arm around her shoulders.

"You're okay now. Just try to relax. Dr. McCarthy will be in in a minute to give you something," Lindsay said, rubbing Lily's arms.

Jake stood in the doorway of the hospital room, growing more and more uncomfortable with each look of gratitude and admiration he received from the two women and just about everyone passing by in the hallway. He'd done his job; that was all. And he wished he were the one driving Carl Phillips back to the Newark detention center, instead of Sheriff Bishop.

Besides the fact that Sheriff Bishop would hardly be a match for Phillips—six-foot-five and all muscle—dealing with victims was something Jacob rarely did. His "bedside manner" in that department was lacking. Once a victim was safe, a situation secured, he was on to the next one. But Lily had refused to let go of him until Lindsay and several other nurses had peeled her away and settled her in the examination room. And even then, she'd insisted he come with her. She was scared and disoriented. He understood that. So he stood where he was, uncomfortable with providing comfort.

Hurried footsteps sounded in the hall, and a second later, Ben and Noah appeared. Noah hung back with Jacob, but Ben rushed forward to Lily.

Instinctively, she pulled away, moving closer to Lindsay.

Ben's expression was one of hurt and concern as he carefully knelt in front of her. "Lily…"

The woman shook her head and buried her face into Lindsay's chest.

"She's still really shaken and a little disoriented," Lindsay told Ben. "Give her a few minutes."

Ben's shoulders slumped as he stood and put his hands in his pockets. "I should have been there with you. I'm so sorry, Lily."

Lily continued to shake, avoiding everyone's gaze but Jacob's.

Great. Survivor attachment. He'd stayed long enough. She was surrounded by caring, supportive people. She would be okay. Now, he had to shift the focus and shift back into his police officer role. Going into the room, he touched her shoulder and felt her flinch slightly. On purpose, he left a hand there, making her just slightly uncomfortable with him. "I'm going to need a full statement in the morning, okay?"

She nodded.

"You're safe now. Lindsay and the doctors will take good care of you, and Ben's here."

The man beside him visibly relaxed.

"I'll see you tomorrow," Jacob said, turning to leave.

"Sheriff Matthews," Lily said weakly.

He stopped. "Yeah?"

"Thank you."

He touched her shoulder again and left the room.

The look in Lily's eyes had reminded him why he'd transferred from a patrol position to being an undercover agent. Rescuing people from immediate danger meant that the victim and their family would often offer praise and admiration—sometimes sending cards or gifts to the station—and while most of his coworkers relished the heroic spotlight, Jacob felt uncomfortable with it.

Doing the right thing, according to the rules of the law, always had another side that no one thought about. Every time he put someone in jail, the victim was relieved, but what about the perpetrator's family—the innocent children or the spouses who got left behind, the mothers who loved their children regardless of the fact that they went down the wrong path in life. Those people suffered. His own family had suffered when he'd had to put his father in jail. Doing the right thing then had come at a cost.

When the department had revealed their offer to assist the FBI in their investigation into the corporate fraud claims against Wallace & Johns, where his father had been a stockbroker for thirty years, his first instinct had been to walk out of the briefing room and request not to be put on the case. But the badge on his shoulder reminded him that he didn't get to choose who he put away for crimes and who he let walk.

So instead, he'd volunteered to solicit a confession from his father, and several bourbons and ill-placed trust on his father's part later, Jacob had read his dad his rights. The look on his father's face was one that would forever be etched in his mind as he'd remained silent as instructed, knowing he'd already said too much.

After the sentencing, his sister had slapped him, accused him of tearing apart the family and hadn't spoken to him for almost three months.

The department had promoted him and congratulated him on a job well done.

He'd found himself caught between pride for having done his job and a sickening self-loathing for having deceived his father and causing his family pain.

Going undercover in the narcotics division had eliminated the issue. Posing as a member of a drug cartel, he hadn't been expected to take care of anyone, and he hadn't been responsible for individual civilian lives. No one ever praised him for being a hero, and yet he knew he was doing more good by helping to take out one of the biggest drug operations in the city than he'd ever done as a patrol cop.

Cops were trained to think of the greater good over individual lives, and it was much easier to do that as an undercover agent.

If he never saw a look like Lily's again, it would be too soon.

"HAVE YOU BEEN home yet?" Sheriff Bishop asked as he entered the office hours later. It was just after three in the morning, but Jacob was still wired. Decompressing after an incident often took him days, and tonight was no different. If he went back to his apartment and tried to sleep, he'd just spend the night tossing and turning and going over the event in his mind. What if he'd gone around the back sooner—could he have saved Lily from the injuries? What if the icicle hadn't fallen— would he have been able to stop her from being abducted without wounding the man? This self-evaluation happened after every call, and then the what-if scenarios started to play themselves out. It was something his superiors were always telling him he had to let go of. Once he'd caught the perpetrator and secured the scene, he'd done his job and should be able to rest easy. Instead, his mind always wandered to what could have happened.

And tonight was worse than most.

This attack was probably the most dangerous thing to happen in this small town in years. The people here didn't worry about incidents like this on a regular basis. Lily had felt safe being in her shop at night alone. Everyone here felt safe. And despite his preaching that they shouldn't adopt a false sense of security, he hoped that this evening's event wouldn't make them all paranoid. Careful, yes. Scared, no.

"I thought I'd get started on the paperwork," he said rubbing his eyes.

Sheriff Bishop retrieved his coffee cup, a mug that read *World's Greatest Grandp*, the *a* obviously having worn off from so many years of use, and filled it with the tar-like liquid from the coffeemaker. He sat down across from Jacob, taking a sip, then placed the cup aside. "I'm sorry I doubted you tonight."

"A small town where nothing ever happens... I get it," Jacob said, but he was annoyed that the situation had been dismissed. He would much rather be sitting here apologizing once again for his overzealous actions than dealing with what could have been this evening's outcome—a manhunt and missing person case...or worse.

"Still. It was wrong. It was against protocol. I don't know what I was thinking really." The man toyed with the rim of his coffee cup. "I'm getting too old for this."

"Nah." Not too old, just complacent in a town where nothing ever happened.

"Yes, I am. If that had been me there tonight, I couldn't have done what you did—chasing him down." He rubbed his stomach. "Look at me. I get winded walking to the vending machine. Can't remember the last time I worked out." He shook his head.

"The icicle got him, not me," Jacob reminded the sheriff, though he'd been fully prepared to shoot again. He doubted the older man would have even fired once.

"But I don't have your instincts anymore. I mean, if I'd been the one driving down Main Street and saw Lily's lights on, I'd have kept driving." He shrugged. "We need new blood around here, someone who's in great shape, still has that edge…and we need them here permanently," he said pointedly.

*Ah.* Jacob stood and reached for his coat, his adrenaline subsiding and weariness setting in. "I see where you're going with this, and I'll stop you right there. I appreciate your confidence…" Not that the sheriff had shown it earlier. "But I never signed on for the long run out here. As soon as I'm cleared to return to the city and my job, I'm on the next plane out of Newark." He hoped the older man understood his position on that.

Sheriff Bishop rose to squeeze his shoulder

as Jacob headed for the door. "Okay, enough said. Good night, son."

Jacob paused and turned back. "By the way, any word on that?" Suddenly he worried that the man with the knowledge concerning his fate might neglect to tell him something...or at least delay the message. This wasn't the first time in four months that the sheriff had hinted about him sticking around. If the courts could bring Lorenzo into custody before the container shipment bust, that would be ideal.

"No." The sheriff stuck his head into the mail room and retrieved a small green envelope. "But you did get more mail."

Again, it was Kyle's handwriting on the front of the envelope. The address was torn off as usual. But this time it wasn't opened. "You haven't read it?"

"I trust you," he said, placing a hand on his shoulder.

Jacob shook his head and handed it back. "I trust protocol. Please, read it."

# CHAPTER FIVE

JACOB WAS STARVING and tired—having been up all night replaying the events in his mind—but mostly starving. As he parked outside Joey's the next morning, he shot a quick look toward Lily's shop. Daisies and Dukes was still dark, and the sign on the door read Closed. He hoped by week's end, business would resume. The best thing for Lily would be to get back into her normal routine as quickly as possible.

He got out of the car and went into the diner, his monitor beeping to indicate his blood sugar was dropping.

Loud applause erupted all around him in the crowded restaurant. Word traveled fast around here. Taking in the smiling, admiring faces, his appetite faded. He could not deal with this this morning.

As Tina came forward, grinning at him for the first time since he'd moved to town, he held up a hand to her open arms. "Sorry, I'm not staying..." he muttered, backing out the diner door.

"Wait..."

The door closed on her protest, and he jogged across the street to Ginger Snaps. Coffee and a muffin would be breakfast today. Unless there was a crowd waiting for him inside the bakery, as well...then he was just going to starve to death.

A bell chimed as he entered, and he was relieved to see the place was empty, except for a man in the corner talking on his cell phone.

"Hi, Sheriff Matthews," Ginger greeted him wryly.

Good. At least someone was treating him normally. "Hey, Ginger, can I get a coffee and muffin to go..." He scanned the choices in the display case.

"What's wrong? The adoring crowd at Joey's too much?" she asked.

So, she'd heard. And she knew about the mob inside the diner. "People around here are crazy," he said.

To his surprise, she laughed. The effect made her look ten years younger. "You're right about that."

Spotting a double chocolate chip muffin,

he pointed to it. "Can I have one…two…of those?"

She frowned. "You sure?"

"Why, are they stale?"

The rest of her smile evaporated. "Young man, I'll have you know, nothing in my display case is ever *stale*." She said it as if it was a bad word.

"Sorry. Yes, I want two…no, three of those." He'd save one for later, in case he couldn't get into Joey's for the rest of the day.

"Are you low?"

He looked at her in surprise, then checked his glucose monitor. He'd barely eaten in twenty-four hours. "I will be if I don't eat. How did you know?"

"Heard your monitor beeping the last time you were in here yelling at me about the walks."

"Wasn't yelling."

"My husband was diabetic, and he had a monitor like yours just before he died." She opened the display case and removed one of the double chocolate muffins. Then, turning to the back display case, she removed two plain chocolate chip muffins. "These are sugar-free," she said.

He made a face. In his experience, sugar-free meant tasteless and chalky. He preferred to just stay away from sugar until he was low and needed something, rather than eat the sugar substitute products. After he was diagnosed, his mother had baked a new sugar-free, diabetic recipe almost every day until her death, and though he'd appreciated her efforts, nothing had tasted as good as the cookies he watched his sister eat, even though she tried to hide them. "Nah, that's okay."

She broke off a piece of one and handed it to him. "Try it."

"No, I don't…"

She leaned over the counter and plopped it into his mouth. The startling gesture almost made him choke on the muffin, but then… *mmm, this was actually good. Delicious even.* "Those are sugar-free?"

Ginger nodded, putting the muffins in a bag. "I told you, my husband was diabetic and he married a woman whose passion was baked goods. Once he was diagnosed, I spent months coming up with new recipes for all of his favorites."

Reaching for his wallet, he swallowed the muffin. "How much?"

"Put your money away," she said.

He shook his head, removing a ten-dollar bill and tossing it onto the counter. "Please, don't start treating me differently. Now that I know these muffins exist, I want to be able to keep coming in here. See ya, Ginger."

FROM THE CORNER booth where she sat with Melody, Brad and their nine-year-old twin boys, Heather watched Jake leave the diner and jog across the street to the bakery.

*Someone* wasn't comfortable being the center of attention, she mused, taking a sip of her coffee.

Across from her, Josh frowned, slapping his homemade "We Love Sheriff Matthews" sign down onto the table. "Well, that sucks. He didn't even notice the sign."

His brother, David—less impressed by Jake's sudden hero status than by his video game—shrugged. "I don't see the big deal. Grandpa saves lives all the time," he mumbled.

Heather hid a grin behind her cup as she met Melody's gaze. David's loyalty to his grandfather was adorable.

"Yeah, that's sorta true…but Sheriff Matthews caught a real-live bad guy, like the ones on TV. I want to be a cop when I grow up," Josh said, stirring his hot chocolate with a candy cane.

Brad frowned. "I thought you wanted to be a guitar player."

Melody shot him a look. "He can be whatever he wants."

Brad kissed her cheek, but then, covering his mouth, he whispered to Heather, "He's going to be a guitar player."

Heather laughed, loving how happy the family seemed together. For too many years, her friend had struggled to raise her boys alone after her husband's death. Melody seemed to be so happy and in love now, and her music career was booming. Heather didn't know anyone who deserved it more. She reached for Josh's sign. "He usually comes into the bar in the evenings after his shift. I can give it to him."

The little boy's face lit up. "Awesome. Thanks, Heather. Hey, do you think you could ask him if I can do a ride-along with him?"

"Grandpa has offered to take you in the squad car a million times." David put his game away as the food arrived.

"I know…" Josh glanced at Heather. "But can you?"

She shook her head, reaching for the ketchup and handing it to the boy, who covered everything he ate in it. "I don't know why everyone assumes we're friends. I don't know him any better than anyone else."

Melody raised an eyebrow. "Really? You two seemed to know one another quite well at the tree-lighting ceremony yesterday."

Heather sighed. Agreeing to ride along with Jake had been a mistake. Opening up to him and catching the briefest glimpse into his life had been a mistake, too. Everyone around town was bound to get the wrong idea about them. "That was nothing…" She glanced across the street through the window and saw him leave the bakery, a muffin in his mouth as he opened the door to the squad car.

He looked her way and smiled when he caught her stare.

No smile should ever have that effect on someone, she thought, feeling her cheeks flush as she averted her eyes quickly.

Across from her, Brad and Melody exchanged looks.

Melody smirked. "Nothing. Right."

"JAKE, THIS IS Cody Kelly. He'll be graduating from the academy in January," Sheriff Bishop said as he entered the station later that day, a tall young man in tow.

Mrs. Kelly's nephew. Jacob had known Cody was arriving today, as his landlady had talked of little else the past week. Luckily, he'd dodged the dinner invite for that evening, but it looked as if he couldn't avoid meeting the man. He stood and extended a hand. "Nice to meet you."

"You, too."

Huh, didn't sound like it.

Sheriff Bishop cleared his throat. "Cody's going to be shadowing you for a few weeks while he's here on break over the holidays."

He *what*? Jacob had not signed on for that. What if Emilio called? Sneaking away to Newark would be a lot harder with the kid around. Jacob looked at the older man. "Why?"

"Well, he needs the field experience…"

Field experience? In Brookhollow? "Are you planning to work here?" A Brookhollow cop and a big city cop's "field training" would be different.

"I was," he said curtly.

Oh. Right. Jacob had essentially taken the

position from the new academy graduate, but in August, Cody had still been in school… and Jacob had been hoping to get out of town sooner. The young man could have the job as soon as Jacob could vacate the position.

Of course, he couldn't tell him that.

He cleared his throat. "Well, there's not exactly much action around here…" The last thing he wanted or needed was to have a partner tagging along with him everywhere he went. "Wouldn't he be better riding along with you?" he asked Sheriff Bishop.

"I requested that already," Cody said, his expression hardening.

"Jake, can we talk for a second? Excuse us for a minute, Cody," Sheriff Bishop said, nodding toward the locker room.

Cody obliged, and the sheriff lowered his voice.

"Listen, I know you're not thrilled about this, but Cody was sort of promised a position here after he graduated. Then you arrived…"

"Hey, I'm not fighting him for this job. It's his as soon as—"

The front door opened, and an obviously pregnant young woman, wearing an oversize winter coat that looked as if it came from her husband's closet, entered the station. Slightly out of breath, she smiled. "Hi, Sheriff Bishop. Cody left without his lunch," she said, holding up a metal lunch tin.

"Hi, Alison. He's just in the locker room. There's no one else in there. Go on in," Sheriff Bishop said.

"Thanks." She shot Jacob a less than pleasant look as she passed.

When she was out of earshot, he said, "I took the position from a guy who's expecting his first child?" This just kept getting better.

"First?" Sheriff Bishop laughed. "Try third."

Jacob blinked. The couple looked to be in their early twenties. He ran a hand through his hair. "Can we afford to pay him while he shadows me?" He said the words through gritted teeth.

"Not a full salary, but we can help him out in the meantime, while we wait…"

That eased his conscience a little. Still, he suspected working with the guy would be a whole lot easier if he was able to reassure him that this was only temporary. "While we wait," he muttered, reaching for his jacket on the back of his chair.

THE SILENCE IN the vehicle was deafening as Jacob and Cody drove the side streets in search of danger.

"Can we turn on the radio or something?" Cody asked.

"I'd love to, man, but it's busted." The old patrol car was from the late eighties, and it was miracle the thing still ran. The manual steering and windows had actually caused Jacob's forearms to ache the first few days he'd driven it that summer.

"Why haven't you taken it into Bailey's Place to see if she can fix it?"

Because he hadn't expected to be driving it long enough to care. But now that the kid mentioned it, it might not be a bad idea. "Well, we can do it now." He turned onto Main Street, and five minutes later, he pulled into the garage parking lot.

Cody was out of the car and in the shop before Jacob could cut the engine and remove his seat belt. At least this awkward working situation was not ideal for either of them. He climbed out and went inside.

"Broken radio? Sure, I can take a look. It could be just a loose connection or something," Bailey was saying. "Hi, Sheriff Matthews."

"Hey, Bailey." Reaching for the coffeepot, he poured the dark substance into a cup and grimaced. "Like it strong?"

She laughed. "A necessity of late nights and early mornings. Cody, you'll remember all about that next month, won't you?"

The young man's face lit up at the mention of the new addition to his family. That was the first time Jacob had seen him smile. "You never quite remember just how sleep deprived you were with the previous kids until you're in the throes of it again, but I don't mind a bit."

"Is Alison on maternity leave yet?"

His face clouded again. "No, not yet… doesn't look like she'll get much time off," he said guiltily, which made Jacob feel ten times worse. "The long shifts on her feet at the grocery store aren't good for her, though…"

The young mother was obviously working to supplement the income her husband hadn't been able to bring in while attending the academy. And now his guaranteed position wasn't so guaranteed anymore.

"Well, I hope you guys are still planning to come for Christmas Eve brunch at our place…

we have a few surprises for all the kids," Bailey said.

"Yeah, I hope so…" He sounded noncommittal. "Anyway, how long should we leave the car?"

"Just give me a few hours. Come back around noon?"

"Sounds good," Cody said.

Bailey glanced at Jacob, and he just nodded. He didn't expect an emergency in the next few hours…or years…

Outside, Jacob turned to Cody. "Okay, so what's the plan?"

"We walk. Don't tell me you've never had to patrol on foot?"

"Okay, we walk," he said.

And they did. In painful silence.

Jacob cleared his throat. "Look, man, I'm sorry about the job. I didn't…" He stopped. Didn't what? How was he supposed to apologize and lie to this kid at the same time? "I'm sorry."

Cody shrugged. "Brookhollow is home for us, but I can't stick around much longer. Alison wants to be near her parents during this pregnancy, but once the baby is born, we may have to move. I haven't told her yet, but I'm considering a position in Boston."

Great. This kid was going to uproot his family and move to a city they didn't want to live in, putting his life on the line every day when he left his home with three children and a wife to consider...and for what? "When would they want you in Boston?"

"In the new year—January 15, right after my graduation ceremony."

That gave him about a month to vacate the position, so Cody could take over. He hated that there was no guarantee he would be out of here by then, but being in this position of authority, close to where the drugs were coming in was important. This kid had no idea how dangerous this job could be or the important reasons Jacob needed to be in Brookhollow. "Don't decide anything too quickly, okay?"

"I'm not sure I have a choice. We've already had to rent out our home, and we're living with Alison's parents." His tone was cold.

"That not working out so well?"

"I take it you've never had to live with in-laws."

"Never been married."

"Do you have kids?"

"Nah." He didn't say that in their line of work, he didn't see where having a family could be anything more than a liability. Not exactly the input a father of three would appreciate.

"But you're here to start settling down?"

That was his story at least, but the lie wouldn't roll off his tongue, so he nodded.

"So, what's it like being a cop in the city?" He looked uneasy; obviously his decision about whether to take the BPD job was weighing on him.

"Different than being a small-town cop, for sure. Every day in the city is different, challenging. It's about being prepared, seeing the potential danger in a situation where other people might not notice anything and never taking chances with your own safety."

"You ever have to shoot someone, other than Carl Phillips the other night?"

He'd lost track of how many people he'd shot. He nodded. "Never killed anyone, though." And he was glad Carl Phillips hadn't been his first.

Cody's eyes widened as if that possibility hadn't even occurred to him. The kid had grown up in a small town, and not even the academy had shaken his roots enough for him to be fully prepared for the life of a big-city cop.

"All I'm saying is, think long and hard about this decision. This life is not suited for—" His words were cut off as Cody hauled them both onto a snowbank just as a truck slid on a patch of black ice and spiraled into the opposite lane, coming within inches of them before it stopped, and Victoria Dawson jumped out in a panic.

"Oh, my God, Sheriff Matthews, Cody— I'm so sorry, that ice came out of nowhere!" she said, helping them to their feet.

Jacob turned to Cody. "There's nothing wrong with your instincts, I'll give you that."

"I'M NEVER GOING to be able to drink all of these," Jake said, sitting on his usual bar stool across from Heather that evening. "You have to stop letting people buy me drinks."

She shot him look. "Yeah, 'cause I'm crazy like that. Are you kidding me? This is the most money the bar has brought in on a Monday night in, I'd say, forever. I'm not turning away money."

"Well, start helping me drink some," he said, pushing a tequila shot her way.

She barely drank, but seeing the occasion called for a celebratory toast to the hero of the hour, she tossed it back. "That's all I'm having."

"Well, if I'm not going to be paying for drinks tonight, can I have my ID back?" he asked.

She removed it from the pile and glanced at it before handing it to him. His birthday was December 7—Friday night. Huh. Interesting. She wondered if anyone else in town knew about it. She doubted it was something Jake had announced. Hiding a grin, she grabbed that day's *Brookhollow View*. "Have you seen this yet?"

He groaned, pushing it away. "Yes."

"Don't like the spotlight?"

"I don't know how many times I have to say it—I was doing my job, that's all." He took a sip of the drink in front of him, then frowned. "Hey, how far-reaching is this paper, anyway?"

"Just local. I think there's an online version, though," she said.

His expression clouded.

"What's wrong? I'm sure this isn't the first time your picture's appeared in a paper for heroic deeds," she teased, but his mood didn't lighten.

"I'd just rather keep things private, low-key."

"Like the reason you moved here?" She still wasn't buying that as his motivation. The man had been bored out of his mind before, issuing warnings and handing out parking tickets, and now he seemed intent on making sure no one started freaking out about crime in Brookhollow. When there actually had been a crime. Odd guy.

He took the paper from her. "Stuff like this shouldn't be headline news. It just convinces the crazies of the world to commit more crimes. Attention is attention, whether it's good or bad."

She scanned the article. Huh, it did focus heavily on Carl Phillips and his previous convictions. There was hardly any mention of Lily at all, except to say she was recovering in the Brookhollow medical clinic. The write-up on Jake was short, too, saying simply that he'd chased the fleeing perpetrator by foot and hit him with an icicle—which wasn't exactly accurate. "I didn't really notice before, but you're right. This piece really does focus mostly on the bad guy."

"Hey, man, can I buy you a drink?" Luke Dawson asked, approaching the bar. Seeing the row of glasses in front of Jake, he added, "*Another* one? It's the least I can do, seeing as how my wife almost hit you with the truck today." He shook his head.

"Seriously, worst driver ever," Heather muttered.

"If you really want to do me a solid, you can take some of these away for you and your buddies," Jake said, sliding several beers across the bar toward Luke.

"Why don't you join us? We're still looking for bowlers for the holiday tournament next week."

"Ah…"

"Yeah, why don't you go bowl? Get off that stool for a change?" Heather teased him when he hesitated.

"What if I like this stool?" he surprised her by saying, his eyes dancing with hers.

Were they flirting again? It certainly felt like flirting. And flirting was not good. It felt good, but it was definitely *not* good. She was determined not to fall for anyone here, especially now that she was leaving. Yet she was still meeting his gaze, and the look in his eyes was definitely flirty.

Oh, no.

"What's happening here?" Luke finally broke the silence with a wide smile, glancing back and forth between them.

Good question.

She quickly turned away, busying herself with the dishwasher. It was empty. Great.

Jake had shifted on his stool and was looking anywhere but at her.

Luke was still studying them. "Are you two…?"

"No!" they both said at the same time.

"You know, I think I'll go bowl," Jake said, climbing down from the stool quickly and grabbing several drinks from the bar.

"Good idea," Heather said, releasing a deep breath as the two men walked away.

What was that? she wondered, watching him join the other guys at their lane. Had she imagined the spark of electricity that had coursed between them?

He shot a quick glance back at her, catching her stare, and the same look of intensity and interest shone in his eyes, even from a distance.

Nope, hadn't imagined it.

What on earth were all of these women doing here? Jacob hesitated before getting out of the car. Through the still-frosty windshield, he spotted Lily among the group...and several other women he recognized from around town. His gut told him to put the car in Reverse and come back later, but he suspected they'd still be there, and he really needed to get more work done on the float. With the events of the past few days, he hadn't stopped by the farmhouse, and he was way behind everyone else. Not that he really cared, but at least it was something to do besides sitting in the station or driving around town all day with Cody in awkward, strained silence.

Luckily, without much else to do, Cody had offered to help build the float. And now it appeared that he might have several other volunteers.

"Why are all those women staring at us?" Cody asked.

"I think we're about to find out," he said, reluctantly opening the door and climbing out. Their boots crunched against the snow as they approached the farmhouse. Besides Lily, there was Long Legs Dawson, Bubbly Betsy, Smiles-a-lot Thompson and several other women he'd yet to have reason to create nicknames for. "Good morning, ladies," he said, to be on the safe side. No way would he get each of their names correct.

"Hi, Sheriff Matthews," they chorused, ignoring Cody, who mumbled an awkward hello. The overly friendly, singsong tone of the greeting and the eyelash-batting battle among the women told him everything he feared was true. They'd gone from disliking him and writing him off as an arrogant jerk to hero-worshipping in less than forty-eight hours. Amazing.

"What are you all doing here?" he asked, entering the barn behind Cody.

All six women followed.

"We heard you were entering a float in the parade and that you didn't have a crew to help you, so we thought we'd volunteer," Lily said.

He glanced at her bandaged hand and her bruised eye. The swelling on her lip had gone down, and she looked much better than the last time he'd seen her. "Should you be doing much? How are you feeling?" It had only been two days. She should probably be taking it easy. Recovering from something like that took time.

If possible, the other women appeared even more enamored by his concern...enamored and a little jealous. What was going on? He was a cop. He'd protected the innocent and done his job. Sure, his work had gotten him a pretty girl's attention in the past, but six? Never. He knew he should be flattered, but it was hard to get a big ego over attention that had nothing to do with him personally. It was all about the badge. And the attention only made him more concerned about his cover being blown. He wasn't that far away from the city, and he was basically hiding in plain sight; staying as low-key as possible was the only way he could prevent his problems from following him to Brookhollow. Every day, he prayed he'd get the call from Emilio, so this could all be over before things got complicated or dangerous.

"I'm feeling much better, and I owe you so much," Lily was saying. "I really want to help, and I won't take no for an answer."

He glanced at the others. "You're *all* here to help?"

They nodded.

"Well, I do need all the help I can get, but unfortunately Mrs. Dawson said each team can only have four crew members…and Cody here has offered to help, as well…" He turned, but the young man had already disappeared into the stall. Great, he was on his own. How was he supposed to decide who stayed and who went? He studied the women. The stronger-looking ones would be his best bet, especially if he was stuck with Lily's busted hand. He suspected she wouldn't be able to contribute much.

Heather entered the barn then and stopped when she saw the group. He smiled and shrugged, but she barely glanced at him. Weird—she was usually the only one who gave him the time of day. Today, she just blew right past him. A memory of their exchange the night before flashed in his mind. Was she annoyed by the casual flirtation they seemed to have going on? Well, she could rest easy; it wouldn't be happening again. A relationship, no matter how casual or fleeting, was the last thing on his list of priorities and top of the list of things that could jeopardize the case. He'd already destroyed Amber and Kyle's life, albeit temporarily, and he wouldn't risk doing that to anyone else.

"Don't worry about crew limit," Long Legs said, interrupting his thoughts and directing his attention away from Heather's back. "I checked with Mom, and she said since you were starting so much later than everyone else, you could have extra team members."

Okay, so Long Legs was Mrs. Dawson's daughter. He knew she had two, Kayla and Alisha…but he couldn't remember which of the two was the younger woman standing in front of him. He had a fifty/fifty shot. "Oh, okay, thanks… Kayla." He mumbled the name, but she beamed.

Phew. He'd gotten it right. "Okay, well, there's lots to do, so are you all ready to see this year's winning float?" he asked, grateful for the extra twelve…eleven hands, even if they were there to help for all the wrong reasons.

That seemed to be the slogan for this float.

THE SOUND OF laughter coming from three stalls over was driving Heather insane. High-pitched cackling and fake bubbliness competed against one another, and she wondered how Jake could stand working amidst the cacophony. She was a few stalls away from the noise, and *she* wanted earplugs. But then the sound of his deep, rich laugh mixed in with the women's voices made things even worse. He was enjoying himself.

Of course he was enjoying himself. In two days, he'd gone from not having a single friend in town, unless she counted, to being the center of adoration for six women. Reaching behind her, Heather turned the volume louder on the portable radio she'd brought along. "Rudolph the Red-Nosed Reindeer" drowned out the laughter. Better.

But seconds later, the giggles once again rose above the music. Oh, come on.

"They must be getting nothing done over there," she said to Candace, the other team member working on the float with her that morning.

"Sounds like they're having a good time, though," Candace said longingly.

"Hey! We're having a good time," Heather said, stapling a strand of white lights to the edge of the float and catching the edge of her sweater beneath the staple. *Shoot*. She removed the staple and pushed her sleeves up, then tried again.

"My hands are numb from gluing these candy canes, and my legs are starting to cramp up. You didn't tell me the barn wasn't even heated."

The truth was, she hadn't known. Nor had she realized how much work went into building these floats. Melody had made running the bar and everything that went with it seem easy. Heather stapled the last set of lights and jumped off the float. "Okay, we'll switch jobs for a bit. But first, I'll go for a hot chocolate run. Whipped cream and cinnamon?"

"Is there any other kind?" Candace asked, getting up and taking the staple gun from her.

"Okay, be back in ten. Don't leave." Candace was the only team member she could actually count on to help. The other two girls who worked part-time at the pool hall on their busier days had survived half a day in the barn and had since found excuses not to pitch in. Maybe she should borrow some of Jake's helpers—he seemed to have more than he needed.

Leaving the stall, she headed for the door, making a face as she passed Jake's stall, where the women were now singing along to the Christmas carols coming from her radio. "Seriously?" she muttered.

"Something wrong?" Jake said behind her, causing her to jump.

"Jeez, Jake. Give a girl a heart attack," she said, turning and continuing on her way, embarrassed that he'd heard her.

He followed. "Where are you going?"

"Hot chocolate run." She hesitated, then sighed. "Does your team want anything?" *Please, say no.*

"I'm sure they do. They've been working nonstop."

Huh, she was surprised they were getting anything accomplished with all the chatter and laughing, but she bit back her comment, knowing how it would sound. And she was *not* jealous that these women were working with Jake and having a good time. Not one little bit. "Okay, I'll be back in a few minutes."

"I'll go with you."

"No, that's okay…"

"You won't be able to carry them all." He shrugged, falling into step next to her. "We can take the squad car."

"Okay, fine." As they left the barn, he said, "So, how's your second-prize float coming?"

She gave him a small shove. "*First*-prize float, you mean. And it's coming along great." Or at least it would be if she could drag her team members out there.

At the car, he opened the passenger-side door for her.

"And yours?" she asked him. "How are your little elves doing?" Wow, even *she* heard jealousy in that statement.

He smiled. "Things are moving a lot quicker now."

"I find that hard to believe with all the giggling and nonstop chatter." What was wrong with her? She was sounding like a jealous girlfriend. She'd never been that girl. Ever. Even when she'd had a boyfriend—and Jake wasn't even close to being a boyfriend. He was…oh, forget it. Trying to define what was going on between them only made her head hurt.

Leaning toward her, he placed a hand on top of her head and gently guided her into the car, as he would a criminal, then said as he bent down to face her. "Don't worry, Talks-a-lot, you're still my favorite."

She opened her mouth to speak, but he shut the door.

*Hmph.*

When he got into the driver's seat, she didn't even pause for a breath. "I don't want to be your favorite. I don't want to be your anything at all. I mean, you really should get to know those other women, seeing as how you came here to settle down and put down some roots. You really haven't been doing a great job fitting in, so this is good…" *Shut up, Heather!* What was wrong with her mouth, that it insisted on moving so much? She clamped her lips tight and sat on her hands, staring straight out the window. *Do not say another word.*

Jake looked amused as he pulled into traffic. "Okay, well, who do you suggest I get to know better?"

Seriously? She wasn't falling into that trap. She cleared her throat. "That's none of my business, or my decision…"

"Come on. You know all of these women. Help me out by giving me the inside scoop. Save me from some of the crazies."

He had a point. Some of these women were a little nutty. She straightened in the seat. "Fine. How about Lily? She's pretty, smart, has her own business to keep her busy, so she won't be needy or clingy."

He shook his head. "She has a boyfriend, doesn't she? And besides, she's not into me— she's just feeling grateful, that's all."

"Maybe, but I'm sure she's attracted to you for more than that reason." She sighed. "Okay, what about Kayla Dawson?"

"Too young."

"She's twenty-five."

"Too young. Next."

Um… "Rebecca Miller?" Personally, she found the bubbly nurse to be a busybody and kind of annoying, but who knew—maybe that was his type.

"Which one is she?"

She narrowed her eyes. "They're helping you, and you don't even know their names?"

"I have my own names for everyone," he said.

So hers wasn't unique. For some reason, that bothered her. She was just another nameless person in town whom he'd dubbed with one of many stupid nicknames. Who cared? She was leaving soon. She wasn't interested in this guy.

Was she?

"Anyway, Rebecca is the dark-haired one with the blond streaks in the front…green eyes…"

He was already shaking his head. "Nope, not my type."

Her stomach turned slightly. *She* had dark hair and sorta green eyes. So she wasn't his type, either? *Seriously, who cares? Leaving, remember.*

She shrugged. "Well, choose one of the blondes, then." She really didn't feel like playing his matchmaker for the last few weeks she was in town. She had her own life to think about and figure out. He could do the same.

"I prefer brunettes," he said. "Ones with hazel eyes and lips that won't stop moving, a fascination for ankle-breaking heels and who hate acting jealous but just can't help themselves." He parked in front of the coffee house and turned to face her. "Know anyone like that?"

Her heart pounded, and she prayed he couldn't hear it. She swallowed hard. Suddenly at a loss for words, she simply shook her head.

"That's too bad," he said, reaching across and tucking a strand of hair behind her ear.

Yeah, too bad. She stared at him dumbly for a second too long. In that second, she almost gave him the answer he'd been hinting at. And that was not a good idea. Complicating things mere weeks before she could get out of Brookhollow was not a good idea. She'd made up her mind to leave and having any reason to second-guess that decision would only make it harder. So why did she have to keep reminding herself of that?

Luckily, Jake broke the spell before she could dive headfirst into complicated. "Heather... I was messing with you," he said with a grin.

An urge to hit him competed with an unexpected pang of disappointment. He was messing with her. Of course.

"Should we go get hot chocolate?"

She nodded, her common sense returning. "Wouldn't want to leave the Sheriff's Angels waiting."

As JACOB WAVED goodbye to his work crew later that day, after successfully dodging three invites to dinner, he breathed a sigh of relief. In eight hours his float had gone from a shell of a design to half-finished. But he wasn't sure the quick pace was worth it. At first the flirty women were funny and his ego had started to inflate a little, but somewhere along the way, they had begun competing for his attention. He sighed. At least their desire to capture his interest had resulted in quick work on the float. At this rate, he'd go from being behind the other entrants to finishing early. He just hoped he could survive the next week with the women. He only had so many excuses not to date any of them.

The main reason—his secret identity— was an excuse he couldn't exactly use. But he knew there was another reason he didn't want to date these women. He was attracted to Heather.

And allowing himself to feel that way was the dumbest thing he could do right now. He was in Brookhollow for one reason only: to get his life back on track and regain his confidence with the container drug bust. Falling for a woman at this stage of his life was not happening. Relationships were hard enough for cops; they were almost impossible with his undercover stints. And right now, being with Heather could compromise this important case and put lives at risk.

Putting the squad car in reverse, he shook

his head. What had he been thinking, flirting with her that afternoon? He must be losing his mind. And then, passing it off as a joke had just been mean. He remembered the look on her face and wished he'd never agreed to go on the hot chocolate run with her. In fact, being around her at all wasn't a great idea. From now on, he'd avoid the pretty brunette as much as possible.

# CHAPTER SIX

"EVERYTHING OKAY?" VICTORIA asked the next morning.

"Huh?" Heather glanced at her friend, who was sitting next to her behind the B and B's front desk. "Yeah, everything's fine. Why?"

"Because you've been stapling those sheets together for two minutes now. I think eight staples oughta do it." Victoria took the reservation file from her and removed several staples before putting it away.

Heather shook her head. "Right, sorry. Spaced out for a minute." A common occurrence lately.

"Thinking about the position with Highstone Acquisitions? 'Cause I am," her friend said, only half teasing.

That seemed like the easiest and safest answer. Sure, she'd go with that. "Yeah, waiting to hear from Mike Ainsley is torture." In truth, the job offer was the farthest thing from her mind. Since the day before, she'd done everything she could to stop thinking about Jake, to no avail. And when he hadn't shown up at the bar last night, it had only gotten harder to forget about him and his attempts to flirt with her. Though he'd claimed to be kidding, she'd felt...what? Connection, sincerity in his words?

"I'm sure you'll hear something soon," Victoria said, as the front door opened and her sister-in-law Kayla entered, stomping her boots on the mat. "Hi."

"Hi, sorry I'm late. I was at the barn working on Jake's float."

Didn't she mean Sheriff Matthew's float? Since when had everyone gotten so friendly? Heather pushed aside her irritation and forced a smile. "How's it going?"

"Good. Though today wasn't much fun. Jake had to work, so it was only a few of us women."

She smiled for real, then quickly looked away. *Don't be stupid*. She couldn't let herself fall for Jake. Not now. So why shouldn't he date one of these other women? Because she said so, that's why.

Kayla removed her coat and hung it on the rack.

"Okay, ready to get started?" Victoria asked.

Kayla had offered to take over Heather's position on the front desk three days a week, while she continued her online studies to become an interior designer. She was here to learn the ropes, but Kayla seemed as distracted as Heather.

"How old do you think he is?" she asked wistfully as Victoria tried to show her the new online guest tracker.

"Who?" Victoria asked with a frown.

Heather knew who the girl was referring to. "Thirty-five on Friday," she said.

"His birthday is on Friday?" Kayla asked, her eyes widening.

Victoria shot Heather a look, which she ignored as she nodded.

"Oh! We should totally throw him a party." Kayla's excitement shone in her eyes.

*We?* "I'm already planning one," Heather said before she could stop the lie from escaping her lips.

HEATHER KNEW EXACTLY who to go to with her new plan. That afternoon, she knocked on Darlene Dawson's front door and waited for the town's event planner to answer, hoping her daughter wasn't around. Other than Darlene, she didn't want anyone else involved with Jake's surprise party at the pool hall. She wanted to do this for him, and it took all her strength not to start asking herself why.

She also didn't want to think of the dent it would put in her savings. She'd better get this job at Highstone Acquisitions soon.

"Heather! What a nice surprise. Come on in," Darlene said a moment later, stepping back to usher her into the family's home.

"Hi, Mrs. Dawson. I was hoping you could help me with something." She bent to unzip her boots, holding the wall for balance.

"Of course," she said. Then eyeing the boots, she added, "I have no idea how you walk on those."

"I've been wearing heels since I was four," Heather said with a laugh. Her mother, a corporate professional with a passion for shoes, had passed down her love of stilettos before Heather could read.

"Come into the sitting room. Would you like coffee?"

"Yes, please," she said, hanging her coat on the brass hook next to the door.

A few minutes later, Heather explained her idea. "I know you're busy with all of the holiday events this month, but I was wondering if you could help me plan a surprise party at the pool hall." Jake would be there like clockwork Friday evening. There was no way she could convince him to go anywhere else without ruining the surprise. Though, he hadn't shown up the night before... She bit her lip. Ah, one night in months, the odds were good that he'd show up.

"Sounds easy enough. For who?"

"Sheriff Matthews," Heather said, desperate to act nonchalant.

Darlene studied her. "You like him, don't you?"

"No... I mean, yes, of course. He saved Lily's life. Everyone likes him now," she said. "But I don't *like* like him, if that's what you mean. Like I'm not attracted to him. Well, I mean, come on, I'd be dead if I wasn't attracted to him, but not in that way..." Oh, God, she really was Talks-a-lot.

"Sure, dear. So, about the party..."

*Yes, let's talk about that. Much easier,*

*much less confusing.* "Well, I was thinking we could keep it simple—just invite maybe fifty or sixty people. I'll close the pool hall side for a special event. We can ask Ginger to bake a cake…"

"What kind does he like?"

How was she supposed to know? Up until a week ago, no one in town knew anything at all about the man. And now all she knew was he had a sister and a nephew and the most beautiful set of dark brown eyes she'd ever gotten lost in. "Chocolate seems safe enough," she said.

"Okay, well with fifty plus people, we'll need at least two—maybe a cheesecake and a regular cake—and then what about catering?" She grabbed her day planner and opened to a blank note section in the back.

Heather remembered what he'd said about Joey's Diner tampering with his food, and she giggled.

"What?"

"Nothing. It's just…they were totally messing with him at the diner last week…" She shook her head, laughing again as she remembered the look on his face when he'd asked if she, too, had been messing with his drinks.

"Yeah, you're not attracted to him at all," Darlene said sarcastically.

"I just thought it was funny," she said quickly. "Anyway, catering should probably be the Fireside Grill. I want him to feel safe eating."

"Yeah, but that could get pricey, dear. Especially on short notice, this time of year."

She hesitated. Darlene was right. The Fireside Grill was the only real fine dining they had in Brookhollow. The five-star restaurant was located on the border of the town park with a fantastic view of the lake. Their menu wasn't cheap. She bit her lip. Her savings were dwindling...but hopefully soon she'd have a new job. Oddly enough, it was that thought that made her feel uneasy. "You know what? Let's do it. The guy saved Lily's life after all, right?" And besides, the revenue the bar would make on drinks at the event would ease her guilt over quitting.

Not to mention she was most definitely not *not* falling for Jake.

WHEN HIS SHIFT ended that evening, Jacob drove straight past the pool hall without stopping. In fact, he sped up a little.

He had to put some distance between himself and the gorgeous brunette whose intense "oh, no, what did we let happen?" expression a few days before had told him everything he needed to know. She was into him, but she wasn't happy about it.

He wasn't exactly thrilled about his attraction to her, either.

He'd always done well keeping things casual with the women he dated. One of the most fortunate aspects of his circumstances when he'd applied to go undercover was that he hadn't been married, seeing anyone or attached in any way. No children or wife who would suffer or cause him any guilt or grief while he focused on his assignment. He'd been capable of going under full-time until the case was solved, which made him the first choice among the applicants. He'd always been motivated by the idea of serving a greater good, so he'd been stoked when he was promoted.

At least until he'd told Amber...

"What do you mean undercover?" Amber's eyes had narrowed over her glass of wine. He'd taken her out to celebrate his good news.

"Exactly what it sounds like. I'm being promoted to the narcotics division," he'd said quietly.

"Promoted?"

"Yes. The pay raise is almost fifteen grand, and my first assignment starts in a few months." His commanding chief officer had been eager to get him on assignment, but first he'd needed to undergo training with a senior undercover officer who had experience with similar cases. The other officer would teach him how to dress, how to act and how to talk like the drug cartel he would be infiltrating. Fitting in would be key to the success of the operation and—most of all—his safety.

"How long is the assignment?" she'd asked.

He'd looked away then, cutting into his steak. "Not sure. Some assignments are a few weeks...others a few years."

"Years?!" Her raised voice had caught the attention of other diners, and he'd shushed her.

"Yes, possibly. Hopefully not." Knowing he'd have little or no contact with Amber and Kyle while he was working the case had been the only drawback, and it was a big one.

Amber had sat back in her chair, her lips set in a thin, straight line.

Jacob had sighed. He'd avoided marriage

and kids of his own to prevent his life choices from being influenced by others, but thinking about what going undercover meant—leaving his sister and nephew—still made him feel terrible and second-guess his choice. But making the streets safer for his family had to be better, right?

"You're telling Kyle," she'd said.

"That's fair." He'd pushed his plate away, his appetite vanishing. His nephew was going to be upset, and the idea broke his heart. He hoped the little boy would understand, if not appreciate, the sacrifice he was making.

The two of them were close. Especially since the boy's grandfather had gone to jail. The little boy's father was an artist whom Amber had fallen in love with in art school, but he'd left for a museum curator's job in Paris shortly after graduating, which he'd claimed was the opportunity of a lifetime. She'd found out a month later that she was pregnant. She'd told him, but he'd refused to believe Kyle was his. Nice guy.

"Look, I'm sorry." He felt like a jerk for leaving them when he knew they depended on him.

Across from him, his sister had been silent.

"Amber, this is my life. I supported your decision to open the art gallery, didn't I?" He'd more than supported it; he'd helped her with the deposit on the building's lease.

Obviously the same thought crossed her mind because her expression had softened just a little bit. "Yes, you did." She'd sighed. "This sucks, Jacob."

"I know." His excitement over the news gone, the full realization of the assignment's implications setting in, he'd begun to worry whether he was doing the right thing.

His sister's ability to read him was uncanny. "Don't question your decision. I never intended for you to be the father figure in Kyle's life—that's not something I meant to put on you. You're right. You have no reason not to accept this promotion." She'd picked up her wineglass in a toast. "To my stupid kid brother and his terrible life choices," she'd said, but her tone was at least partly teasing.

He'd raised his glass. "I'll drink to both."

Jacob climbed the stairs to his apartment now, grateful the house was empty. He rarely had time alone. Cody had mentioned they were having his aunt over for dinner that evening, so Jacob went back down to the kitchen and took his time preparing a sandwich and a pot of coffee.

Once he'd eaten, he went back up to the attic and grabbed a pen and piece of paper. A letter to his nephew was overdue.

Dear Kyle,

Sorry, it's taken me a while to write. It's been so great getting your letters, and I'm so glad you and your mom are doing well.

You can assure your mom I'm not lying around on a beach…in fact nothing could be further from the truth. Tell her I'm sorry that this time apart has lasted longer than I'd hoped, and I'm doing everything I can to get us all back to New York before the holidays.

I'm building a parade float here, and it's a gingerbread-world theme. It reminds me of the houses we make together every year, just much bigger. I wish you could see it. I'll send pictures once it's finished.

Don't give up hope yet. Anything can happen at Christmastime.

Love you guys.

Uncle Jacob

He folded the letter and slid it into an envelope, then he wrote his nephew's name on the front. Sheriff Bishop would fill in the rest. He tucked it into his jacket pocket and sat back against the sofa cushions, thinking about what he'd just told Kyle. Anything could happen at Christmastime. An image of Heather flashed in his mind, and he groaned. Anything could happen. Did that include falling in love?

"I THOUGHT YOU said he comes in every night?" Lindsay asked Heather above the noise inside the pool hall.

It was Friday night, and the last-minute party had miraculously come together, thanks to Darlene. But the guest list had somehow spiraled way out of control. There were at least two hundred people in the small space. For a guy who had rubbed everyone the wrong way just a few weeks ago, Jake certainly had a lot of fans now. Including a lot of young female fans, Heather noticed, eyeing the tables of beautiful twentysomethings whom she was pretty darn sure had not been on the original guest list.

"He used to. This is weird," she said, glancing at the clock. 8:05. This was the fourth night in a row that Jake hadn't sat on the bar stool across from her while she worked. It was driving her crazy, and she was afraid it might have something to do with whatever had passed between them in the squad car…or had it been her rebuttal? He was avoiding her either way, it seemed. "I'll call Sheriff Bishop and see if he's at the station," she said.

Lindsay pointed toward the bowling alley, where the over-fifty league was taking advantage of the empty lanes to practice for the upcoming holiday tournament.

"Well, I guess he can't help us," she said.

Lindsay reached for her cell. "I'll call Noah. He's on shift at the fire hall tonight." She disappeared toward the washrooms, where it was quieter, and there was better cell reception, for some reason. Heather continued to watch the front door.

Come on. She couldn't believe he was avoiding her. Actually, she could believe it. It was probably the smart way to handle things, as annoying as that might be. She'd received a call from Mike Ainsley earlier, for an interview on Monday morning. Things were progressing, and she needed to keep her focus on what was important. A fling with a man who insisted he was done with city life, even though it seeped from his every pore, was not a good idea. She needed to worry about her future. If and when she decided to start dating again, it had to be someone with similar goals, similar life plans and a similar zip code, preferably.

"Yeah, he's there," Lindsay said, returning a moment later. "Noah told me the squad car is parked out back, and he's in the office. Do you want me to fake an emergency call or something?"

Heather sighed. "No, he'll see through it." She grabbed her coat, scarf and hat from behind the kitchen door. "Just keep everyone here, and I'll be back as soon as I can."

"There's still food and cake, no one's going anywhere," Lindsay said, reaching for a bacon-wrapped scallop.

Heather looked around the packed pool hall. It was true. The catering was going over quite well, with the guests, if not her credit card. She just hoped she could drag Jake back here while there was still some decent food left, so he wouldn't be stuck with the usual bar pretzels.

THE OFFICE DOOR OPENED, and Jacob looked up to see the one person in Brookhollow he was desperate to avoid. He jumped to his feet, spilling his steaming coffee down the front of his jeans. *Ow, hot...*

Heather's gaze darted there, then she quickly averted it. "Hi."

"Hi," he said, reaching for a paper towel and dabbing at the stain. "What are you doing here?"

She shrugged. "Well, since the first day you arrived in Brookhollow, you've been occupying a certain stool at my bar. And the last four nights, not so much."

"So you came to get me?" he asked, irritation seeping into his tone unintentionally. That was a first. Someone in town actually wanted him to be somewhere.

"Are you working?" she asked, ignoring his grumpy mood and glancing at the paperwork on the desk.

His cell phone sat on top, "Candy Crush" illuminating the screen. He reached for it and tucked it into his pocket. Damn, he'd almost completed Level 156. Not being at the bar the past four evenings, he'd had plenty of time to catch up on his candy crushing addiction. "Sort of…"

"Well, what time are you done?"

"Why?" He squinted at her. She was up to something. Was she about to ask him out? Obviously, she'd felt the spark between them, but he'd hoped she would be just as eager to put it out as he was, not allow it to turn into a flame.

She shifted from one foot to the other in her higher-than-usual boots. Red leopard-patterned boots that reached her midcalf over dark blue skinny jeans. Brookhollow or not, Heather Corbett was all New York. And for once her mouth remained closed, forcing him to ask again, "Why do you want to know when I'm off?"

"I just thought you might stop by the bar for a drink…like you used to do *every* night." He could tell she was upset, but he wasn't a mind reader. He had no idea what he'd done wrong. Had she been expecting him to act on the feelings he was developing for her? Was she peeved that he hadn't? She was leaving town soon, and he had his own agenda.

"Um…no, probably not. I'm going to try to finish up the paperwork from Lily's statement…" And try not to think about her in those skinny jeans and red boots. He reached for the file.

"Can't it wait?"

Okay, Heather was definitely not the type to beg for a date, so that couldn't be it. He stood, hands on his hips. "What are you up to?"

"Nothing," she said, taking a step back as he came around the desk to study her.

"You should know I specialized in interrogation. I will get the truth," he said, moving closer.

She backed up until her butt reached the edge of Sheriff Bishop's desk. She met his gaze defiantly but refused to speak.

He stared at her, waiting… The silent staredown continued for several seconds, until he couldn't remember who was trying to shake whom.

"Fine!" she said, just as he was about to cave and follow her anywhere she wanted him to go. "I'm throwing you a party at the pool hall."

He blinked. A party? Why? For rescuing Lily? That was kinda extreme…

"A *birthday* party," she said, when he didn't respond.

"A bir—" He stopped. Oh, no. His fake ID listed his birthday as December 7. Today.

"Yes. There's like two hundred people there right now eating the expensive food I bought and waiting for the guest of honor to arrive, the man who never failed to show up at the pool hall before a couple of nights ago, before whatever weird connection or spark we had obviously freaked him out. But you don't have to avoid me—you have nothing to worry about because I feel nothing for—"

"Talks-a-lot, stop talking for once," he said, before grabbing her waist and pulling her close. He trailed a hand along her cold cheek, brushing several strands of hair away from her face.

Her breath was ragged as his fingers touched her slightly swollen lips. "Jake…what are you doing?"

What was he doing? He shook his head and let his hands fall away from her. "Sorry," he mumbled.

She seemed slightly disappointed as she cleared her throat. "Anyway…the party. You have to come."

He shook his head. "No, I really don't." The last thing he wanted was more praise, more attention... For the past week, his blood sugar had been on a permanent spike from all the cookies and desserts people kept dropping off at the station. Pretty soon, he would be in a sugar coma. A party with more tempting food and a certain tempting brunette was sure to kill him.

"Jake, please."

He dropped his gaze and sighed. He was in Brookhollow for one reason only, and he hated that he'd let someone get this close to have this guilt-inducing effect on him. "I can't, Heather, I'm sorry."

HEATHER ANGRILY REACHED for the door of the pool hall ten minutes later, her heart still racing and not from the brisk four-block walk from the station. She couldn't believe him. After all the effort and money she'd put into throwing him a party, he refused to show up? Unbelievable.

Everyone in town had been right to think he was a jerk. She sighed. A jerk who'd just sent her heart into overdrive. What had happened back there? Had he been about to kiss her before she'd opened her mouth and ruined the moment? Typical.

"Where is he?" Lindsay asked her.

"He's not—" she started, but her words were drowned out a second later.

"Surprise!" Everyone shouted as Jake entered the bar.

He was here?

Her gaze locked with his, and he faked his shock, but not before Heather noticed a brief look of annoyance. *Sorry*, he mouthed at her.

She swallowed hard, nodding, then turned away quickly to start pouring drinks. The guest of honor was here. "Let's get the party started," she mumbled.

IN THE THIRTY seconds after Heather had stormed out of the station, Jacob had battled with his thoughts and emotions. Finally, he'd come to the conclusion that it would be a jerk move not to attend his own birthday party, even if it wasn't his real birthday. Heather had gone through a lot of trouble for him, and that thought had made him feel even worse. So he'd sucked it up and headed for the pool hall.

In three hours, Jacob had met more Brookhollow residents than he had since coming to town. But his thoughts and his gaze kept returning to Heather. Of course, she'd tried to act as though she were ignoring him while she poured drinks for the party guests, refilled the food trays and played DJ, but he could sense her looking his way throughout the evening. Just being in the same room as her, there was an electricity, something he'd never felt before ripping through him.

His relationship history consisted of one awkward three-month experience in high school followed by a period of casual dating. The closest he'd come to a real relationship hadn't even been real. His first year undercover, he'd fallen for Leo Gonzales's younger sister, Maria.

She'd been twenty-four and in way over her head. She was beautiful, smart and funny. She didn't belong in the drug cartel world, but she thrived on the danger of it. She never used the drugs she imported; she got her high from the uncertainty and fast-paced situations she found herself in. The thrill of the danger appealed to her, and her intensity had appealed to him. He'd tried to stay away from Maria, but he'd had an overwhelming urge to protect her, to convince her to leave the family business without blowing his cover. What had begun as a fake attraction to get close to her had ended up developing into real feelings.

The closer he'd gotten, the harder he'd fallen until he was desperate to get her away from Leo and the cartel. So desperate he'd considered giving up the undercover assignment by offering her a confessional agreement. Six months in jail for her previous involvement in the crimes in exchange for evidence that would get her brother locked up.

But his offer hadn't come quick enough. Maria had been arrested in Mexico, bringing a new supplier's goods across the border, and she'd died two months later from a stab wound in jail before US authorities could bring her back to the country.

The experience with Maria had taught Jacob not to get close. Not when he was pretending to be someone he wasn't. There was no way for a real relationship to develop under those circumstances.

He looked across the bar at Heather. Now was no different. She could still get hurt from not knowing the truth, from getting caught up in all of this with him.

Walking away from her would be the best

thing for both of them. But suddenly, he knew that wasn't going to be so easy.

"Well, that's it. Party's over—get out," Heather was saying as she emptied the dishwasher.

The last guests were putting on their coats near the door, and he turned to wave at them as they left. "Need some help?" he asked.

"Nope. Just going to cash out and then head home myself."

"I'll wait with you," he said, even though he was desperate not to be alone in the empty bar with her.

"It's okay. My car is parked right outside. And besides, I don't have any crazy ex-con ex-husbands who could be stalking me," she said, opening the register and removing the cash. She started to count.

He cleared his throat. "About earlier—at the station," he began. "I'm sorry. I'm not sure what happened there."

She sighed. "It's fine. Nothing happened." She started counting again.

"Right. Okay, well, I promise nothing will."

She started counting a third time. "Good. I'm glad we both agree that it was just some weird, awkward moment that meant nothing."

Had he said that? Not exactly. Though he wasn't about to complicate things by correcting her. "Right. Okay…so you're good. You're sure?"

She nodded.

He climbed down from the bar stool and grabbed his jacket.

She put down the bills. "The thing is—I told you, I'm leaving Brookhollow. And you've said you plan to stay. Whatever personal reasons you have for that, I don't need to know them. But I'm just not interested in getting involved at this point."

Right. That was smart. He smiled tightly. "I totally agree."

"So, we're good?"

"Absolutely." He waved as he headed toward the door.

"Happy birthday, Jake," she called after him.

Guilt for letting her go through all of this for a fake birthday made him pause. He turned back. "You really shouldn't have gone to so much trouble."

# CHAPTER SEVEN

"COFFEE?"

"Check."

"Interview clothes?"

"Check," Heather said, grabbing the garment bag that held her new light gray suit from Lily's, the one Jake had picked out.

"Impossible-to-walk-in-for-anybody-but-you shoes?" Victoria continued.

"Check. I think I'm ready." Heather glanced at her watch. She had three hours to get to New York, change in a Starbuck's bathroom and show up at her interview at Highstone Acquisitions.

Victoria hugged her, squishing baby Harper between them. "I'm not."

"I'm sorry, Vic," she said for the millionth time. The only thing she felt bad about was leaving Victoria and the B and B. At least that *was* all she'd been feeling bad about…until last night. The time with Jake was changing everything. At first, she'd been able to dismiss their casual flirting as some much-needed excitement in her small-town life experiment. But now...well, she could no longer deny she had feelings for him. The question was—how strong were those feelings? Would they linger after she'd left Brookhollow, make her long to return? Or would they disappear the moment her stiletto heels clicked down the sidewalk in Manhattan?

Man, if someone had told her a month ago she'd be dealing with a dilemma like this, she'd never have believed them.

"No, *I'm* sorry," Victoria said, cutting into her thoughts. "This is a good thing. You deserve this opportunity. Now, go before you're late." She glanced through the curtain. "Looks like the snow hasn't started yet. Just be careful."

After losing her friends in a highway car accident, Victoria worried whenever someone else she loved left the Brookhollow town limits. "I will," she said, pulling on her UGG boots and sliding into her thermal jacket.

"Are you sure you wouldn't rather take the truck?" Victoria still looked concerned as she surveyed the darkening morning clouds. "The four-wheel drive would be safer if the snow does start…"

"No, in case I decide to stay overnight at my sister's place, I wouldn't want to leave you and Luke with my crappy old sedan. Besides, Bailey just put new all-season tires on it, so I should be fine." She hoped she sounded more confident in the run-down used vehicle she'd bought just to get around town.

"Okay. And your cell phone is charged?" Victoria asked.

Oh, no. *Was* her cell phone charged? She rummaged around in her purse until she found it. Half battery. Not great, but it should last until she could charge it in the city. "It's good enough," she said, hugging her friend again. "Wish me luck."

"Even if I don't mean it?" Victoria teased.

Heather laughed. "I'll see you guys either later tonight or tomorrow. Bye, Harper," she said, waving to the little girl, who was busy yanking Victoria's blond hair from her head.

A few minutes later, Heather backed her tiny car out of the B and B parking lot. She turned on the radio and found the local all-day Christmas music station and got ready for the long drive ahead of her. The first few snowflakes began to fall, and she took a deep breath.

"Don't panic. It's only snow. You got this," she said, sitting straighter in the seat, already feeling her back tighten. She'd never actually driven on the highway in winter before…but it was fine. She had three hours. She'd just take her time. Everything would be fine.

She had an MBA. This couldn't be that difficult.

As she reached the stop sign on the corner, she heard a police siren and spotted red-and-blue lights in her rearview. She frowned, her heart racing. *Please, let it be Sheriff Bishop.* The last thing she needed was to see Jake right now. It was bad enough that her every waking thought the past few days had been about him, but then sleep had eluded her the night before, and she'd lain awake thinking about him and his easy agreement that nothing could happen between them. She glanced at the side mirror.

Fantastic, it *was* him.

She quickly checked her reflection before rolling down the window and turning the volume down on the radio.

"Oh, it's you," he said, a look of awkward surprise on his face.

Wow. Nice greeting. "Good morning to you, too."

"Sorry—good morning," he mumbled. "Can I see your driver's license and registration, please."

"Are you serious right now, Jake?"

"Yes."

She huffed as she opened her purse and handed him the license and registration.

"Do you know why I'm pulling you over?" he asked, scanning the registration.

"Well, I couldn't possibly have been speeding yet, since I'd just left the driveway, so, no. No idea." She shivered as a cold breeze blew snow onto her lap. She reached forward and cranked the heat.

"You have a taillight out. I saw the New York plates and thought you were a guest from the B and B heading back to the city."

"Well, I guess technically I am. I have my job interview today at Highstone Acquisitions." She checked the time on the dash. "And I have to get going, or I'll be late. I'll take the car into Bailey's Place to get the taillight fixed as soon as I get back."

He nodded reluctantly, but studying her

driver's license, his brow creased. "Um... Heather?"

Oh, no. Stay calm. Act cool. "Yeah?"

"Is this your current driver's license?"

"Yep," she said, reaching for it.

He moved it out of reach. "It expired two years ago."

"No, it didn't." Could it really have been that long since she'd renewed it? She didn't drive in the city...and Brookhollow roads didn't count as real driving. There was only one stoplight.

He showed her the expiration date.

Yep, two years. "I'll renew it as soon as I get back," she promised.

Unlikely. Once she returned to New York, it was subways and taxis for her. This piece of crap car that had caused her nothing but trouble could stay right here in Brookhollow.

"Heather, I can't let you drive to New York without a valid license. I *should* be giving you a fine right now," Jake said.

"Jake, I have to get to this job interview. I'm begging you to let me off with a warning this time and let me continue on my way."

"I can't."

She sighed. "Look, just because there's a

connection between us doesn't mean you can pull this on me right now," she said.

"Hey! It's *because* there's a connection between us that I'm not dragging your butt into the station."

She stared straight ahead, fighting the tears she felt forcing their way into the corners of her eyes.

"Look, I'd like to give you a break but, Heather, two years? You've been driving without a license for *two years*? Come on—you have to know that's not a good idea."

She slumped against the seat. What was she going to do now? If she called and canceled the interview, would Mike Ainsley allow her to reschedule? Their office closed the following week for the holidays.

So much for the weather being her major challenge this morning.

JACOB STARED INTO space next to Heather's car, hands on hips, wishing he'd never pulled her over. His night shift *was* technically finished. Could he let her go? Pretend this never happened as long as she promised to renew the license right away? Could he ignore protocol and all of his gut instincts this one time?

Who was he kidding? If she got stopped on the highway or in New York, the officers there wouldn't be so kind. She could face huge fines. Or worse, if she had an accident, she could be in a lot of trouble.

He couldn't allow her to go.

But she needed to get to this interview. It would really suck if she lost the job opportunity because of this. "Hey, I'm sorry. If I could go back ten minutes and not pull you over, I—" He shook his head. "No, that's not true, I'm glad I did. Heather, you're lucky I'm the one talking to you right now and that this wasn't an accident or something."

"Lucky? Ha!" She folded her arms, staring straight ahead. Her pretty pink lips, set in a thin straight line, said it all.

"Is there anyone else who could drive you?"

"No. Luke is on a job site, and Victoria has to stay at the B and B. There are guests checking in any moment, and she has Harper to take care of."

"What about Melody and Brad?"

She shook her head. "They're in Newark giving a benefit concert this evening."

He sighed. "Is there anyone else you could ask?"

"I really don't have many close friends around here. Not ones who would drive three hours to New York and back."

He was afraid of that.

"What about a taxi?"

"A taxi from here would cost a fortune, and I spent all of my disposable cash throwing *someone* a birthday party," she said tightly, still refusing to meet his eyes.

A birthday party for a fake birthday. He still felt guilty about that. "I'm sorry, Heather... I'd drive you myself, but..." He couldn't go to New York. He'd promised that he'd stay away and try to keep a low profile. And if he got hurt and couldn't testify, who knew when his sister and nephew could return to their home? Their lives? There was so much at stake. And he couldn't tell Heather any of it. His jaw tightened, and he wanted to kick something.

"But?" She looked at him expectantly.

The pleading and disappointment in her eyes was too much.

He stared at the darkening sky for a long moment, going back and forth in his mind a million times.

Screw it. "Turn the car around, and I'll meet

you at the B and B. I'll drive you." He could drop her off, wait in the car for her, then head straight back. His next shift didn't start until that evening. How long could an interview take? An hour? No one had to know he was there, and Sheriff Bishop didn't have to know he'd left town. Cody was spending the day with his wife, since it was her due date, so he wasn't tagging along that morning. No one would know. Everything would be fine.

When her face lit up, there was no changing his mind anyway. "You will?"

"Yes. Meet you at the B and B," he said, tapping the roof of the car.

He must be out of his mind.

Or falling in love with her.

Fan-freaking-tastic.

SITTING IN THE passenger seat of her car a few minutes later, Heather removed her jacket in the warmth of the vehicle.

That was a close one. For a second, she'd thought she might not make it to the interview. Jake's offer to drive her was actually a good thing because she really was nervous about the slippery highways. By the time she arrived, she would've probably been too stressed to be at her best.

Still, his offer had taken him quite a bit of thought, and she couldn't help but wonder what that was about.

"A little underdressed for an interview, aren't you?" Jake asked, glancing at her as he put the car in reverse.

"My interview clothes are in the backseat. I don't think I'd be getting the job if I showed up wearing this."

He slowly scanned her white tank top and navy yoga pants. "I'd hire you."

A rush of heat soared through her. "Just drive. I'm going to be late," she said, turning her attention out the window. Suddenly, spending hours in the car with Jake seemed like a terrible idea. If things went well, soon she would be leaving Brookhollow…and if her schedule was half as busy as it had been at Clarke and Johnston, she wouldn't have time to visit often, if at all. She wondered if she should say something…but she couldn't decide if it was necessary or not. Since his party, she hadn't seen him; he hadn't shown up at the bar again, and despite the intense look of interest he'd just given her, he seemed to have taken her instructions and had turned his focus strictly to driving.

Kicking her feet free of her boots, she tucked her legs beneath her.

He cleared his throat then turned down the volume on the Christmas music. "So about the other night."

"At the party?" Okay, so she was going to pretend she didn't know what he was referring to.

"No, at the station."

She waved a hand and scoffed. "That was nothing. Don't sweat it," she said, hoping she sounded convincing. In truth, she'd thought about that "nothing" for two days straight.

He nodded, looking slightly relieved. "Okay."

"Okay."

"Yeah, but it kinda wasn't nothing, and I feel like I should apologize again and explain…"

She swallowed hard. "There's nothing to explain, Jake. Neither of us is looking for a relationship right now."

He still looked frustrated, but he nodded. "Okay. So we're still good?"

"We're good. Besides, December 7—that would make you a…Sagittarius."

He shrugged. "If you say so."

"I'm a Virgo."

"Okayyy…"

"It just further proves that we're incompatible. So even if I wasn't leaving Brookhollow and you weren't so closed-off and antirelationship-y, this would never work." Well, that solved that. Even the stars didn't align for them—it was a sign. Too bad her heart was beating the crap out of her common sense.

"Incompatible, huh?" Jake asked, swerving quickly into the outer lane and pulling to the curb. He released his seat belt and reached for her.

Her eyes widened. "What are you doing?"

"You have your way of determining if we're compatible. Let me show you mine," he said, placing his hands on her face and kissing her.

She blinked in surprise, then quickly gave in, closing her eyes and wrapping her arms around his neck. His fingers tangled in her hair, and she didn't even care that she'd spent over an hour painstakingly flat-ironing it to perfection. His mouth exploring hers was bound to be wreaking havoc with her lip liner, but again, she couldn't care less. She deepened the kiss, moving closer to him until the gear shift was pressing into the side of her leg. She barely felt it, enjoying the way his tongue teased her bottom lip. She moaned softly, and he pulled away reluctantly.

"Care to reevaluate our compatibility?" he asked, sounding more than a little annoyed at the outcome of his test.

She was in trouble. The stars could say what they wanted, but Jake's compatibility test said so much more.

"How can they close a Starbucks?" Heather stared wide-eyed at the sign on the door three hours later. "I assumed Starbucks were like churches—always open and there when you need them."

Jacob leaned over and read the notice. "Says they're closed due to flooding," he said, rubbing his hands together and blowing on them for heat. The forecasted snow had started, and the temperature seemed to have dropped ten degrees since they'd left Brookhollow. Even the Sixth Avenue skyscrapers looked frosty, and rather than block the violent wind ripping through his jacket, the buildings seemed to channel it.

They climbed back into the car, and Heather sighed. "Great."

"Can't you change in the bathroom at the Highstone Acquisitions office?" he asked, cranking the heat.

"No. How lame would that be? I'll walk in dressed like this, announce I'm there to see Mike Ainsley, and then ask if they have a bathroom I can use to prepare?"

He wasn't seeing the problem, but he shrugged. "You're right. Crazy idea." He shook his head. His sister was correct; he'd never understand women.

"I'm just going to have to change in the backseat," she said, climbing out and quickly getting in the back.

Was she serious?

"Promise me you won't look," she said, already reaching for the hem of her tank top.

"Oh, no. Definitely not," he mumbled, opening the door. "I'll wait out here, try to block a window for you or something." He was only a man. There was no way he could sit in the car while she changed her clothes without sneaking a peek.

Shivering, he leaned against the back door, using his body to block the view of Heather getting changed from people walking past.

Standing on the busy streets, he felt more relaxed than he had in months. He missed the city, craved it even, and he prayed he could get back here soon. Months away from everything familiar, the place he'd grown up in and barely ever left, was far too long. It was worse than when he'd been undercover, because at least then he'd been able to stay in New York. He might have been pretending to be someone he wasn't, but the city, his surroundings, had all remained the same.

Down the street, a family stopped among the dense crowds gathered in front of the Macy's holiday window display—a winter wonderland theme with mannequins posed inside large inflatable snow globes, and he sighed. He took Kyle shopping there every year to buy a present for his mom. It was already December, and so far, he'd heard nothing about the court case and still no word from Emilio. He didn't think their annual shopping trip would be happening this year.

Nor would the skating at Rockefeller Center or the horse-drawn carriage rides through

Central Park. He wondered if Heather would partake in those holiday activities again, once she was back here…and with whom?

"Okay, I'm ready," she said, opening the door he was leaning against, pushing him out of the way to clamber out.

"I think you only showed your butt to about—" He stopped as he took her in. In skinny jeans and boots, Heather was a knockout; in yoga pants and tank top, she was nearly irresistible. But dressed in a gray pencil skirt and jacket, the lace of a red camisole revealed at the top, she knocked him on his butt.

"You were saying?" she asked, raising one eyebrow.

He did a quick scan down to the six-inch black heels she wore, then he quickly averted his gaze. Who knew what he was saying? He could barely remember his own name right now. And that was not good. Not good at all. He had to pull it together. "You look…fine."

"Would you hire me?"

He'd do more than just hire her. He nodded. "Without a doubt. You got this."

She licked her lips and let out a deep breath. "Thanks, Jake. I really appreciate it. I need this job."

Right. This job. The one that would take her away from Brookhollow, away from him... and right before Christmas, a holiday he'd been dreading. Spending it by himself now seemed even more lonely and depressing. "You'll get it." He checked his watch. "But you said this guy is a clock-watcher, right?"

Her eyes widened. "What time is it?"

"Three minutes to ten. Hope you can run in..." He moved away and gestured to her heels, but she was already sprinting down Sixth Avenue. "Impressive." He was in trouble.

HEATHER STOPPED FOR a breath outside of the office two and a half minutes later. If Ainsley's clock was fast, she was doomed. She hadn't exactly factored in being hauled over by police, or a make-out session, or having to change into an impossibly tight pencil skirt in the cramped backseat of a car. But she doubted she should mention any of those things to her potential new boss.

She walked into the reception area, where two young women sat behind a desk, headsets on, taking incoming calls. Heather waited for one of them to end her call and glance at her.

"Hi, I'm Heather Corbett. I have an interview with Mike Ainsley Sr. at ten o'clock."

The blonde swiveled in her chair to check the large wooden clock on the wall behind her beneath the Highstone Acquisitions sign.

"I'm on time," Heather insisted quickly. Gone were the days at Clarke and Johnston when she could stroll in whenever she felt like it. Dating the boss had really enabled her non-morning-person habits, if nothing else. Oh, well, she could be a morning person. She just had to try harder. This new position—this new start—would be worth it. Besides, Mr. Ainsley had mentioned a lot of travel, so at least she wouldn't be in the office much… No, that wasn't the right way to go into this position. Attitude-check time. Unlike at Clarke and Johnston, where she'd relied on her relationship with her boss to keep her employed, this time she was going to work hard and get the better cases on her own merit.

"Please, fill this out and I'll let him know you're here," the receptionist said, typing a mile a minute.

"I, uh…submitted a résumé already," she said, scanning the three-page application. Mr.

Ainsley had all of this info already. Couldn't she just write *See Résumé* across the front?

"Yeah, he probably hasn't read that. And HR will need all of this filled out if you do get the job." She didn't sound confident that Heather would. "So, just fill this one out," she said, answering another call.

Heather smiled politely as she carried the clipboard over to a dark leather couch. But a second later, the woman stood and said, "Heather, he says he's ready for you now. You can just head down the hall—his office is the last one on the right. Oh, and be careful when you open the office door," she said.

Heather frowned as she stood. "Be careful opening the door?" she asked, but the woman had answered the phone again and had gone back to ignoring her. "Okay, then," she mumbled, walking toward Mr. Ainsley's room.

The offices on either side were composed of glass walls, and each side had a different yet fantastic view of the city. Each had a large mahogany desk and leather chairs, bookshelves built into the walls, small sofas near the window and wall-mounted fireplaces. Cozy and inviting, but professional. Her excitement rose. She'd missed this: the high-powered career, the beautiful offices in a high-rise in the most exciting city in the world, the sea of yellow taxis on the streets below and the crowds of people rushing from one place to another, lattes in hand.

She'd been missing the city, but she hadn't realized just how much until she was here, remembering everything it had to offer—success, fulfillment and excitement. And takeout at any hour.

When she reached Mr. Ainsley's office, she glanced in through the glass but didn't see the man at his desk. She knocked.

"Come in," he called.

Slowly, carefully, she opened the door.

Mike Ainsley Sr. stood on a step stool on the other side, hanging bright red garland on the wall above the door. He struggled to reach the far corner.

"Hi, I'm Heather Corbett," she said.

He glanced at her and nodded. "Perfect. You're tall."

*Huh?*

He climbed down from the step stool, letting the piece of garland dangle. "Would you mind hanging this? Just secure it in that far corner."

Was he for real? He wanted her help decorating his office? They hadn't even shaken hands yet.

Well, whatever it took to get the job... Within reason this time, of course. "Sure." She handed him the clipboard. "Sorry, I just got here, so this isn't filled out yet."

"That's why you should always plan to arrive at least ten minutes early," he said, setting it aside.

She carefully climbed onto the top rung of the ladder, reaching for the end of the garland. Ten minutes early? She'd driven all the way from New Jersey...give her a break. Maybe she should have driven out earlier...but she'd wanted to throw the party for Jake. "Yes... you're right," she said politely, remembering her commitment to changing her outlook on her career. She easily reached the corner and fastened the garland in place, noticing the rest of it lying on his sofa, along with Christmas tree decorations and window hangings. *Please, don't let him ask me to decorate his entire office*, she thought as she climbed back down. "There you are."

"Great, thank you," he said, and to her relief he went around his desk and sat, gesturing at the chair across from him. "Have a seat."

"Thank you. Beautiful offices."

"We like to make our staff comfortable, since they work long hours when they aren't traveling."

She sat. "Thank you again for seeing me."

"Your brother-in-law gave you a high recommendation," he said, reaching for a file folder of résumés on his desk.

"He really enjoys working here. He's told me nothing but good things about the company." Of course, she'd always countered that Clarke and Johnston was better…but her opinion may have been clouded at the time.

"He's one of our best agents." Mr. Ainsley scanned her résumé. "So your last position was with Clarke and Johnston Acquisitions almost two years ago—is that correct?"

"Yes."

"And what have you been doing since you left there?"

"Actually, I took a little break from the city for a while. I've been helping to run a B and B and a local pool hall in Brookhollow, New Jersey." She hoped her work ethic showed, if nothing else. She wished the gap after the job at Clarke and Johnston hadn't been so long; she could have fudged the dates a little.

"A B and B and a pool hall…" He said the words as if something didn't add up.

Probably because they didn't. *She* couldn't believe how her life had been going for the past year and a half; how could she expect this man to? She swallowed hard. "Well, opportunities in the small town are limited, but I'm a hard worker and dedicated—"

The office door opened, and she almost sighed in relief to have her desperate explanation cut short. She turned to see a younger man walk in.

"Hi. Sorry to interrupt. Dad, Amy said you were looking for me," he said, his gaze locked on Heather.

*Dad.* Mike Ainsley Jr. The complete opposite of his father: tall, muscular and handsome. And judging by his confident smile, Armani shoes and faux hawk—which was almost inappropriate for an office, yet somehow seemed as professional as his designer suit—he knew it.

"Yes, I was. I needed you to hang something, but Heather was kind enough to do it," Mike Sr. said. "But since you're here, why don't you join us? This is Heather Corbett, Rob Ashley's sister-in-law. She's interviewing for the acquisitions position opening in the new year."

"Oh, great. Rob mentioned you would be stopping by. Nice to meet you," Mike Jr. said, coming closer and extending a hand.

"You, too," she said, feeling her nervousness grow. An interview was intimidating enough; being interviewed by two men, one of whom looked like a GQ model, was deeply unnerving.

The younger executive pushed the holiday decorations to one side of the sofa and sat.

Mike Sr. glanced at her résumé once more. "Where were we?"

Heather remained silent. No sense reminding him of her current irrelevant employment status.

"Right, your work experience. What were your reasons for leaving Clarke and Johnston?"

Oh, no. She'd known that one was coming. She also knew there was no point in lying. Mr. Ainsley had probably already heard the answer. Staff changeover was high in this industry, and agents moved around—they talked. "I was fired," she said, slowly.

He frowned. "Rob said you took a leave of absence."

Crap. "Oh…well, that's probably what I told him…" Her cheeks flamed. "I mean, who wants to admit to their family they were fired, right?"

He frowned and scratched his forehead.

Mike Jr. coughed behind her.

"I mean, especially given the circumstances…" Oh, this was not going well. Stupid Rob. He should have told her he'd lied on her behalf. Now they both looked like morons.

"Why were you let go?" Mike Jr. asked behind her.

This kept getting better and better. She should just thank them for their time and leave now. Her palms were sweaty as she clutched them together on her lap and willed her knees to stop shaking.

No. She wanted this job. She hesitated before answering. Honesty was always the best policy, right? She'd soon find out. She turned in her chair so she could see both men. "Well… Mel Clarke, my former boss, said it was due to numbers not being as high…"

Mike Sr. sat back in his chair, and his expression changed to one of disinterest.

"B-but that wasn't the real reason, I assure you. My numbers were just as high as anyone else's. He fired me because he'd dumped me the same week, and it was awkward working together," she said quickly. There, the truth was out.

Mike Sr. sat forward again, his expression now unreadable. He folded his hands and studied her. She refused to even glance at Mike Jr.

In the brief, awkward silence that followed, her heart echoed in her ears. This was a disaster. How was she ever going to secure a new position in acquisitions with her previous history? The two-year break was bad enough, and the fact that she'd been fired from her most recent relevant position didn't bode well, especially when she had to decide whether to tell the truth or let them assume she wasn't capable of the job. A no-win situation that she had no one to blame for but herself.

"You were in a relationship with your boss?" Mike Sr. asked finally.

"Yes." Her shoulders slumped.

"And he fired you and dumped you in the same week?"

"Yes."

"What a jerk," the older man said.

Heather's head shot up in surprise, but Mike, Sr. was already scanning her résumé again.

"So, how much travel did you do before?" he asked.

She sat straighter. They were moving on? The interview wasn't over? "Oh…um…about fifty percent," she said, her confidence returning. If her dismissal and relationship with her boss weren't deal-breakers, maybe she would get this position after all.

"And you're willing to do that again? No family obligations in the way?"

An image of Jake flashed briefly in her mind before she punched it in the face. "No, sir. None."

JACOB JUMPED AT the sound of the passenger-door handle snapping what felt like only seconds after he'd closed his eyes. Heart pounding, he straightened quickly and reached across to unlock the door. A shivering Heather climbed into the car.

"I swear it's even colder out there now than it was when we got here. Brrrrr!"

Reaching into the backseat, he grabbed her jacket and wrapped it around her shoulders. "So, how did it go?" A quick glance at the time on the dash revealed she'd actually been at Highstone Acquisitions for more than an hour. Hopefully that meant it had gone well.

Hopefully? Of course hopefully.

While she'd been inside, he'd come to the conclusion that Heather moving back to the city was ultimately a good thing, and the sooner, the better. He couldn't afford any distractions or unwanted complications. When Emilio called, Jacob was moving in. And there was no predicting how that bust would go. He and Heather would both be much better off once she was gone.

"Good, I think," she said, sliding her arms inside the coat. "I can never tell... I mean it started off awkward, but then it got better... I think." She bit her lip. "I don't know."

"I'm sure you did great."

Her forehead wrinkled, and she looked about to say something, but for once her lips remained shut.

For all of nine seconds.

"You're not bothered by this? Me getting a

job in the city…leaving Brookhollow?" she blurted out.

Jacob sighed. He was making a mess of things. His actions must seem crazy to her. His flirting, his kissing and then his support and encouragement about the job. How could he explain it when he really didn't fully understand it himself? "The thing is, even if you were staying, you said it yourself—I'm not a relationship guy. My job makes it…hard to get close to people."

"Maybe when you were in New York, but in Brookhollow? It should be a little easier now, right?"

He hesitated. "Maybe… I don't know. But either way—you're leaving, right?"

She nodded.

He checked his watch. "We should get on the road…we could stop for food if you want, or coffee…" He was hungry, and he knew he should probably eat before starting the drive back. He pulled the car back out into the sea of traffic.

"Um, actually, I'd like to stop somewhere else real quick…"

He had to get back to Brookhollow. He shouldn't even be here at all. He checked the time again, then rubbed his palm across his face. "Okay, but real quick. Where?"

"My sister's office."

## CHAPTER EIGHT

EVERY INSTINCT IN Jacob's body told him to turn around and go back to the car. But his sugar levels were dropping, and he wouldn't be able to drive if they dipped even lower. So his feet kept moving behind Heather as she climbed the front steps to his lawyer's office building.

She gave him a reassuring smile as they entered. "Don't worry. It will be fine. She doesn't bite."

Still, from what he knew of her track record in court, Cameron's bark could be pretty intimidating.

Heather walked over to the security desk, and he reluctantly followed, keeping his head down and his gaze away from the building's surveillance cameras. He was crazy for doing this. Driving her to the city was bad enough, but this was just plain stupid. "Hey, I really think I should just find something to eat and then go back to the car," he said.

She linked her arm through his and pulled him closer as she announced her visit to the security guard at the desk. "Heather Corbett here to see Cameron Ashley."

"Which office?" he asked, picking up the intercom phone.

"Third floor...the entire third floor," she said with a shrug and an I-hope-that-helps smile, which of course, the guard accepted.

"Just a minute, ma'am," he said, dialing third-floor reception. A second later, he covered the receiver and glanced at Jacob. "And you are?"

"Uh...um..."

"He's my driver, Jake," Heather said with a playful grin.

The guard nodded. "She'll be down in a minute."

"Thank you," Heather said, leading Jacob away from the desk.

He scanned the lobby, uneasiness creeping up his spine. He could be recognized so easily here. He swallowed hard and ducked his head as several lawyers he recognized from court passed them. Being here was a big mistake, getting bigger with every moment. "Heather, I—"

"Ah, there she is," she interrupted, staring past him toward the elevators.

Oh, no.

"Relax. Just be cool," she whispered, as she turned him around to face his lawyer.

Cameron's smile faded so quickly he thought he'd imagined it when her gaze landed on him. The sound of her high heels against the marble floor kept time with his pounding heart. His breath caught in his chest, and he fought the urge to flee. Though it was probably more the death grip Heather had on his forearm keeping him in place.

"Hey, sis," Heather said, finally releasing him and giving her sister a hug.

Cameron's arms remained limp at her sides, as she shot Jacob a panicked, annoyed, quizzical look over Heather's shoulder.

Now was his chance to escape, but rushing off would be way too hard to explain to Heather, and he was afraid of how Cameron would handle things if he left them alone. So, eyes wide, he shrugged and gave what he hoped was a stay-cool-she-doesn't-know-anything-this-is-all-a-big-crappy-coincidence expression.

"Who's your friend?" she asked a second later, as Heather stepped away.

"This is Sheriff Matthews—Jake." Heather smiled.

How could Heather not feel the suffocating tension in the hallway that threatened to make the entire building implode? "Hi," he said.

"Jake?" Cameron repeated, eyeing him.

He nodded. She knew he hated being called Jake. He had the feeling she was going to be using this shortened version of his name a lot.

"And what are you doing here, *Jake*?" she asked.

Heather glared at her sister. "Be more rude!"

Cameron ignored her as she continued to stare at him, waiting for an answer.

"No, it's cool," he told Heather. His mouth felt chalky as he turned to Cameron. "I, uh… drove Heather to her interview."

"From Brookhollow?" Realization dawned on Cameron's face.

Next to him, Heather nodded. "Yes. My driver's license expired…"

"Two years ago—yes, I know. I've been harassing you to get it renewed for that whole time, remember?" Cameron said, finally taking her eyes off him to scold her younger sister.

He could breathe again. Heather was still oblivious, so if he and Cameron could just keep acting as if they didn't know each other, everything would be fine. And as long as Heather never found out they were both deceiving her, then, yes, everything would be fine, he thought wryly.

"I told Jake I'll renew it as soon as we get back to Brookhollow, okay, so you can both relax."

Relax—ha!

Heather picked up her bag of clothes. "I'll be back in a minute…"

"Where are you going?" they both asked in unison.

Heather glanced between the two of them. "What's going on with you two?" Her eyes widened. "Did you two used to date or something?" Now it was her turn to go pale.

"No!" Cameron said, and Jacob shook his head.

Man, this was a big mess. One he needed to get out of quickly.

"Okay…well, I'm going to change, then I desperately need coffee."

He watched her disappear down the hall,

resisting the urge to grab her leg and beg her not to leave him alone with Cameron. Barely.

"*What* is going on, Jacob?" Cameron seethed, advancing toward him the second Heather disappeared from sight. "Or should I say, *Jake*."

"This was not my fault. I insisted I wait in the car while she visited with you," he said.

Her mouth gaped. "You think *that's* the problem? You shouldn't even be in the city at all." Her voice rose, and he motioned for her to quiet down. "And not to mention that there are people in this city who want you dead. Are you trying to get killed before the court case?" Hands on her hips, she looked as if she didn't know whether to hit him or hide him somewhere.

"No, of course not. It was stupid coming here—"

"You think?"

"Shh! Heather doesn't know who I am. Let's just get through the next hour, and then I'll be back in Brookhollow, and we can pretend I was always there, okay?" He touched her arm.

"We are so close, Jacob, to getting this guy. *You* are our key witness. I need you alive. The department needs you alive. You, of all people, should know how important it is that you continue to breathe." The case was her first priority; he understood that. At least someone was thinking clearly. But while his lawyer might have a lot of time and energy invested in this case, she wasn't the one who'd been exiled to the middle of nowhere, separated from the only family she had and forced to live lies without a clue how long it would be necessary. Not to mention a dangerous secret backup plan.

"I know. Just please don't say anything to the department or the head of witness protection." If they found out, they could cut Amber and Kyle's protection, and then there would be no way to ensure his family's safety. "Please, Cameron."

She sighed. "How on earth did my sister convince you to do this?"

"It's a long story," he said, noticing the bathroom door opening. "She's coming."

His lawyer studied him with perceptive eyes. "You're falling in love with my sister," she said, her tone annoyed but not entirely surprised.

He remained silent. Heather was getting closer…and well, he really didn't know what to say. The truth was, he was falling for Heather. Of course, he had zero intentions of acting on that. Right…'cause the kiss they'd shared was really a sign of him restraining himself.

"Oh, jeez, Jacob. That doesn't complicate things at all." Cameron smacked him in the back of the head and forced a fake smile as Heather rejoined them.

"All set—you guys ready to go eat?" Heather asked.

Jacob cleared his throat. "You know, you two haven't seen one another in a while, so I'll let you both catch up. I'll just wait for you in the car."

"Are you sure? It's totally fine…"

Cameron nodded. "Actually, if Jake doesn't mind, I really could use some one-on-one time…try to talk some sense into you," she added in a mumble.

Jacob frowned.

"Huh?" Heather asked.

Cameron shook her head. "Just about getting your driver's license renewed," she said quickly. "Let's go."

Jacob followed the women outside.

"Are you sure?" Heather asked him again,

as Cameron practically dragged her down the street.

He nodded. "Go eat."

As he climbed back in the car a moment later, Cameron's words played on repeat in his mind. Was he falling in love with Heather? He liked her. A lot. More than he'd liked any woman he'd met in a long time. It just sucked that he was meeting her under these circumstances...when he couldn't be completely honest with her about who he was.

But did that option ever exist in his life? In his chosen career? He hadn't thought so, which was why he'd decided to remain single instead of complicating his life and someone else's. Going undercover with a wife and family waiting and worrying back at home hadn't seemed fair.

He doubted that things could ever work between him and a woman. Just the idea that being with him could put yet another person's life in danger was enough for him to stay away.

Jacob drove away down the crowded street, not realizing the direction he was headed until ten minutes later, he parked across from his sister's gallery—Amber Marx Studios. Paintings were still displayed in the window, but the open sign was off and stacks of old newspapers littered the step. Through the front window, the place looked dark and deserted. Such a stark contrast to the lively showings and artist events his sister had held there regularly. Since opening the gallery four years before, Amber had made quite a name for herself in the art world, and her studio had been on its way to becoming the spot to discover new talent in New York.

Guilt washed over him. Amber had given up so much for the safety of her son—and herself. A predicament he'd put them in. Telling them they would have to go into witness protection had been the hardest thing he'd ever had to do and one of the worst things their family had had to face.

He remembered that day five months ago well…too well.

The terror in his sister's eyes when she'd opened the door to their apartment and dragged him inside was a punch to the gut. He couldn't remember ever seeing Amber afraid. Mad—yes. Annoyed—most of the time. But scared—never.

"Where's the note?" he'd asked, glancing

around the apartment. If these guys had gone to his nephew's school, they wouldn't hesitate to show up there. The thought had made him nauseous, and the idea that these dangerous men would go anywhere near his family had made his blood run cold.

Her hand shaking, Amber had taken the note from the pocket of her sweater and handed it to him.

The threatening words were written in crayon, but this was no schoolyard prank. The L.G. at the bottom of the page was a signature he'd seen many times and would recognize anywhere. And he knew what it meant—his family was being targeted. Gonzales's men liked to toy with people, make them afraid, then strike. But even though they prolonged the torturous suspense, they always struck. He knew. He'd been forced to strike with them.

Maybe this was retribution for the pain and suffering he'd been a part of. He couldn't mess with other people's lives and not expect some form of punishment. Good or bad, lives were lives, and hiding behind his badge and the idea that one less criminal on the street was best for everyone didn't change the fact that now his family was suffering the consequences of his failure.

"It's for real, isn't it?" Amber had asked, pacing the living room.

He'd nodded.

"Damn it, Jacob—what are you involved in?"

He hadn't answered. She knew he couldn't tell her anything about the cases he worked on. Instead, he'd dialed his commanding officer's number. "I've got to get you both out of here."

"What do you mean? A hotel?"

"No, that's not safe enough. They're watching. These guys have eyes everywhere." His boss's phone had continued to ring while Jacob pried open two slats in the blinds and checked outside. The cartel could even have been watching at that moment. He couldn't get his family out of there fast enough.

Amber had reached out and snatched the phone away, disconnecting the call, just as his boss had answered.

"Amber."

"We're not leaving New York, Jacob." She'd wagged his cell phone at him, angry tears glistening in her eyes.

"You don't have a choice. These guys are not messing around. They know where Kyle goes to school. They more than likely know where you both live, where you work…" It didn't take these men long to gather all of the information they needed on someone.

"Okay, so we'll move into your apartment for a few weeks until this all blows over."

His sister hadn't understood. "This stuff doesn't just blow over. I've been undercover on this case for two years…" He'd run a hand through his hair, unsure how much he could and should reveal. Enough to convince her this was serious. "My cover was blown last night…and I know far more than they'll allow me to live knowing." He'd put his hands on his hips and sighed. "I need to get you both under witness protection as soon as possible." Like yesterday. They'd already stayed there long enough. He'd never forgive himself if anything happened to his family.

Her eyes had widened. "Witness protection? No way. I've been busting my butt to get ready for my biggest gallery showing of the year in two weeks, and Kyle just started making friends at his new school—you know how hard that is for him."

Jacob had cringed. His nephew suffered from a mild form of autism and was often misunderstood by teachers and bullied by peers. To hear he was doing better, then turn around and ask them to uproot, tore a hole through him. Kyle making friends and his sister's gallery showing were important, but nothing was more important than staying alive and safe. "You're both in danger."

"Because of you and your job," she'd said angrily.

He'd bitten back the argument rising within him—his job had almost torn the family apart when he'd been forced to arrest his father. Jacob had been the one responsible for putting him behind bars three years ago, and he knew his sister blamed him for dismantling the family. "I'm sorry. I realize this is unfair, but I need to think about your safety."

Defeated, his sister had slumped into a chair. "I can't believe this is happening. Where are we going to go?"

He'd gently taken his phone away from her and hit redial on his boss's number. "I don't know and I won't know." The best option he had for protecting them was not to find out where they were going. Then he couldn't reveal any information—under any circumstances.

"You're not coming with us?"

"No."

"We have to leave, but you get to stay in the city?" Her anger had returned.

"No. I'll be sent somewhere else."

Tears of frustration had gathered in his sister's eyes once again, breaking his heart. "What am I supposed to tell Kyle? He's going to hate this."

"I'll talk to him." The boy's father had left when he was just a baby…then Jacob had put his grandfather in jail. Would the boy understand he wasn't leaving him by choice?

"When will we be able to come back home?"

"I don't know," he'd said as his boss answered.

Staring at the gallery now, he knew he'd done the only thing he could to protect his family, but still the guilt plagued him. Amber had never approved of his decision to go undercover, and at the time he'd felt his life choices didn't really affect her.

How wrong he'd been.

"WHAT IS UP with you? I thought you'd be happy to see the sister you haven't seen in months," Heather said, struggling to keep up with Cameron on the slushy sidewalk. Her sister took mastery of heels on snow to a whole other level.

Cameron sighed. "I am… I just wasn't expecting…"

"Jake?" Heather frowned. "I told you, he's the new local sheriff in Brookhollow. Well, actually, he's been there now for about five months. By law, he couldn't let me drive out here for the interview with an expired license, so he offered to drive me."

Her sister stopped in front of their usual lunch meet-up, a café on the corner of Wall Street—one Heather had missed terribly. Her expression was unreadable. "And that's all there is to it? He was just being neighborly instead of giving you a ticket? You're sure?"

Cameron was perceptive. Three minutes of seeing her with Jake had obviously set her spidey senses tingling.

Still, she lied. "Yes." A memory of his kiss on the side of the highway almost betrayed her, so she moved past her sister into the café. "Come on, I'm starving…and I do have someone waiting on me." The thought of the road-trip back with Jake brought a small smile to her face.

"Right there! That smile—I knew it," Cameron said, selecting a turkey sandwich from the cooler and a low-fat bran muffin from the basket on the counter.

Heather reached for a ham sandwich and a double-chocolate cookie. "You know nothing. You're reading way too much into this."

They paid for their orders and found a table near the fireplace in the corner of the café. "How well do you know this guy?" Cameron asked, unwrapping her sandwich.

Heather shrugged. "I don't know. He comes into the bar every night…"

"Great, he's turning to alcohol," Cameron mumbled.

Heather frowned. "What?"

"Oh, I mean—he's an alcoholic," Cameron said quickly.

"No, he's not. He has one drink…sometimes not even." She shook her head and bit into the sandwich. Why was her sister so intent on talking about Jake?

"Okay, what do you know about him?"

"Not much—he's from Manhattan, he has a sister and a nephew…"

Her sister was watching her intently.

"He was abducted by aliens and has visited Neverland with Peter Pan... Come on, Cameron. He's just some guy. Can we talk about something else, please?" Normally she'd be excited to share information with her sister about a guy she was interested in, but this time it was different. She had no idea where things stood with Jake, and the last thing she needed was her sister thinking that once again she planned to let a man control her future. That wasn't happening.

Her sister sighed. "Fine."

"How's Dylan?"

"Excited to have you with us for Christmas this year." She pointed at her. "So, you better make sure that this 'some guy' doesn't change our holiday plans...or your life plans."

Wonderful. They'd come full circle in less than three seconds. Heather took another bite of her sandwich and avoided her sister's eyes. "Of course, Cameron. Give me some credit—I know what's important, and I'm not planning to lose sight of that." Besides, hadn't Jake said just an hour before that a relationship wasn't something he'd consider right now?

# CHAPTER NINE

As HEATHER BUCKLED her seat belt in the car almost an hour later, she tossed Jake a sandwich. "I wasn't sure what you might like, so I took a guess."

"Thank you. Sorry about skipping out on you like that—I just got the feeling your sister really wanted to spend time with just you." He unwrapped the sandwich, then pulled out of the parking spot.

"Sorry about her. She was extra sisterly today," she said, rolling her eyes.

"It was totally fine. She's…nice."

"That's a stretch, but I like her." She removed her boots and put her feet up on the dash. "She's working on a really big case right now, and it's making her a little crazy, I think." But while she'd tried to dismiss her sister's qualms about her feelings for Jake and his feelings for her, Cameron wasn't wrong in her assumptions.

"What's the case about?"

"She can't talk about it, as usual—at least not until it's all over, but I think it has to do with that high-profile drug dealer, Leo something or other, who was arrested this summer," she said. She didn't know much about the case, just how much it was stressing her sister out. She'd never seen her so wound up about work before. Cameron was always passionate about her cases, and her long hours were normal, but Dylan had said more than one morning he'd woken to find his mom asleep at the kitchen table, still in her work clothes from the day before.

And it hadn't escaped Heather's notice that Cameron's clothing was hanging off of her or the fact she'd consumed twice as much coffee than she normally did and ate next to nothing of her lunch. "I'm worried about her," she admitted.

Jake reached across and took her hand, giving it a squeeze. "I'm sure things will get better soon. The holidays are coming, so I'm sure she'll get a break then."

"I hope so. It's one of the other reasons I would love to have this job before Christmas. I'd like to be out here with them for the holidays and be able to help with Dylan. Rob is great, but he works as much as Cameron does, and he travels a lot."

"Will you be traveling a lot once you get the job?"

"*If* I get the job, then, yeah, about fifty percent of the time." She bit her lip. The travel had never bothered her before…and it shouldn't bother her now.

She heard a beeping noise and turned to face him. "What's that?"

Reaching into his pocket, Jake took out a small black monitor. "My glucose monitor. My blood sugar levels are low, so it's telling me to eat. The sandwich will help," he said.

"You're diabetic?" She'd had no idea.

He nodded.

"Since when?"

"I was diagnosed at eight."

"Wow. Sorry to hear that. I always associate diabetes with older people."

"Juvenile diabetes sucks. There were even younger children at the hospital with me when I first found out. I was in there for a week until my blood sugars balanced, and I learned how to help control the highs and lows." He turned onto the highway, then bit into the sandwich.

"Which is worse? Highs or lows?" She really knew nothing about the disease.

"They both cause problems. Too many highs can destroy your liver and other organs, while the lows can make you kinda loopy, almost like you're drunk, and in severe cases they can lead to blackouts, coma or death." His voice hardened as he said it, and she noticed his grip tightened on the steering wheel.

"How does the monitor work?" she asked, hoping the discussion wasn't bothering him. She longed to know more about it…about him. Whatever he revealed about himself, it was never enough, but she also didn't want to push or pry.

He lifted his jacket and shirt to reveal a plastic device on his skin, keeping his eyes on the road. "This sensor has a tiny needle inside that sends readings continuously to the monitor. It beeps when my blood goes above eight or below four. In between is where I need to stay."

"Does it hurt?"

He shook his head.

"Is it hard to control the highs and lows?"

"It was at first. I was hospitalized a few times in high school—the last thing on my mind at fifteen was making sure my blood sugar levels were balanced. I was on every sports team at school, so my father bought me the monitor to help me stay on top of it. Once I was diagnosed, he kinda made it his life mission to try to fix me. As soon as new technology was available, I had it. Clinical trials..."

Something in his voice made her think his father was a hot topic, but her desperate craving for information about him made her ask anyway. "Are you and your dad close?"

He stared straight ahead. "We were. Really close actually, before I sent him to jail for ten years for corporate fraud."

Her mouth dropped open. "I'm so sorry, Jake. It was none of my business..."

He glanced at her quickly. "Now do you understand why I try not to get close? My job will always mean that personal relationships come second to the greater good."

She nodded. She did now.

HEATHER STAPLED A row of white lights along the base of her float at the barn the next morning. Kayla was looking after the B and B's front desk to see how well she could handle things while Heather was still in town as backup, and so far she'd only called her once with a question. Heather was starting to feel better about leaving Victoria and the Brookhollow Inn. Kayla was smart and eager to learn—the front desk was in good hands.

So was the bar. Candace had readily stepped in to take over, and the bar's owner had already approved the latest transfer in management. Vacating both positions was going without a hitch, making it easy for her to leave.

Which should be a good thing. So why was the idea upsetting?

She wondered if Jake would find a replacement for her as quickly and easily once she left. It wouldn't be hard now, with all of his new admirers in town...

His revelation the day before about his father had shocked her, but it had given her insight into the mysterious man. It definitely explained his standoffish attitude and his unwillingness to get close to people. She couldn't even imagine how tough it must have been to have to put his own father in jail.

The diabetes, too, had surprised her. She hadn't been aware that people with the disease could even be on the police force. When she'd asked him about it, he'd said the process hadn't been easy and required a lot of persistence, but he'd proven that he could control his blood sugars and that it wouldn't be an issue. But something in his tone and the way he'd quickly changed the subject after that made her think that maybe there was more to it than he was revealing.

The brief glimpses into his life hadn't satisfied her curiosity one little bit; they had only sparked it further.

He'd also mentioned that his sister owned an art gallery on East 7th Street. How many could there be on East 7th Street? She bit her lip, reaching for her cell phone. She could look it up…maybe learn a little more.

Sitting on the edge of the float, she opened the Google app and typed in "art gallery on East 7th Street in New York" before she could change her mind.

She frowned as the information loaded. Amber Marx Studios was closed. Marx? She'd expected his sister's last name to be Matthews. A married name she'd kept, maybe? She opened the website and scanned the page. "Closed until further notice." Since when? Jake hadn't mentioned that.

She clicked on the About Us page, and an image of Jake's sister appeared, standing outside the gallery. Heather leaned closer to the phone. The brother and sister could be mistaken for twins, they looked so much alike. Same dark hair, dark eyes, thin nose...

She quickly scrolled through the rest of the pages. The art collections were amazing— mostly colorful abstract pieces, but also several framed scenic photographs that looked like refinished images of older shots.

She hit the contact page and stared at the phone number, wondering if the calls were being forwarded.

This was crazy. She was not going to call Jake's sister.

No, but she could call Amber, the art gallery owner, about one of the paintings...

But why? What was she hoping to learn?

Anything!

Dialing the number, Heather stood and paced the floor. If someone answered, she would just ask about when the gallery would be reopening. Simple.

The phone continued to ring, then the voice mail clicked on. "Thank you for calling Amber Marx Studios. Today is July 29. The gallery will be hosting a private event this evening and will be closed to the public, reopening on Monday, August first—"

Heather hit End on the call. July 29? That was the last recording? And by the sound of it, Amber had had every intention of going back to business as usual the following week. This made no sense.

July 29…around the same time Jake had arrived in Brookhollow.

Her eyes widened. Oh, no. Her stomach knotted.

Was his sister…dead?

Was that why he was here? To regroup after a family tragedy? But he talked about her as if she were alive.

Oh, no—was the guy crazy? That would be her luck, to fall in love with an insane guy.

But he didn't seem crazy. He seemed lonely, troubled…secretive, closed-off at times…

Her cell phone chimed with a new text message, making her jump.

Her hand flew to her heart. She was scaring the crap out of herself with her own overactive imagination.

She glanced at the phone. A message from Jill? That was odd. She barely knew the fitness instructor, except to see her at the bar with Jim sometimes…where she drank lemon water and gave Jim heck if he consumed too many beers.

Any chance you're available for dinner at our place tonight? Need guinea pigs.

Wow. Way to sell it, Jill.

She hesitated. She wasn't working at the bar that evening, and her only other plans were to sit around and make herself crazy thinking about Jake. She sighed as she texted back.

What time should I be there?

"Hi, Jake, is Sheriff Bishop around?" Cody asked, entering the station.

"No, he's off this morning. Taking his grandsons ice fishing," he said, grabbing his radio and squad car keys. "Ready to head out?"

"Actually, I'm not planning to ride with you today. The baby isn't feeling great, and Alison has been at the clinic all night, so I'm going to head over there once I get the other kids to school. I just stopped by to drop these off," he said, setting a file folder on the desk.

The young man looked tired and stressed. "Everything okay with the little one?"

He nodded slowly. "She's struggling with some fluid on her lungs. Dr. McCarthy wants her to stay in for a few days."

"Okay, well, I hope she gets better soon."

Cody nodded. "Can you just ask Sheriff Bishop to fill out the forms inside the folder and mail them when he gets a chance?"

Jacob narrowed his eyes as he caught the Boston Police Department's logo on the corner of the file. "That your recommendation letter?"

"Yeah. It's the last thing I need filled out before they'll schedule an interview and physical."

"Right. I'll let him know."

"Great. Thanks."

He watched the young man leave the office and saw him climb into an old minivan. He sighed as he opened the folder. The kid's academy grades were above average. He was smart and fit. With a good recommendation from Sheriff Bishop, there was no reason he wouldn't get the job in Boston. The big-city departments were often desperate for new re-cruits.

He tossed the folder back onto the desk and stuck a note for Sheriff Bishop on the front of it.

The door to the locker room opened, and Jim Bishop, Sheriff Bishop's oldest son, came through, talking into his cell. "Yes, Jill, I'll invite him…I'll do it right now if you let me off of the phone."

He turned to look at Jacob as he hung up and slid the cell into his pocket. "Women. I swear…" He shook his head. "Hi, Jake."

"Hey, man, everything okay?"

"Other than the fact that my girlfriend is so stressed about hosting Christmas dinner at our place this year she's decided to hold a test run tonight? Then, yes, everything's great."

Jake laughed. He'd met Jill once when she'd stopped by the fire hall. She was…a little high-strung, and he still couldn't wrap his head around the couple. Jim was so laid-back, Jacob often felt like checking him for a pulse. Maybe opposites really did attract.

"Anyway, she wanted me to invite you, if you're not doing anything."

He was being invited to fake holiday dinners now? "Um…"

"It's just Ethan and Bailey and us…she said she could use an 'honest opinion' or two," Jim said.

"And she thinks I won't hold back to save her feelings the way the rest of you will?"

Jim shrugged. "Well, would you?"

"No. You're right." He laughed. "If you want honesty, you've come to the right place." He stopped. Unless of course he was undercover or hiding out in a small town. When was the last time he'd actually been a hundred percent honest with anyone?

Yesterday, when he'd told Heather about his father and his condition…and Amber and her art gallery. He shook his head, uneasiness in the pit of his stomach. He still couldn't believe he'd told her any of it.

Jim was waving a hand in front of his face. "So you will be there? Six o'clock?"

He nodded. "Sure. Why not?" If nothing else, it gave him an excuse to avoid the pool hall and the one person he'd already let get too close.

HEATHER PARKED HER vehicle outside of Jim and Jill's house later that evening and struggled with the urge to turn around and drive back to the B and B.

A squad car was across the street, and she said a silent prayer that it was Jim's father, Sheriff Bishop, and not the other sheriff in town.

"Of course it's not Jake," she told herself, as she climbed out of the car. "Why would Jill invite Jake?"

"Probably the same reason she invited you—honesty."

His voice behind her made her jump. "Jeez, Jake!" She slapped his arm. "Don't sneak up on people like that."

"You were the one talking to yourself and not paying attention to your surroundings," he muttered, looking about as pleased as she was at this turn of events.

"You know what? I'll go."

"No, I'll go. They're your friends," he said.

Were they? She barely knew them. The invite to dinner had been unexpected. Seeing Jake here was even more unexpected. She sighed. "Too late," she said as the front door opened and Jill waved at them.

"Hey, you two, get in here. Dinner's almost ready."

"She is way too perky," Jake mumbled.

Heather hid a smile. "And Jim's semi-comatose all the time."

"I know!" He smiled at her. "Glad to know I'm not the only one noticing how odd these two are." He stopped as they reached the step. "Heather, I'm sorry."

"Jake, it's fine. I get it. You have a dangerous job, and you don't want anything to compromise that." She swallowed hard. "Like your sister and nephew."

He frowned. "What?"

*Just say it quickly.* "Jake, I looked up your sister's art gallery—it's been closed since July."

"You were snooping around in my life?"

"I wouldn't have to if you'd ever give me the full story for once. You reveal bits and pieces and leave me to fill in the blanks."

"You're right. I shouldn't have told you anything at all."

"Then why did you?" she challenged. "I was doing just fine planning my escape from Brookhollow, and then you started complicating things with your hot and cold, back and forth, drawing me in and then pushing me away." Her voice rose.

"What do you need, Heather?" he asked,

moving closer, his dark eyes boring into hers, his warm breath on her cold cheek. "Do you need me to say it?"

She swallowed hard.

"Do you need me to tell you that I like you? That you're the first woman I've been attracted to in a long time, the first person I've gotten close to in even longer? Would that make it less confusing?"

"Yes." The word escaped before she could stop it.

He sighed. "The problem is, I shouldn't be acting on those feelings, giving in to the urge to kiss you and let you into my life." He touched her cheek. His hand felt warm, but still a shiver danced down her spine. "My world isn't something you'll want to be a part of."

Moving closer, she wrapped her arms around his neck. "Why don't you let me decide that?" Standing on tiptoes, she placed her lips to his, ignoring the voice in the back of her mind that told her she still hadn't gotten any answers from him. She wasn't even sure she was going to.

And unfortunately, her heart continued to fall in love with him anyway.

## CHAPTER TEN

THINGS WERE GETTING COMPLICATED, and that wasn't good.

He'd successfully skirted Heather's questions about Amber the night before, but he knew that wouldn't be the end of her mission to find out more about him. And the biggest problem was that he wasn't sure he wanted to continue hiding things from her. He'd revealed so much already. A few more Google searches and she could probably figure everything out on her own.

The thought that she'd snooped made him a little uneasy, but he'd created this anti-trust situation by holding back.

Opening his locker, he saw a dark green envelope with his sister's handwriting on it. He closed the door to the room before opening it and removing a holiday card. Handmade. A beautiful abstract snowflake design on the front, and inside, a message from Amber.

Jacob (my pain in the *** brother)
Sorry it's taken me so long to write, but
it's taken me this long to stop being stubborn and see this situation for what it is—
you doing what you believe is right and as
always, keeping us safe, if not together.
I just wish you could have sent us somewhere warmer, but I digress.

I hope wherever you are, you are
happy. I am. I've met someone here in
the place that can't be named or the authorities will tear a hole in my beautiful
homemade card. For the first time in my
life, I'm truly happy.

Wow. He had to reread the words. Amber
had met someone? Since Kyle was born, he
could count on one hand how many dates
she'd had. Always putting her son and her art
career above everything else. But now, in the
oddest of circumstances, she'd met someone.
Just as he had.

He's wonderful. And Kyle adores him.
He teaches at Kyle's school. Of course I
can't tell him anything, which is really
annoying—

He knew all too well.

—but he has a good heart, and I'm hoping that if and when I can eventually tell him the truth, he will keep loving Kyle and me anyway.

It's Christmas, after all, the time of year to put our faith and trust in one another.
Take care, little brother,
Love, Amber.

Jacob closed the card and slid it back into the envelope. Faith and trust. Could he put his faith and trust in Heather? He wasn't sure he had any other choice. For once, he refused to do the "right" thing and walk away from her.

"SO I'M THINKING I need a tree," Jake said as he sat with Heather on his tiny love seat in the attic apartment two days later.

They'd been almost inseparable since the kiss outside of Jill's. Heather wasn't sure what had caused Jake's sudden change of heart, but she refused to question it. She also refused to ruin it by asking him anything else, even though her questions were burning a hole in her mind.

She scanned the twenty-by-twenty space that served as his home. With a single bed in one corner, the love seat and television in the middle, and the kitchenette on the other side, there was hardly room for a sprig of mistletoe, let alone a tree. "Where on earth do you think you can fit a tree in here?"

He removed her legs from his lap and stood.

"Hey, get back here. I was comfy," she said with a pout.

But he was clearly on a mission. Without waiting for her to get up, he pushed the love seat toward his bed until it touched, making a few extra feet of space.

"That's better."

Not really. "How are you going to get out of bed?"

He shrugged. "I'll climb over the back of the sofa."

Every morning? That would get old soon, she thought, an amused smile on her face as he continued to move his furniture around the apartment, hunched slightly as the six-foot ceiling was just a little too low to accommodate his height. "Why did you rent this place, anyway? You barely fit in here."

He set the tiny table in the corner of the kitchenette, then lifted the old television from the floor and placed it on top of the dresser, shoving aside his deodorant and hairbrush. His only two grooming products. "The price was right," he said.

"But it's just temporary, right?" He couldn't possibly be planning to stay here for too long. He'd have a permanent neck cramp. No wonder he didn't spend much time at home.

He stopped and turned to look at her. "What's wrong? You don't like my place," he said, coming toward her, tickle fingers active.

Oh, no. She hated being tickled. "No, Jake...don't. I'm sorry, I was kidding. Your place is wonderful. Perfect!" The last word was a high-pitched squeal as he went for her ribs.

She folded her arms tightly to prevent the attack, but he was too strong, pinning them above her head on the couch with one hand as he continued to tickle her with the other. She was laughing so hard she could barely breathe.

"Besides, you live in a B and B," he reminded her, leaning against her legs to stop her flailing.

"I know…stop…please… I'm going to pee my pants!"

"That would be hilarious," he said, continuing to tickle.

"I'm serious, Jake!" She wiggled and squirmed until he finally stopped.

"Be nice to my apartment now?" he asked, still holding both of her wrists as he pulled her to her feet.

"Yes," she said as he wrapped an arm around her waist.

He released her hands and touched her flushed cheek. "Besides, what else could I possibly need in here?"

She knew what he meant, and her heart beat wildly in her chest. Things were heating up between them, that was for sure. But it was more than that—their feelings were getting stronger. She knew it when she caught him looking at her and by the affectionate way he touched her. She also knew it by the excitement she felt whenever she was going to see him and the nausea in the pit of her stomach every time she remembered she was leaving.

Like now.

She took a deep breath and stepped away. "A tree. You need a tree."

"HEY, YOU GUYS!" Melody greeted them as they arrived at the Monroe family tree farm an hour later. She and her two boys were handing out handsaws and hot chocolate to customers in front of the tree lots. Homemade wreaths and poinsettias for sale sat on the table in front of them, and Christmas music played over speakers above the trees. Multicolored Christmas lights decorated the fence and hung between the large lights illuminating the tree farm for the after-dark crowd. According to Heather, the tree farm had been in the Monroe family for decades.

"Hi, Mel. Hi, David and Josh," Heather said, bending to accept hugs from Melody's children.

Jacob wasn't even going to try to figure out which of the twin boys was which, so he just smiled and waved to the family.

"What brings you two by?" Melody asked, glancing between them, interest showing in her dark eyes.

If Heather noticed her friend's curiosity, she

ignored it. "Sheriff Matthews here needs a tree."

Melody laughed as she turned to him. "I heard you were renting that attic apartment in Mrs. Kelly's house."

"Yes, I am," he said, accepting a handsaw from one of the boys.

"Can you even fit a tree in there?"

"Oh, don't worry," Heather said, hiding a grin. "He's moved some things around."

"There's always room for Christmas," he said with a shrug, wrapping an arm around her. He could never satisfy his need to be close to her, which was really going to suck when she left town.

"That's a man after my own heart," Brad said, joining them. He was dressed in a pair of jeans, cowboy boots and hat, a large silver belt buckle reflecting the late afternoon sun, almost blinding the group. He looked nothing like the baseball-hat-wearing guy he'd met at the tree-lighting ceremony.

"What's with the outfit, Brad?" Heather asked, sizing him up.

A sliver of jealousy ran through him at the sight of her staring at the music star.

"It's for the bachelor auction at the community hall tonight," he said, rolling his eyes. "Mrs. Dawson really should go into politics."

Melody's eyes widened. "Better not say that around her. She used to date Mayor Parsons years and years ago. I think she did have political aspirations at one time."

"Bachelor auction? But…uh…aren't you two…?" Jacob was confused as he glanced between the couple. He'd been certain the two of them were together.

Melody wrapped an arm around Brad's waist. "Yes, we are. Well, I think we are… I mean, nothing's official or anything," she teased him, holding up her empty ring finger.

"Like it, put a ring on it," Heather agreed, winking at Brad.

The poor cowboy looked uncomfortable as he shifted from one foot to the other. "Quit pressuring me," he said. "Anyway, I have to head over to the community center early to get assigned a number for tonight. You guys are all coming?"

Melody nodded, then kissed him. "Yes, but I'm not paying money to date you."

"I've already given Mrs. Dawson a blank check," he said.

When he left, Melody turned back to them. "Are you two planning to attend?"

"Maybe, if we get the tree set up..." Heather said.

Jacob nodded, relieved that somehow he'd escaped Mrs. Dawson's radar. Guess she figured no one would pay to spend time with him up until the incident with Lily a few weeks ago. Hey, whatever worked. "As long as I'm not being auctioned off, I'm there."

Ten minutes later, he spotted the tree he wanted. Holding it up, he called to Heather, "I think this is the one."

She laughed when she saw it. "Where are you planning to put it? The front yard? Jake, that tree is seven feet tall." She shook her head. Glancing around, she selected a different one. "This is more the right size, I think..."

He eyed the teeny, tiny Charlie Brown tree. "That one's so small." How was he supposed to decorate that? Not that he had any decorations yet.

"Have you seen your apartment?" she asked, effortlessly cutting down the short evergreen.

"Fine. I guess that's the one."

"Okay, let's go buy decorations." She picked up the tree with ease. "I think about six ornaments oughta do it."

"MY HANDS ARE still sticking to everything I touch," Jake said, removing the napkin stuck to his palm as they sat at the table with Melody and Brad's family at the bachelor auction later that evening.

"Tell me about it. I swear I have sap in my hair. Who knew a three-foot pine tree could produce so much of this stuff?" Heather said with a laugh. Putting up the tiny tree in his tiny apartment had taken no time. Cleaning up the pine needles and hiding the fact that they'd gotten a real tree—which went against his rental agreement with Mrs. Kelly—had been the real challenge.

Actually, the real challenge had been keeping her attention on decorating the tree and not on watching *him* decorate the tree. He'd insisted on glass ornaments in red, green and gold, claiming he was a traditionalist when she'd suggested a blue-and-silver color theme. He'd also bought strings of gold garland and an angel for the top.

After all his grumbling about her decorations at the bar, she'd been amazed watching him work—he'd placed every ornament strategically, and she'd even caught him moving some of the ones she'd put on. An hour after they'd started, the tree rivaled those in the window displays at Macy's.

"Where did you learn to decorate?" she'd asked as they'd plugged in the lights in his only outlet. They'd had to unplug his coffeemaker and microwave.

He'd shrugged. "I'm a natural, I guess."

"Come on, seriously…" She was dying to get to know him better, but so far, he'd refused any real conversations.

He'd pulled her onto his lap on the sofa and said, "Everyone in our family is kinda creative I guess." He'd paused, pushing her hair away from her neck, and placed a soft kiss on her collarbone.

She'd been tempted to once again bring up his sister and the art gallery, but she was starting to think that ignorance really was bliss. She was having such a great time with him, and she didn't want to ruin things. He'd already revealed a little bit about himself; the rest would come…when he was ready.

"Ah, here he is," Mel whispered, bringing

Heather back to the present as Brad took to the catwalk. Brad was the last of this year's ten contestants; the number of eligible men in town was dwindling. But Brad's participation was guaranteed to bring in the necessary funding to make the charity event for the local medical clinic worthwhile. And while he'd told Mel he'd given Mrs. Dawson a blank check for Mel to claim him, she'd told them she had zero intentions of doing so. Though Heather suspected she'd change her mind quickly if one of the young, single girls in the crowd somehow outbid the older women for Brad's attention.

As he reached the front of the stage, he removed the cowboy hat and winked at Mel. The collective *ahhh* across the room made Melody's cheeks light up. "He's such a performer," she said, but Heather knew her friend loved the man up on the stage—the man who had given her another shot at her own dreams of performing.

The paddles flew through the air so quickly that Mrs. Dawson had trouble keeping up at the podium, and when she finally stopped the bidding at eight hundred dollars, she was out of breath. "Sold to… Mrs. Norris…for eight hundred."

"Mrs. Norris always gets the good dates," Heather said, collecting her coat and purse.

Melody stood, as well. "I guess I should go tell him to have fun," she said with a smile, obviously relieved the group of younger girls in the front row had run out of funds at five hundred.

"Um, excuse me, everyone," Brad said, taking the microphone from Mrs. Dawson.

Everyone stopped moving and turned toward the stage.

"Before I go on my date, there's a question I'd like to ask Melody Myers, if you could all indulge me for a second," he said.

"Oh, my God." Melody went pale next to her.

"Is he about to propose?" Jake whispered at her side.

"Shhh," Heather told him, her eyes glued to the stage.

"Mel, you know I love you…and Josh and David. This last year, having the three of you with me on tour, performing with you and watching you shine, I've just fallen more and more in love with you…every day. So, Melody Myers—will you finally stop being so stubborn and marry me already?" He jumped down from the runway and dropped to a knee in front of her.

"For real?" Melody asked.

"I've asked you four times already—you should know by now it's for real," he said, reaching into his pocket and producing a Tiffany's box.

"Mel, that's a Tiffany ring. Say yes or I'm going to," Heather hissed when her friend hesitated.

"A Tiffany ring, huh? That's all it takes to get a yes? Thanks for the tip," Jake whispered in her ear, wrapping an arm around her waist. Her pulse quickened, and she barely heard Melody's acceptance. Her mouth went dry as she glanced over her shoulder at him, but he'd directed his attention back to the proposal.

He'd been kidding. Of course. He was just messing with her, as usual. That's what they did, after all. Right?

She watched her friends kiss and smiled and congratulated them when they finally broke away from each other.

"Thank you," Melody said, absolutely glowing as she extended her hand to show Heather the two-carat solitaire diamond.

Then, as a crowd gathered around the newly engaged couple, Jake led her away. "So, what's their story anyway?"

"Melody was married to Patrick Myers, Brad's best friend and bandmate, but there was an accident four years ago, and Patrick died." Heather didn't feel the need to add that the accident had been Brad's fault. It was a long and tragic story, and tonight was about love. "Anyway, last Christmas Brad was home filming a holiday special, and the two fell in love."

"Didn't Victoria and Luke fall in love while she was in town for the holidays, as well?" he asked.

She nodded as they stepped outside into the cold night air.

"I'm sensing a pattern," he said, taking her hand.

She laughed. "Apparently Christmas in Brookhollow has a way of making people fall in love."

He stopped when they reached the car, and placing his hands on either side of her face, he gently lowered his lips to hers. "Then maybe you should have gotten out of town sooner."

# CHAPTER ELEVEN

*SHOULD HAVE GOTTEN out of town sooner.* Yes, it would have made things a whole lot easier, Heather thought, if she'd left town before she'd started to fall for a man who could break her heart.

Now, she was staring at the ringing phone in her hand the morning after the bachelor auction. Highstone Acquisitions' number lit up the call display, and she was torn about answering. She wanted this job. But she also wanted Jake—even if he turned out to be damaged and delusional. And if he refused to leave Brookhollow and return to the city with her, she had a choice to make. An impossible one.

"Can you get that? Your ringtone is driving me crazy," Victoria said, poking her head around the corner. Her eyes widened. "Is it about the job?"

Heather nodded.

"Answer it!" She rushed to take the empty seat behind the desk, obviously planning to listen in on the call.

"Can I have some privacy?"

"I haven't had privacy to pee since Harper was born. Why should you get any? Come on, hurry up," she said, her knees bouncing.

She cleared her throat. "Hello?"

"Heather?"

"Yes, this is Heather."

"This is Mike Ainsley calling. Have I caught you at a bad time?"

Three weeks ago would have been better. Before she'd started to get to know Jake, started to fall for Jake, kissed him several dozen times. "No, not at all."

"Well, I'm sorry it's taken so long to get back to you, but I was away for a few days."

"No problem at all."

"Anyway, I'm calling to offer you the position, starting January 4."

She couldn't pinpoint any particular emotion. Happy and excited—yes. She was finally going back to New York, to work for a fantastic company in a fantastic office with a fantastic view of the city, fantastic health benefits...

But she was also disappointed and anxious. January 4 was less than three weeks away.

"You are still interested in the position?" he asked when she was silent.

"Did you get it?" Victoria whispered.

She nodded, answering them both.

Victoria did a silent squeal of delight, and Mike spoke. "Heather?"

"Yes, sorry, sir. Yes, I'm definitely still interested. Thank you for this opportunity." Victoria was going to kill her for what she was about to say next. "Um, is it okay if I have a few days to think about it?"

Victoria's mouth dropped open, and Heather stood and moved away from her.

"Oh…okay, of course. I'll have Amy draft up the official offer for you this afternoon. If you could let us know by early next week, we would love to have you join us for our holiday party on the twenty-third and have you sign off on the position that day, as well."

The twenty-third…seven days… January 4 had seemed too soon. "Of course, I'll get back to you as soon as I can. Thank you again for the opportunity, Mr. Ainsley." She disconnected the call and faced Victoria, preparing for a what-were-you-thinking speech, but to her surprise, her friend was smiling.

"What?" Heather asked.

"You're in love with Sheriff Matthews."

It wasn't a question, and she almost wished her friend had yelled at her for not taking the position immediately. This conversation would be worse.

"I'm not," she said. Apparently all she could muster at the moment was a two-word lie.

"You totally are. Why else would you need to think about taking the position?"

She scoffed. "I didn't want to seem too eager..."

"Does this mean you're actually thinking about staying?"

"I haven't thought about anything yet. I mean, this is stupid. Who chooses a potential relationship over a definite career?"

Victoria's eyes narrowed. "This girl right here." She pointed to her own chest.

"That was different. You and Luke were made for one another." And Luke wasn't a closed-down, guarded man who refused to talk about anything near to personal. "And besides, you loved your job, but when you came back here, you knew it was the right thing to do."

"No, I didn't. I was terrified. I had no idea if I was doing the right thing."

"So why did you do it?"

"Because I love him, and everything else worked itself out."

"So you think I should stay?"

"I can't give you an unbiased answer to that, so all I'm going to say is—do what your heart tells you to do, but don't sacrifice who you are." She stood.

"Hey, where are you going?" *Now* she was giving her privacy?

"To leave you to decide between your heart and your head."

VICTORIA MIGHT NOT have been able to give Heather an unbiased opinion about what she should do, but her sister had no trouble. "I can't believe you asked for time to think about it," Cameron shrieked into the phone later that day.

Clearly, news traveled fast in the Highstone Acquisitions offices. And Rob had wasted no time ratting her out to her sister. They were going to have to set some ground rules if they were going to be coworkers. Work stayed at work, family stuff was personal. "I'm—"

"You're killing me, that's what you're doing. For the last six months, all I've heard is how bored you are out there, and how you're desperately looking for a job in the city. Then Rob puts his neck out for you…"

*Puts his neck out?* "Hey, I'm a good agent. Rob didn't put anything on the line recommending me." Where was her pep-talking sister? The one reminding her how she was wasting her talents in Brookhollow? She'd liked that one better.

"Maybe not. But how do you think it will reflect on him if you turn the job down? They were considering three other applicants," she said.

Heather bit her lip. She had to get an answer to Mike Ainsley soon. She couldn't leave him or the other applicants waiting. She wished she knew what to do.

"Call him right now and tell him you want this job."

"Cam, it's not that simple anymore…" Her sister was career-driven and focused. Her family had almost happened by mistake; she would never understand Heather's current dilemma.

"If this is about Sheriff…"

"Matthews."

"Yes, him," Cameron said tightly, "then I think you're a fool to be stalling."

"Cam, not all of us are made of steel, okay? I have feelings for him, and as much as I'd like them to go away, I can't just reduce them to a minor inconvenience and move on. I'm not like—" She stopped.

"Me? You were going to say me."

The hurt in her sister's voice made her wince. "It's not an insult. You're amazing at what you do because you put it first, but I'm not sure I'm that driven. I kinda want to find that…balance between work and home."

"Only since you met *this* guy!"

"I've never cared about anyone this much before, I guess." It was true. Her relationship with Mel had consisted of one weekend together a month, if they were lucky, and she'd been okay with seeing him that infrequently. She should have recognized that maybe that was telling her something. She saw Jake almost every day, yet leaving him sucked. The more time she spent with him, the more time she wanted to spend. Whatever this was with him felt different than anything she'd experienced before. It felt right. And she wasn't ready to give up on it...even if he was impossible to figure out.

Her sister sighed. "Look, I get it. But I can't say this strongly enough—making a decision about your future based on a guy you only started to have feelings for a few weeks ago is a mistake, Heather. Trust me. I know what I'm talking about."

She didn't doubt for a second that her sister was right, but she had a feeling her common sense would take a leap off a New York high rise the moment she saw Jake later that evening...

"WE ARE NOT supposed to be here," Jacob said, as Heather picked the lock on the barn door. "And what you're doing is illegal, by the way." He shifted his weight nervously, glancing around the dark property.

"So, arrest me," Heather said with a teasing smile that made him want to lock her up and throw away the key. "Ta-da!" She held up the lock and opened the door.

"I can't believe you talked me into breaking and entering," he muttered, following her inside.

"Oh, come on. It's not like we're going to vandalize other floats…or worse, work on our own after the permitted hours," she said with a laugh. "I just want to see yours. The ladies are all whispering about how wonderful it is."

He sensed jealousy in her tone again and couldn't help but play on it. "They think *I'm* wonderful."

She flashed him a glare. "Watch yourself, buddy."

He reached for her hand and drew her to his chest. Staring into those hazel eyes he couldn't seem to get enough of, he said, "I think you're wonderful."

"You think I talk too much."

"That's true. But we figured out a cure for that, remember?" he whispered, lowering his lips toward hers.

She pushed away from him.

He frowned. "Hey! Get back here." He reached for her, but she ran toward his stall.

"Not until you show me your float."

He sighed. If that's what it took to get a kiss, so be it. And the quicker they got out of there, the better. Getting caught breaking the law was the last thing his reputation needed. He raced after her and opened the door to his stall. The float was almost finished. Having the extra workers had really helped make it happen. "Here it is," he said, moving aside to let her in.

Her mouth fell open when she saw it.

"Like it?"

"How did you do this?"

"Impressed?"

"Not at all," she said, recovering and plastering on what he assumed was her best competitor's face. "I mean, it's okay…" She touched a gingerbread man eating a candy cane on the back of the float, and shook her head. "I can't even pretend this sucks—you suck!" She hit him. "You didn't tell me you were actually good at this stuff. Though I should have started to worry after I saw your tree."

He laughed.

She continued to circle the float, taking in the gingerbread house and all the colorful candies, the white sugar draped from the roof that looked like candied snow. "Okay, I know you said your family was creative, but this is unreal. Where did you even come up with this idea?"

He shrugged. "As a kid I loved candy."

She shot him a look.

"Hey, you can't get type one diabetes from eating too much sugar!" he said. "Anyway, one year when I was about five or six, my dad—on one of the rare occasions he wasn't buried under a pile of work—took my sister and me to a gingerbread-house contest." He walked around the float toward her. "After that, I was hooked. Every year, I spent weeks designing my own and entering them in every contest I could afford."

"Did you ever win?"

"Not at first, but after a while, I got better and better, and then no one could beat me," he said with a cocky smile.

"Of course not. Why doesn't that surprise me?"

He shrugged. "I'm a bit of a perfectionist when I get fixated on something."

"I've noticed," she said. "You certainly seem fixated on me."

He wrapped his arms around her. "Is that a problem?"

"I'm just not sure what you're going to do when I leave."

"I'm not worried. I'm sure I'll find something else to fixate on."

She went to smack him again, but he caught her hand, bringing it to his lips. "I was kidding," he whispered. Her not being around wouldn't change how he felt or how he thought about her every waking moment when they weren't together. Being apart was only going to make it worse.

Her eyes searched his, and she opened her mouth to say something, but for once, she didn't speak.

"Okay, come on—show me yours." Keeping her hand in his, he led the way out of the stall.

"No way...not now. Mine needs more work first."

"Thought you said it was done?"

"I thought it was, until I saw yours."

"Fine, I'll wait, but can we please get out of here before we get caught by Mrs. Dawson? I wouldn't put it past her to be sitting guard."

Heather shook her head. "No. That's what the cameras are for."

His stomach flip-flopped. "Cameras?" He

glanced at the ceiling. He didn't see any cameras. Maybe they were hidden in the beams, or... When he looked back at her, she was laughing. "Okay, and then you say *I* suck?" He grabbed her and started tickling.

"You really are a goody-goody, aren't you?" she said between bouts of laughter, wiggling away from him.

"I don't know. Is this a kiss that a goody-goody would give you?" he asked before covering her mouth with his.

JACOB PULLED THE squad car onto the parking lot of the community center the next morning. "There you go," he told the young boy, Troy, in the passenger seat. The sixteen-year-old had been hitchhiking along the highway, and he'd picked him up, recognizing him as one of the kids who mentored other kids at the center. His car had broken down.

"Thank you, Sheriff Matthews. I appreciate the ride."

Jacob nodded. "Don't forget to call the tow truck once you get inside. You'll want your car towed to Bailey's before the heavy snow falls, and it gets buried."

"I will, sir. Thanks again." Troy grabbed his backpack and climbed out of the car.

Through the windshield, Jacob noticed Luke Dawson and several men from the bowling league near the side entrance, carrying boxes into the center. He hesitated momentarily before shutting off the car. He raised the collar on his jacket against the blowing snow and wind as he crossed the lot.

"Hey, Sheriff Matthews," a boy clearing the steps said.

"Hi…uh…"

"Dominic. You busted me for graffiti a few months ago, remember?"

Jake frowned, trying to reconcile this young man with the tall, skinny, scared teenager he'd caught defacing the community center wall back when they thought the place was going to be torn down. The kid appeared to have matured a lot in the past few months. "Sorry, I haven't seen you here much." And he'd been looking. His daily patrols included several tours around the center, where some of the town troublemakers tended to congregate, though their meet-ups hadn't been as common lately.

He had to admit Heather was right: Noah

did keep a close eye on the Turnaround program kids. But Jacob was happy his extra presence seemed to be helping, as well.

"I was away at college in Boston," Dominic said proudly. "Just back on winter break to spend the holidays with my mom."

"That's great."

"What brings you by?" the kid asked cautiously. "Someone in trouble? Troy?"

"No. Nothing like that. His car broke down. I just picked him up." He kicked at a lump of snow at his feet. Why was he still here? He wasn't exactly sure. All he knew was that since he'd loosened up a little and started participating in things around town, living in Brookhollow had become more bearable. Heather had a lot to do with his sudden change in mood, but she'd been right about getting involved with the community. "I noticed the guys bringing in a bunch of stuff, and I thought I'd see if there's anything I could do to help."

Dominic smiled. "That's awesome, man— uh, I mean, Sheriff Matthews."

Jacob laughed. "Believe it or not, I prefer 'man.'" He tapped the boy on the shoulder as he went inside.

The community center was busy with teens

pinning up holly and colorful garlands. Glittering silver snowflakes from the bachelor auction still hung from the ceiling, and Christmas music blared from the stereo system. Luke Dawson and his nephew Steve were carrying long tables in through the side entrance, so Jacob made his way over to them and held the door open. "Hey, guys, what are you setting up for now?"

"The Christmas craft fair is this weekend, and we need to get the vendor tables set up so people can start bringing in their sale items."

Noah joined them. "Thanks, guys," he said, before turning to Jacob. "Sheriff Matthews, how are you?"

"Good... I thought I'd see if you guys needed a hand." He shrugged.

Noah nodded. "Awesome, that's great. All the kids are on break until after Christmas, but we could certainly use your help in the new year..."

New year... Noah had misunderstood. Jacob hadn't meant to volunteer with the Turnaround program. He hoped to be back in the city before the end of January, at the latest. He just nodded, though. "Sure."

"But since you're here, we could use an

extra pair of hands setting up," Noah said, as Luke and Steve went back to Luke's truck to grab another table.

Jacob removed his jacket. "What can I do?"

"I think those guys could use some help with the Santa staging area." He pointed to the corner of the room where a group of teens struggled to place a red velvet underlay beneath the big green Santa chair and Christmas tree.

"No problem," he said, rolling up the sleeves of his sweater.

"Thanks, Jake. It's good to see you finally settling in."

Jacob paused. He was far from settling in. In fact, that was the last thing he wanted to do. Especially when the woman he was falling in love with was leaving the small town and taking his heart with her.

HEATHER PRINTED OFF the job offer from Mike Ainsley, and sitting at the B and B's front desk, she reread the details. Eighty thousand to start, until her commissions started rolling in, and then a base of fifty thousand and a ten percent commission on her deals. Within six months, she would be back to making over a hundred thousand a year. She could easily afford her own place within a month of getting back to the city. Full health benefits and a gym membership. Company business expense card when traveling. The offer was exactly what she'd been hoping for.

This decision should be a no-brainer. Her bank account had recently dipped into her overdraft. She couldn't stay here, basically unemployed, for much longer.

Besides, this was what she'd wanted. Still wanted. She just wanted it not to come at the cost of the man she was falling in love with. She shook her head. She couldn't be falling for Jake that fast, could she? She'd only known him for five months, and most of that time, she'd paid little or no attention to him. He'd made it easy to not like him.

Then things had changed. He'd changed. Yet he knew she was planning to leave, and they hadn't discussed what would happen next. She should be grateful he wasn't asking her to stay or trying to get serious. How could she fall for a guy she didn't really know that well? How could she possibly miss him when she left?

Unfortunately, the knot in her stomach told

her she would. She would miss him, and she was definitely falling for him.

Her cell phone chimed with a new text, and she smiled at the picture of Jake standing next to his three-foot tree on her screen.

She needed to talk to him. She had a huge decision to make, and while her common sense—and her sister—told her she couldn't base such an important choice on Jake, she wanted to give him one last chance to open up, to tell her exactly what was going on with him. She needed to know she'd be making the right move by listening to her head and leaving, when her heart was demanding that she listen to it instead. She needed to have the confidence to reboot her career in New York without a shadow of a doubt that she was where she was supposed to be, doing what she was supposed to do.

And she couldn't have that confidence without being certain this thing with Jake wasn't going anywhere. That a future with him was not possible. If he still refused to open up and be honest with her, if he refused to tell her why he wouldn't go back to New York—not for his family and not for her—then that was it. It would be over, and she would move on.

Finally, she read the text. Be there in five. Dress warmly.

Obviously their date was something outside. She went to the front closet, debating her choices: warm and frumpy thermal coat that kept her toasty but made her look like a marshmallow or stylish and slim-fitting wool that accentuated her waist but left her mind-numbingly cold? "Vic, how cold is it outside?" she asked her friend as Victoria entered the B and B a second later.

Victoria was bundled in a long parka, a hat, scarf and mittens, and she was still shivering as she set the baby's car seat on the floor. Baby Harper's eyes were the only thing visible beneath layers of clothing and the blanket wrapped tightly around her. "Let's just say my breast milk has ice cubes in it."

"That's pretty cold." She reached for the thermal jacket and her matching cashmere hat and glove set. She was wearing a flattering V-neck sweater and jeggings and her peppermint body lotion—Jake's favorite. She just had to make sure they went somewhere indoors at some point so he could enjoy the sight and smells beneath the Michelin Man costume. If this was her last chance to get some clarification from the guy about his feelings and where he saw this going, she wanted to use everything she had to persuade him to say the words that she longed to hear.

Which were what? The thought made her pause.

"Where is Jake taking you?" Victoria asked. She removed her warmer layers and put her boots against the heater in the hallway to dry.

"He wouldn't tell me, which makes it impossible to get dressed."

A sound of a car pulling into the driveway made her stomach flip. "He's here."

"Tonight's the night, huh?"

She nodded. "I've been putting it off long enough. I have to tell him."

"What do you think he's going to say?"

"I really don't know." That was the most terrifying part. If he was upset about her taking the job in the city, she'd be torn, wondering whether she should accept the position or not. But if he wasn't upset…that would be so much worse. They hadn't exactly told one another how they were feeling yet, but she was pretty sure he was falling just as hard and fast as she was.

"Well, try not to worry about it and just enjoy your evening," was her friend's advice.

But Heather knew she had to say something, and maybe it was like pulling off a Band-Aid—better to do it quickly and get it over with right away. Otherwise, it would weigh on her all evening.

As she opened the door to the B and B and stepped outside, she prepared her speech. The only part she was unsure of was her time frame for leaving. They wanted her there for the twenty-third to sign off on the position and attend the corporate Christmas party, but…

A snowball hit her arm, breaking into her thoughts, followed immediately by another one to the chest. "Hey!" she said, forgetting everything she'd been rehearsing as she stooped to gather a handful of snow.

Jake hid behind the open driver's-side door of the squad car, and she could see a pile of snowballs on the ground in front of him.

"That's not fair! You need to let me get my own stack," she said, forming balls quickly, but not as quickly as he was making more and launching them toward her.

"There're no rules in a snowball fight," he said, tossing another one just as she bent to gather her own handful. The snow landed above her collar, and cold, wet slush seeped down the inside of her V-neck sweater. "Oh, my God—cold!" she said, trying to scoop snow away from her neckline.

Laughing, he moved toward her, removing his gloves. "Sorry. Here, let me help."

Instead, she grabbed his shoulders and tripped him, dropping him on his butt. "For a cop, you're awfully trusting," she said, staring down at him.

Without a word, he reached for her leg, knocking her off balance and pulling her onto the snowbank next to him. In an instant, her butt and legs were soaked. "Great, now we are both wet and freezing," she said, standing and dragging him to his feet.

"This is nothing. I wasn't kidding when I said to dress warmly. This is just the beginning."

TEN MINUTES LATER, they stood at the top of a steep, icy hill at the edge of the town park. "Are you kidding?" Heather asked.

He *hadn't* been. Now he wasn't so sure. He'd heard the kids at the community center talking about this epic sledding hill, and he'd thought they were exaggerating. Now, standing at the top of a hundred-foot slope with a forty-degree incline, he was starting to believe the outrageous stories the kids had been telling. "This is nothing," he said, hoping he sounded brave, placing the two-person toboggan he'd borrowed from Mrs. Kelly's shed on the ground and climbing on. Now that he'd brought her here, he couldn't exactly wimp out. "Climb on."

"No, thanks."

"All of those little kids are doing it," he said, amazed that it was true. On the hill, kids who looked as young as five and six were jumping on their sleds with excitement and sailing down at breakneck speed.

Kids were fearless...or dumb.

"Peer pressure doesn't work on me." She watched with a horrified expression as two kids flew off of their sleds and rolled several feet, when they reached the bottom of the hill. When they stood up, laughing and high-fiving, she muttered, "Children are insane."

"Come on. You're not going to make me be the only adult sledding, are you?"

A long row of parents stood at the side of the hill, watching in terror probably, sipping hot chocolate while their children participated in the winter sport.

She shrugged. "This was your idea—go nuts."

"Look, it's safe. We even have a steering wheel," he said, wiggling it. It came loose and broke off in his hands. "*Had* a steering wheel."

"How old is that sled, anyway?"

Wooden with metal skids, it had to be at least forty years old. Mrs. Kelly had said her own kids had used it. "I don't know. Just get on." He was starting to lose his nerve, and if he didn't do this soon, he wouldn't at all.

"You go first. If you survive, I'll think about it," she said.

"Fine." He put his feet up.

"Want a push?" she asked, going behind him.

"No!" He put one foot back out on the ground and turned to face her. "But I'll take a kiss in case I die."

She laughed as she leaned forward to kiss him, and in an instant, he'd grabbed her and placed her on the sled in front of him.

Panicking, she flailed, and in her desperate attempts to get off, she sent the sled in a spiral. A second later, they were headed down the hill...backward.

His heart raced as they picked up speed, and Heather's scream grew louder. "Relax, I'll try to turn us around," he said, shifting their weight to the left and eventually righting the sled.

Seeing where they were going didn't make things much better. The ground flew by beneath them, cold wind and powder blowing up into their faces. The snow was too firm from all the other kids going up and down, so that digging his heels in to slow them wasn't working.

"Trees," Heather whispered, her voice full of terror. Through her gloves, her nails dug into his hands at her waist.

He glanced up. They were headed straight for a group of trees at the edge of the hill. "Grab the steering," he said, trying to keep the note of panic out of his voice and failing. Big, snow-covered pines were getting closer by the second.

"You broke it!" She threw her feet onto the ground, but the movement sent them spiraling again.

Faster and faster the sled went, as they descended the hill and approached the trees. They were only a few feet away from the thick trunks. They were going to hit. "We need to bail."

"What?"

"On three, go to the right," he said in her ear, his grip tightening on her waist, ready to yank her off with his own body weight if she refused to jump.

"Jake—"

"One, two, three!" he said, as they both hurled themselves off the sled.

They rolled several feet as the sled continued and crashed into the pines, breaking into two pieces. Sitting up, they stared at it.

"That was fun," Heather said.

He wrapped an arm around her, and she rested her head against his shoulder. He kissed her hair, her hat lost somewhere on the hill. "Ah, they say surviving a near death experience only makes a relationship stronger." Relationship? Where had that word come from? Maybe she hadn't noticed.

But she'd obviously picked up on it. Heather stiffened at his side, pushing off of his shoulder to turn to face him. "I was offered the job in New York."

His stomach clenched, as if he'd been punched, but he shook it off. He had been expecting this. He'd had no doubt she'd get the position. This was good. She was going back to the city, where *he* would be again one day. Hopefully, soon. But the thought only made him feel ever more uneasy. Here in Brookhollow, he'd been able to let go a little and follow his heart for once; but back in the city, back at his high-danger job, things would be different. He forced a smile. "That's wonderful. Congratulations."

She didn't appear happy at his response. "They want me to start January 4, but they'd like me in the city by Deccmber 23."

Before Christmas. That sucked. The longer Heather had been waiting to hear from Highstone, the more hopeful he'd become that she'd at least consider staying for the holidays, or at least until Christmas Day. But that wasn't fair, either—he knew she wanted to spend Christmas with Cameron and her family.

He took a deep breath. "This is amazing, Heather. It's what you wanted." There were so many reasons why this opportunity was great for her…it was just hard to keep them at the forefront of his mind when disappointment threatened to strangle him. When she left, he'd be alone in his tiny apartment, with his tiny tree, surrounded by memories of her and the peppermint smell she'd left on his sofa cushions. He cleared his throat. "Now you can spend Christmas with your sister."

"I know... I had just been hoping to spend it with you," she said softly.

It was exactly what he'd been hoping for, as well. And hearing her say it... But she couldn't pass up this opportunity. She had been dying to leave Brookhollow, and she'd been eager to get this job. He couldn't be the reason she stayed. Especially when he had no plans of staying himself. He struggled to choose his words carefully. "I'd like that, too, but you can't stay if your new boss is expecting you there. You want to make a good impression. And your family is waiting for you, too."

She studied him for a minute. "Would you come to New York for Christmas?"

Crap. He knew that must have taken a lot for her to ask. Putting herself out there, allowing her emotions to show, being vulnerable. He sighed before shaking his head. "I can't."

She touched his shoulder. "Jake, I haven't brought any of this up over the last week because I've been having too great of a time with you, but I need to know…is your family… I mean, your sister…is she…alive?" she whispered.

His eyes widened, and he snapped up his head to look at her. "Yes, of course she's alive." He ran a hand through his hair. This was a disaster. She was staring at him as if she wasn't sure whether or not to believe him. He had to say something. He took a deep breath. "She's alive," he said softly. "She and Kyle just moved out of the city for a while…"

"Around the same time you came here?" She eyed him with open curiosity.

Her imagination was probably running wild, but he truly felt no information was better than lies. "Yes. Things are complicated, Heather."

"Okay." She breathed a sigh of relief. "Well, I'm sorry I assumed the worst."

He nodded.

A long moment of awkward silence passed before she spoke. "So, will they be coming to see you at Christmas?"

His gut tightened. "I'm not sure…" It wasn't a complete lie. And he didn't know what else to say. He saw a lonely Christmas in his future. In fact, he was starting to see a lot of loneliness in his future. Lying to people he cared about, never being able to be completely truthful about himself wasn't fair to anyone. Getting involved with anyone when he lived the life he did was wrong. He wished he could shut off the feelings he had for Heather, but he couldn't.

She turned to face him, her eyes unreadable, illuminated by the pole lamps at the edge of the toboggan hill. "Fine. If you don't want to tell me anything else, just answer this one question—what happens to us?"

His heart was torn. He took her hands and held them firmly as he slowly shook his head. "I'm not sure. But I do know you should take the job in the city."

Her mouth gaped, then she clamped her lips shut. "Oh," she muttered, looking away.

God, how was he supposed to do this without hurting her? "I just know how much you want this job…"

"What if I want you more?"

His heart stopped. She was falling for him as much as he was falling for her. Fantastic, wonderful, terrible, devastating. Could he tell her the truth? Could he trust her with his life? His family's well-being?

He'd known her less than six months. Her sister was his lawyer, and she'd lose it if he told Heather. But what was he supposed to say at this exact moment when she was looking to him for answers? For confirmation that what they had was real.

"Heather..."

"Jake, I realize you think you're doing the right thing by letting me go, but the truth is I'm falling in love with you. In the end, what good is a career when I'm coming home to an empty apartment every night? I've never met anyone who's ever made me feel the way you do. How do I walk away from that? I don't *want* to walk away from that." She stared at him, waiting, silently pleading with him to give her the answer she wanted to hear.

This wasn't fair. He wanted to grab her, kiss her, tell her to stay...

"Heather, this thing between us...we both said it was just...fun." He choked on the words. This wasn't just fun. This was as torturously real as it got.

Her eyes glistened, and she pulled her hands away. "What are you saying, Jake? That you don't feel the same way about me? That I've misread everything going on between us? I'm not buying it," she said, but the confidence in her voice wavered.

*Just tell her the truth. Believe in the woman you're falling in love with. Trust in her.* He urged himself to say the words and hope she could forgive his deception. But he hesitated, an image of Amber and Kyle, of Leo Gonzales, and of Cameron's angry look playing on a maddening loop in his mind.

"Jake?"

Her heartbroken expression was too much. Turning to face her, he took her hands in his. "Heather, I haven't been completely honest with you."

She sighed. "I know!"

"No, I mean about everything—the reason I'm here, my past…" He searched her face, wondering if she would understand once he told her the truth. He swallowed hard before continuing. "Amber and Kyle are under the witness protection program."

She sucked in a breath.

"So am I, sort of…" He paused and ran a hand over his face. So much rested on his trust in her. "Six months ago, I was undercover working a drug case. My cover was blown, and I had to leave the city." That was as far as his confession would go. There was no way he could tell her the rest—that he'd decided to come to Brookhollow to be close to Newark. Or that he was waiting on a call to once again put his life on the line for the case.

"Who are you?" she whispered, looking at him as though she didn't recognize him anymore.

He held her hands tightly. "I'm still me... my name isn't Jake Matthews, it's Jacob Marx, but everything else I told you was true." He paused. "Except my birthday..."

Her eyes widened. "I threw you a party for a fake birthday?"

He nodded. "My birthday is actually in February."

Heather tore her hands away and scrambled to her feet.

He stood. "Heather, I'm sorry I couldn't tell you. My family's lives were in danger..."

"So why tell me now? You've lied this long, why not continue?" She folded her arms across her chest and backed away from him.

He sighed. Maybe he should have. Maybe he should have just continued the lie and told her he didn't love her so that she would take the job. "Because I trust you and I didn't want you to give up this opportunity in the city, when I'm hoping to get back there someday myself." He reached for her, but she shook her head, so he jammed his hands in his pockets instead. "Heather, please…"

"And then what? What happens when you get back to New York?"

He knew what she wanted to hear, but he refused to lie to her anymore. "I go back to my job as an undercover cop." Keeping people at arm's length and never allowing himself the pain of falling in love…ever again.

THE DRIVE FROM the sledding hill to the B and B was painfully slow and silent. Heather kept her gaze locked on the world outside the passenger window. Her jaw was clenched, and her fists were balled on her lap as she willed herself not to say anything, not trusting her voice or the words that might spill out. But when Jake passed the Brookhollow Inn's driveway without pulling in, she finally spoke up.

"That was the B and B."

His knuckles were white as he gripped the steering wheel, and he glanced at her quickly before turning his attention back to the empty road ahead. "I know. I'm just not ready to drop you off yet. I can't help but believe this will be the last time I get to be with you."

She pressed her lips together. He was darn right about that. If he thought he could drop that kind of bomb on her all of a sudden and that she would just forgive him for lying to her, he was wrong. "Please, drop me off."

Instead, he pulled the car to the side of the road.

No way. Not again.

She reached for the door handle, but he stopped her. "Wait, please."

She pulled her arm away, moving closer to the door and away from him, away from the touch she craved. She'd find no comfort there now. "I would like to call it a night." A crappy night that she hoped she would be able to forget sooner rather later once she was back in the city...

"I'll take you home. I just want to try to explain first." His expression was pained as he leaned against the steering wheel and ran a hand through his hair.

She was silent. She didn't think there was anything he could say that would ease her troubled mind and conflicted heart, but she waited. Hoping.

He sighed and sat back. "I don't even know what to say."

Well, that was enlightening. "Okay, then…" She reached for the door again.

"Talks-a-lot, please…"

Hearing his nickname for her made the tiny crack in her heart break wide apart, and she swallowed a lump in her throat as she got out. He wouldn't see her cry. "It's fine, Jake. There's nothing to explain. You're not a backstory guy, and you're not a future kind of guy, either." With that, she closed the door, and, head forced high, she made her way back to the B and B.

# CHAPTER TWELVE

"SLOWLY…SLOWLY," HEATHER SAID, guiding the parade float out of the barn. She suppressed a yawn as she sipped her coffee and struggled to keep her tired, swollen eyes open. The night before she hadn't slept at all, lying awake, wondering how she'd completely misinterpreted this thing with Jake. His lies and his reluctance to get close, she could sort of understand and forgive—he'd been trying to protect his family. But his unwillingness to admit that there was something real between them, something she hadn't felt in a long time… made her chest ache.

She hadn't misinterpreted anything, she thought angrily. He'd been playing her. She shook it off as she watched Luke hitch the trailer to the truck the pool hall had rented. She went over to thank him.

"No problem," he said, handing her the keys. "Who's driving this?"

Not her. She still hadn't renewed her license as she'd promised. And she was actually relieved to have an excuse to avoid the parade; she wasn't feeling very festive this morning, and her plan was to go back to bed as soon as the float was on its way. "Candace said she'll do it. She should be here any minute."

"Great. May the best float win," he said with a smile as he headed toward the B and B float at the other end of the parking lot.

She raised her coffee cup, lacking all enthusiasm. She no longer gave a rat's bum about the float competition. If it was up to her, she would already be on her way to New York. But Victoria had insisted that they couldn't miss the parade, and sans valid driver's license, Heather was at the mercy of her friend's schedule. She'd agreed to stay until the following morning, but she hadn't promised to go to the parade.

She glanced across the parking lot to where Jake's gingerbread float sat hitched up to Sheriff Bishop's truck, relieved that he hadn't shown up. It made avoiding him easier. And for the next twenty-four hours, that's exactly what she planned to do.

He'd been lying to her all along. And though

he had a really great reason, she still felt stupid. The worst lie was the one she'd told herself—that he was in love with her.

She saw Cody climb into the driver's seat and pull away to get lined up at the edge of Main Street.

Candace waved as she approached. "Hey, sorry I'm late," she said, out of breath.

"No problem. Here are the keys to the truck. Enjoy." Heather drained the contents of her coffee cup, not feeling any more awake or alert.

"You're sure you don't want to drive along the parade route?" Candace asked, studying her. "I mean, this float was your baby."

She shook her head. "I'm sure."

"You okay?" the girl asked as she got into the cab.

"Yeah. I'm fine." She wasn't, but the sooner she could get out of Brookhollow, the faster she could be on her way to fine.

JACOB WASN'T GOING to attend the parade. He'd been more than happy to let Cody drive the float from one end of Main Street to the other. But he hadn't counted on getting stuck behind it as it crept slowly down the street. Almost everyone in Brookhollow was out on the side-walks, waving and smiling and enjoying the Christmas sights and sounds. He checked the time. It was after noon; he'd thought the parade would be over by now.

He cranked up the heavy metal rock station to try to drown out the sound of Melody and Brad, dressed as Mr. and Mrs. Claus, belting out "Rockin' Around the Christmas Tree" on the float in front of him—Heather's float.

He could see Joey's Diner...so close, yet so far.

Walking might be faster, he decided, parking and getting out. He'd already taken his insulin, so if he didn't eat soon, he'd be low.

The festivities surrounding him as he walked did nothing to help his mood. He'd been miserable since dropping Heather off the night before, and he'd been too much of a coward to show up at the barn that morning. As much as he regretted it, he hadn't been lying when he'd said that once all of this was over, he was returning to whatever life was waiting for him in New York, and that a relationship didn't really fit into that world.

But he'd known that going in. So why did the thought feel like a punch to the gut now?

As he passed through the crowd, he glanced at his float. Sheriff Bishop's nephews were throwing candy canes to the spectators. At least they were having a good time, he thought, remembering how much Kyle enjoyed the Macy's Thanksgiving Day Parade. The poor kid had missed out on so many of their holiday traditions this year, and it was all his fault.

Noticing a man standing across the street, Jacob froze.

Lorenzo?

The familiar, knee-length wool coat, black leather gloves and brimmed hat made Jacob's pulse race. He peered through the gap between the floats. The man was turned slightly, but he was alone and looked out of place. He couldn't be sure. But his gut was telling him all he needed to know.

A float stopped in front of him, blocking his view, and he muttered under his breath. Jacob pushed his way to the curb, trying to see around it. Why wasn't it moving?

Without another thought, he climbed up onto the float and stumbled over the wires hooked up to the speakers. The music stopped, and several large candy canes fell over. He ignored the confused, annoyed look from Danielle O'Connor, the owner of Dog Eared Books, as he made his way across her float, knocking over several other decorations. His foot stuck to the white foam bedding that was supposed to be snow, and the sound of crunching glass made him wince as he crushed a bulb and all the lights went out.

"Sheriff Matthews, you're destroying our float," Danielle said.

"Sorry," he mumbled, jumping onto the street on the other side and scanning for Lorenzo. Where had he gone?

He saw him a block away…and a little farther down the street, he saw Heather walking toward the B and B. His heart hammered in his chest. How did they know where he was? How did they know about Heather? He started to run, pushing past the families on the sidewalk, ignoring their protests as he hurried to catch up to the guy before he could reach Heather.

The guy was six feet tall, his dress pants and expensive shoes out of place on the slushy sidewalk. Definitely Lorenzo. Jacob saw him reach into his coat and picked up speed, as the man touched Heather's shoulder.

She turned, and her surprised expression gave Jacob the energy to sprint the rest of the way, drawing his gun as he ran. He leaped and tackled Lorenzo to the ground, flipping him over and holding him at gunpoint.

Heather gasped. "Jake? What are you doing?"

His mouth dropped open as he studied the man he'd pinned to the ground. It wasn't Lorenzo. In the guy's hand was an envelope, not a gun.

"Jake, get up!" Heather said, grabbing his arm.

He shook his head as the other man continued to stare up at him in shock and fear. Quickly, he got to his feet and extended a hand to the fellow, but he didn't take it as he stood.

"Sorry," Jacob said.

"Put the gun away!" Heather told him.

He holstered it and once again apologized. "I'm sorry. I thought you were...someone else."

Heather released an exasperated sigh. "Jake, this is Mr. Ericksen—the owner of the pool hall."

Her annoyed tone said everything. She thought he was insane.

Maybe he was. Maybe the stress of all of

this was finally getting to him. But the guy had looked… His monitor beeped. Damn, and now he was low.

"Mr. Ericksen, this is Sheriff Matthews," Heather told the other man as he stood and wiped snow from his coat. "He's a little overprotective," she said with a forced laugh through clenched teeth.

Jacob extended his hand again, but the man ignored it. Instead, he gave Heather the envelope. "Here's your final paycheck… I wanted to give it to you myself and thank you for everything," he said tightly, an eye still on Jacob, seeming ready to defend against another attack.

Jacob couldn't possibly feel like more of a jerk. He stood back as the two of them talked for another minute, and then the man walked away quickly.

"Heather, I'm—"

"Crazy? Overzealous?" she said, arms folded across her chest.

He couldn't help but notice that she looked as tired and confused as he felt. "Yes. And yes. I thought…"

"What? That he was one of the bad guys? Here in Brookhollow?" she scoffed, looking past him toward the crowd that was no longer watching the parade but staring at them. "You just ruined the parade for all of those people. Poor kids are totally freaked-out," she said, pointing to two kids hugging their mother's legs, hiding from him.

He sighed. "I made a mistake." He swallowed hard. "I made a lot of mistakes..." His monitor beeped again.

"You're low?" she asked.

He nodded.

"You should probably go take care of that before it leads to even more clouded judgment," she said, turning on her heel.

He wanted to run after her, but she was right. He did have to take care of it. He had to take care of a lot of things before he could even think about them being together.

# CHAPTER THIRTEEN

"I KNOW YOU and I have had our moments over the years—" Luke began as he carried two of Heather's suitcases to his truck. Victoria was sitting eagerly behind the wheel, waiting to drive her to New York. "—but I just want to say thank you for all your help around here, in the last few months especially."

"It was nothing, Luke." She faced the man who looked terrified as he gazed at his wife, who was singing off-key to the holiday music on the radio. "Don't worry," Heather said, touching his shoulder. "I'll be sure to send her back."

He laughed, but it was tense. "I know I'm being stupid, I'm just not sure I can compete with New York."

Heather hugged the man for the first time ever, the awkwardness of the action overshadowed by her need to reassure him that Victoria had chosen love once before, and she always would…just as Heather would have, given the opportunity. She gulped as she pulled away. "New York is no competition for you, Luke. She'll be home tomorrow, I promise."

"All right, travel safe…good luck with the new job. And if you ever need anything or a place to crash…"

She shook her head sadly. "I won't be back. So let your beautiful girls visit me in the city once in a while, okay?"

He nodded. "This town left a mark, huh?"

Not Brookhollow. Jake Matthews—Jacob Marx—had left a mark. A scar so deep in such a short period of time. "I'll be fine. I'm like a cat—always land on my feet."

"Don't you mean six-inch stilettos?" he asked, touching her arm. "Good luck, Heather."

"Thanks, Luke."

As she climbed into the truck, Luke tapped on the driver's-side window. Victoria rolled it down, and he drew her face toward him for a long kiss.

Seriously? Heather had just gotten her heart broken two nights ago. *Have some compassion for the unlucky in love*, she thought. Leaning forward, she wailed on the horn, causing both of them to jump. "We need to get going," she said.

"Right. Sorry. Bye, Luke. Take care of my baby…"

"I'll be fine." He sounded anything but.

Victoria laughed. "I was talking about Harper," she said as she rolled up the window.

Luke waved to them as they pulled out of the drive. "He's totally freaked-out," Heather said, envying her friend's relationship, not for the first time.

"He'll survive. I'm coming back…maybe," Victoria said, teasing. Then she added, "What about you? Do you think you'll be back to visit at least?"

"I don't know, Vic. I think it's better if you visit me."

"Are you sure about this—leaving?"

She nodded. "Absolutely." The fact was, what she felt didn't matter. Jake had made it clear that eventually he would be returning to the city himself…and to his job. They had no future together. There was no point sticking around only to be disappointed and heartbroken in the end anyway.

JACOB TOSSED A football up into the air and caught it. He threw it up again and caught it…

the same thing he'd been doing for the past hour and a half. Putting the football on his desk, he stood and stretched. He could work out again or do yet another circuit of town in the squad car. It didn't matter. Nothing he did would make the time that had seemed to come to a complete standstill since Heather left go by faster. And nothing he did could stop his mind from wandering to her.

He was dying to call her to find out how she was, how she was adjusting to life back in the city, whether or not she'd found an apartment yet…what she had for breakfast—anything. He didn't care. He just wanted to hear her nonstop voice.

He could block his number and call her. Just to hear her say hello or no doubt ream out the prank caller, he thought with a smile, the temptation to do it growing even stronger.

He couldn't. There was no way he would be able to remain silent on the other end. Not when there was so much he wanted to say.

The front door opened, and Cody entered the station.

"You did this, didn't you?" Cody demanded angrily, as he waved a piece of paper inches from Jacob's nose.

"Hey, take it down a notch, man. What is this?" he asked, taking the paper.

"They are refusing my request for an interview and physical."

Jacob quickly scanned the letter from the Boston Police Department. "Why?" All the letter said was that his application had been denied.

"You tell me," Cody said, leaning across the desk.

"Okay, you need to back it up a little," Jacob said, advancing toward him. The kid had picked the wrong day to accuse him of something.

Cody straightened and took a deep breath. "Go ahead and deny that you didn't fill out those forms I left here for Sheriff Bishop."

The forms? Oh. The recommendation letter. The kid thought he'd had something to do with this? True, he didn't want Cody to take the job in Boston, but he hadn't seen those papers since the day he'd left them on Sheriff Bishop's desk.

"You can't deny it, can you?" Cody said when he hesitated. "I knew it. You kept saying that I should wait, hold out for a position here.

Why, Jake? Did you want the job in Boston?" His eyes flared with anger.

Okay, this was getting crazy. "Cody, I had nothing to do with this." He handed him the letter. "And I didn't try to take your job in Boston." He sat. What a disaster this week was turning out to be. He could use a beer. Unfortunately, he couldn't go anywhere near the pool hall anymore. Reminders of Heather were everywhere in Brookhollow, but especially there.

"Well, if you didn't sandbag me, who did?"

"I did," Sheriff Bishop said, entering through the fire hall.

Both men turned.

"What? Why?" Cody asked.

"Because there's a position opening up here," he said quietly, filling his "Best Grandpa" mug with coffee.

Jacob straightened, and his eyes widened. Did that mean…?

Sheriff Bishop shook his head briefly. "I'm retiring in the spring," he said, and Jacob's shoulders sagged. Not what he'd been hoping to hear.

"But, I thought you were planning to stay on for at least another couple of years," Cody said, his anger dissipating.

"Things lately have taught me that maybe it's time for me to go now," the older man said.

So obviously Sheriff Bishop assumed Jacob wouldn't be leaving Brookhollow anytime soon. Fantastic. This day could stop getting worse any moment now.

"So you can start as soon as you graduate." He extended a hand to Cody, who still looked a little shocked but definitely relieved.

"Thank you, sir." Then he turned to Jacob. "Sorry…"

Jacob shook his head. "We're cool, man." He pocketed his keys. "I think I'm going to head out, do some rounds…" He needed air and some time alone.

Sheriff Bishop nodded, following him outside. "Let's go for a walk," the older man said as Jacob reached for the door handle on the squad car.

Jacob paused. "What's going on?"

"I got a call this morning. They caught Lorenzo, and they've set a court date," he said quietly.

Relief flowed through him. "When?" *Please, say soon.* He couldn't last much longer here…especially without Heather.

"Two days from now."

December 22. "Oh, that's amazing news," he said, wanting to kiss the man. Two days. He could last two days. Barely, but at least he knew when he could get out of here. Two days was better than two weeks or two months. In the grand scheme of things, two days was a blink, yet it still felt excruciatingly long. Two days from now would be two days before Christmas Eve.

"How on earth was Cameron able to get a date that close to Christmas?" In his experience with the justice system, everything came to a complete stop the third week of December up until the new year. He hadn't expected to hear anything until January or later. He'd resigned himself to spending the holidays alone in Brookhollow...without his family. Without Heather.

"Christmas miracle is all I can figure," the older man said with a shrug, zipping his coat against the cold wind.

"I'll take it." Jake laughed. "Oh, thank God," he said, turning to lean up against the squad car.

Sheriff Bishop looked less happy as he shuffled his feet in the snow.

"I'm sorry, I know I sound like I can't wait

to get out of here." He was being insensitive. The department had postponed hiring a full-time, permanent staff member so he could fulfill the role until his case reached the judge. And now with Sheriff Bishop retiring in the spring, they would be once again looking for a replacement.

But the sheriff just laughed good-naturedly. "But you really can't wait to get out of here."

"I know, I'm dying here." No sense lying about it. He'd been pretty obvious about his feelings before.

"You know, Brookhollow's a great place. Less danger, slower pace, you could raise a family with confidence here. You can't do that with your position on the force in New York," he said.

The older man had a point. The small town would be a wonderful, safe place to settle down and start a family. Enjoy the lack of serious crimes and laid-back atmosphere. He was fitting in better now. And here, he didn't have to keep looking over his shoulder.

He sighed. "Brookhollow does offer a level of peace and security, but the city is where I belong." It was all he'd ever known, and his position on the NYPD was important to him.

Important enough that he'd let the one woman he'd ever truly loved walk away.

Sheriff Bishop nodded. "I never expected you to stay…but we sure could use you around here." He tapped his shoulder. "Good luck, son."

"Hey, Sheriff Bishop—thank you." The older man had welcomed him when no one else had. He'd been his only confidant this whole time. Jacob felt he owed him a lot. "I promise I'll help you find a replacement." There were several older men on the force in New York who might be perfect for the position. Once he got back to the city and settled his court case, he would spread the word about the opportunity in Brookhollow.

"Thanks, Jake. I'd appreciate you sending someone this way." Sheriff Bishop made his way inside.

Alone, Jacob smiled. In two days, he was going home. He would testify against Leo Gonzales and Mario Lorenzo, and then he could get on with his life. He just hoped he still had a life waiting for him in New York.

RETAIL THERAPY ON Fifth Avenue made everything better. The hustle and bustle of the holiday shoppers, the businesspeople rushing from one meeting to another in the lead-up to the festive season, the decorated lampposts and the holiday music escaping the shops as doors opened and closed almost made Heather forget her heart was broken.

Two days away from Brookhollow—away from Jake—and already she was missing him. She hoped that the old adage "absence makes the heart grow fonder" was a lie and that as time passed, it would get easier to adjust to her new life without him.

It had only been three weeks since they'd kissed the first time—could she really have fallen so hard so quickly? The concept amazed her, but the ache in her heart told her she'd done just that.

As she exited the change room at Saks on Fifth Avenue, she slid her hands along the dark charcoal pencil skirt. "Do you think it's too dark? Was the light gray better?" she asked her sister.

"It's winter, and you already have the light gray," Cameron said, handing her a navy blue suit. "Try this one next," she said, before returning to the chair to watch Heather's new career wardrobe fashion show, while typing furiously on her iPhone.

Heather turned in front of the mirror back inside the stall. The suit was fine. It was everything else that wasn't.

She removed the jacket and replaced it on the hanger, then reached for the zipper on the skirt.

As she shimmied out of it, she heard her sister's phone ringing for the millionth time that day.

"Seriously? Doesn't your office realize a day off means a day off?" Her sister had surprised her with her availability for a shopping therapy day, but now it seemed that she was still essentially on call.

"Sorry, I have to get this."

"Do what you gotta do, sis," she said, pulling on her jeans and sweater and gathering the items she planned on buying. Four new suits at a cost of a thousand dollars each—an early Christmas gift from her sister—should be enough to dull her heartache for a little while, at least. The frozen yogurt store would be their next stop, she decided.

But as she zipped her heeled boots, she

heard Cameron's voice grow frantic. "Sorry, Heather. I have to get to the office."

Heather stepped out of the stall. "What? No! You promised me ice cream to help brain-freeze away my depression over Jake," she said. Though it would take a lot of low-fat, low-carb, low-taste chocolate fro-yo for that to happen.

"I know, but trust me, this is really important." Cameron looked apologetic as she opened her purse and retrieved her credit card. "Everything's on me. Go shoe shopping, too," she said, handing it over.

"You think you can bribe me?"

"Hoping?"

Heather sighed. She should have known her sister having a day off was too good to be true. Cameron had worked both the morning of her wedding and while she was in labor with Dylan. "Fine. Go."

"I'll make it up to you, I promise."

As Cameron hurried through the front door, she dropped her office swipe card.

Heather rushed to pick it up and pushed open the store door. An alarm sounded.

"Hey! You need to pay," the store clerk yelled.

Shoot. She hurried back to the counter and set her items down. "Hold these for just a second, please." Then she rushed outside.

She spotted her sister turning onto a side street a block away. "Cameron!" she called.

Her sister turned, her cell phone to her ear.

"Your swipe card," she said, waving it as she jogged closer.

Then she gasped. A van stopped in front of them, and a man in a hooded sweatshirt jumped out, grabbed Cameron around the waist and tossed her inside. Heather dropped the swipe card and willed her legs to run away from the big man, but she was frozen in place.

A second later, she was kicking against his hold, terror flowing through her. Then she was dumped into the back of the vehicle next to Cameron. She searched her sister's face, seeing her own distress mirrored there, as the guy tied their hands behind them. "What's going on?" she croaked.

Her sister's face disappeared beneath a cloth bag before she could answer, then suddenly her tears were soaking the cloth at her own cheeks.

"Cameron! What's going on?" she called

again, shaking in the dark. The van started to move. "Where are they taking us?"

"I don't know, Heather," she said, her voice steady but laced with fear.

"Is this about a case or something?"

"This is about Jake's case," her sister said quietly.

Heather's blood ran cold. Jake's case? Her sister was working on his case? She blinked as a wave of nausea hit her. Oh, God! The drug bust...what was going to happen to them? Trying not to throw up, she choked on a sob and jumped as she felt something touch her arm.

"It's just me," Cameron said, moving even closer.

Heather rested her head against her sister's, and the two of them huddled together, desperately seeking comfort in the terror and confusion surrounding them. "What's going to happen to us?" she whispered.

"I don't know."

JACOB REMOVED THE last few items from his locker at the station the evening after his talk with Sheriff Bishop. He could hear Ethan, Jim and Noah playing poker in the fire hall, and he quickly stashed the letters from his nephew into the side pocket of his bag, then hung up his sheriff's jacket for the last time.

He sighed, unsure what he was feeling. He wasn't upset that he was leaving. Brookhollow was a great place to live and raise a family, but his heart was in the city. Heather was in the city, and soon he would be, too. He'd always stayed away from relationships and commitments that could complicate his career choices, but now he was ready to try something different, even if it meant reevaluating the danger he put himself in at work. He just hoped he could convince her to forgive him and give them another chance.

Hearing the guys' laughter made him wish he could say goodbye, at least, but until the court case tomorrow, he had to keep his departure a secret. He was so close. He couldn't risk ruining things by letting something slip.

He'd send the guys all an email from the city in the new year. Or maybe he'd visit. As he closed the locker, his cell rang. His heart raced at the sight of Emilio's number lighting up the screen. His palms sweated as he held the phone, counting the rings. Two, three… Nine rings before the call was disconnected.

Nine o'clock that evening. That's when the

container would arrive. Of course, Lorenzo's guys could show up anytime to collect the shipment. Jacob's mouth was dry as he sat on the bench, contemplating his options. Lorenzo was in custody. He could go to New York, testify and hope that his statement was enough to put the man behind bars.

But what if it wasn't enough?

His skin tingled as he thought about the coincidental timing of his capture. Being brought in the day a shipment was arriving? Was it just a way to ensure that the heat was removed from the surveillance on the dock that evening?

If he went to the dock, and busted Lorenzo's men in the act of collecting the drug shipment, it would give the necessary backing evidence to his testimony... And the video surveillance footage would be more than enough to put the man away.

His legs slightly unsteady, Jacob stood, knowing what he needed to do.

NOISE COMING FROM his bathroom made him pause when he entered the apartment. The lights were off, except for the one in the short hall at the top of the stairs, and slowly, quietly laying his bag on the floor and keeping his back to the wall, he moved further into the room. Mrs. Kelly was at bingo, so who the hell was in his apartment? He stopped to listen again, and the sound of the toilet flushing made him frown. Someone had broken into his apartment to pee?

As he rounded the corner, his hand on his weapon, his common sense told him to remain calm. That his hypersensitivity right now came from the knowledge of where he was headed later tonight and the danger waiting there for him.

Still, his shoulders relaxed when he saw Cody.

"Hey, man." Jacob paused, noticing his unlicensed, loaded weapon in the guy's hand. "I'll take that," he said.

Cody shook his head as he moved it out of reach. "Not until you tell me exactly who you are and why you have an illegal weapon hiding in my aunt's toilet."

"Technically, I'm renting that toilet, so I can put anything I want in there," he said, but he knew he was stalling.

"I'm not messing with you, Jake," the young guy said, palming his walkie-talkie.

Jacob sighed. He didn't have time for this right now, but he also didn't want Sheriff Bishop involved. The older man thought he was heading back to New York to go into temporary custody until the trial the next day. "Fine. Just give me the gun, and I'll explain."

"I'll hold the gun while you explain."

Smart kid. Annoying, but smart. "I'm Detective Jacob Marx. I was undercover in New York until earlier this year."

Cody's eyes had widened, and he was nodding. "The Lorenzo case."

"Right."

"Your family went under witness protection, didn't they?"

Jacob nodded. "And I came here instead. Look, Cody, I have to go." It was already after seven.

"They just brought him into custody—I saw it on the news this morning."

"Yes, they did, and I'm going back to testify."

Cody's eyes narrowed. "You're heading back right now?"

"Yes," he lied. "I just came to get…"

"This?" He held the gun out to him.

Jacob took it. "Yes. Thank you." Removing

the weapon from the plastic, he checked the chamber—full.

"Your hands are shaking. Where are you really headed, Jacob?"

"There's just something I need to take care of."

"I'm coming with you," he said, leaving the bathroom.

No way. The kid had a wife and three children. Jacob refused to drag him into this. The case was barely his anymore, let alone a rookie cop's who had no training in the field and no experience with crimes at this level. "No, you're not."

Cody's eyes burned with determination. "We are partners until you leave, which means I'm going with you."

"Cody, this is not some graffiti bust, man." Jacob advanced toward him, ready to knock him out if necessary to keep him there—safe.

"Jacob, I became a cop for the same reason you did—to make a difference. For the sake of my family, I've decided to stay here in Brookhollow, but for tonight, I'm a real cop, and I'm coming with you."

"Cody, no."

The kid reached for the walkie again. "Fine.

Well, the minute you leave, I'll tail you and call it in. Wherever you're going, I'm pretty sure you don't have jurisdiction, and you sure aren't under the NYPD undercover unit's protection anymore."

Damn. "So, if I won't let you come with me, you're going to rat me out?" Didn't they teach brotherhood and loyalty in the academy anymore?

"Yes."

He stared at the kid for a long moment, wasting time he didn't have. "Fine. You drive. And you stay in the car at all times—understand?"

Cody nodded.

This was a mistake. He already knew it.

"PULL IN OVER HERE," he told Cody as they arrived at the dock. They'd ditched the squad car for Cody's truck, and after another attempt to talk the kid out of this, they'd headed to Newark, and he'd filled his new "partner" in on all the details of the bust. There were few. He knew the container was arriving at nine, and that Lorenzo's two main guys would be there to accept the shipment, now that Lorenzo had been taken into custody. And that was it.

To his credit, Cody's hands were steady on the wheel as he drove.

But a second later, as he cut the engine, the beep of Jacob's glucose monitor made them both jump.

He held out a hand. "Don't check yourself for bullet wounds, it was just my monitor." He knew without looking that the thing was beeping for a different reason this time. His levels were high. Not ideal, but at least he wasn't going to pass out.

"You okay?" Cody asked.

His diabetes was the least of his worries right now. He nodded. "I'm good. Cut the headlights." He buckled his bulletproof vest and handed an extra one from the station to Cody. "Put this on, but stay in the car."

He seemed as if he was about to argue, but when Jacob lowered his visor and pointed to the picture of Cody's family hanging from the rearview, he silently pulled on the vest.

As Jacob stepped out into the snow, Cody said, "This is a bad idea—you know that, right?"

"Absolutely." He shut the door. His boots left dark footprints as he walked casually toward the back shipping area.

Approaching, he saw Emilio's office light on and heard the cranes unloading the container from the boat. Adrenaline made his heart beat faster, and he forced a breath in, then out. Hand on his weapon, he moved slowly toward the trailer.

Sounds of voices. Emilio's and two others… Jacob recognized them both and was almost relieved to hear Guido, the man who'd been with him the day they'd been sent to take care of Emilio. With any luck, the guy was still as squeamish about shooting people as he'd been a year ago.

Rounding the corner, he saw a van and a larger cube van parked near the dock. He watched as they opened the container. It was nearly empty, except for about two million dollars' worth of cocaine. Emilio entered the container, two guns pointed on his back, and he waited…

Jacob needed to see the transfer of goods. Once the product switched hands, he could close in. He inched closer to the van, hiding behind the back wheel. Now, all three men were inside the container. The sound of voices in the van startled him, and he ducked lower, peering in through the back window.

He couldn't see much in the dark, but he made out two figures sitting on the floor, arms tied behind their backs…and a pair of red leopard-print boots that he'd recognize anywhere.

Heather.

His mouth went dry, and he blinked back a wave of dizziness. This bust just got much more dangerous. And much more important.

What could they possible want with *her*? How did they even know she was connected to him? Had they been tailing him? Had they known all along where he was?

The revelation hit him like a two-by-four—Cameron. Cameron was the other person in the van. Lorenzo might be in custody, but without the lead prosecutor on the case, the trial would be delayed. His blood ran cold as the men's voices drew closer.

"Lorenzo sends his thanks," he heard Guido say. "He apologizes he couldn't be here to tie up loose ends himself."

Loose ends? Emilio. Cameron and Heather. Not tonight.

Moving quickly, Jacob swung around to the front of the container. "Police. Hands up where I can see them," he ordered, gun pointed, quickly taking inventory of the guns at both men's waists.

Harris, a longtime employee of Lorenzo's, eyed Jacob and slowly raised his arms. "Marx," he growled, "nice to see you again."

"Wish I could say the same." Jacob inched closer, quickly grabbing the guy's weapon and tossing it out of the container. "Guido." He nodded at the other man and grabbed his gun, as well. "Hands behind your backs and turn around—both of you."

"A little out of your jurisdiction here, aren't you?" Harris said, turning slowly.

"Shut up and put your hands behind your back." He caught Emilio's eye. "Go pick up their weapons and clear the chambers," he said.

The other man looked nervous, but he rushed off to follow Jacob's instructions.

Keeping his gun pointed at Guido, Jacob handcuffed Harris, knowing the bigger man would be harder to take in hand-to-hand combat. The fact that Harris didn't try to pounce on him made him even more uneasy. He cuffed him quickly and faced Guido.

"Drop the gun, Jake," Emilio said, standing

at the edge of the container and training both weapons on him. He was shaking.

Jacob kept his gun pointed on Guido as he said, "What are you doing, Emilio?"

"I'm sorry, Jake, but I'm too far into this mess... I have a family to protect..."

"And you think these guys are going to let you live? Emilio, put down the guns...or better yet, point them at these guys."

What was happening? Trusting a criminal and learning his lesson the hard way was what was happening. He swallowed hard. "Emilio, please. I can get you out of this—"

Guido's right hook staggered him, and he scrambled for his footing as the guy stole his gun back from Emilio and continued to point it at Jacob.

"Drop it, Marx. I won't hesitate to shoot you," he said.

"Really? You got over that weak stomach issue?" he asked, hoping to buy any time he could. He felt sick with the knowledge that he was on his own. No one was coming to save him.

Unless....

His eyes widened as Cody hit Guido in the head with the barrel of his gun. He quickly kicked the man's gun out of reach and gestured for Emilio to step inside the container.

Jacob's shoulders relaxed as he rushed to hoist Guido over his shoulder and place him inside the container with the other men; then he joined Cody, and they held their weapons on the criminals. "I told you to stay in the car," he said, but his voice was only full of relief.

"Thought you could use a hand," he said, the sound of sirens filling the quiet night air. "And I also phoned in backup."

Jacob's heart rate started to slow. "Good call, kid." With the immediate crisis under control, he could deal with Heather and Cameron. "Think you could be a hero to a couple of scared women in that van?" He wanted to go to her himself, but he was better trained to stay on the criminals.

With a nod, Cody handed him the gun and went to the van, just as several cop cars arrived.

"Hands up! On the ground!" one of the officers called, and Jacob readily complied.

STILL IN SHOCK, Heather sat shivering in the backseat of the police car despite the warm blanket wrapped around her. Her mind raced, yet the rest of her was numb. The past eight hours had been the scariest of her life. She'd thought for sure she was going to die.

"Here, drink this." A nice officer she barely noticed handed her a cup of hot water, and she accepted it with a shaking hand, her gaze still fixed on the loading docks, where Jacob, Cody and Cameron stood talking to the Newark police, as the criminals were taken into custody.

He'd saved them.

The man she was in love with had just saved her life. But mixed in somewhere among the relief and gratitude was the heavy realization that this was exactly what Jacob had meant when he'd said that his job didn't allow for relationships and marriage. Heather now knew firsthand that people could be hurt because of his chosen profession.

He glanced toward the car, his expression flitting between concern and affection.

Tears gathered in her eyes, and she tore her gaze away.

He was right. They couldn't be together.

# CHAPTER FOURTEEN

JACOB PACED THE witness room at the back of the courthouse early the next day. The day he had been waiting for for five months had arrived, two days before Christmas. He'd given up hope of having all of this resolved before the holidays. Soon, his testimony would put Mario Lorenzo behind bars, and his sister and Kyle could return to their lives. In a few short hours, all of this would be behind him. Of course, that wouldn't be the end. Going into a bust without jurisdiction, without backup, without any right to do so was going to cost him.

Cameron entered, and he walked toward her eagerly. "How's Heather?" he asked.

"Take your mind off my sister, and focus on your testimony," she said, tying her long dark hair in a tight bun on top of her head.

Long dark hair...like Heather's...

"You're right. I'm sorry," Jacob said, determined to keep his mind on the case. He couldn't think about the woman he was in love with just yet. Still... "But how is she?"

Cameron sighed. "You broke her heart, and then she just went through the most traumatic experience of her life yesterday. How do you think she is?"

Hurting Heather was the last thing he'd ever wanted to do. And he desperately wanted to hold her and tell her that everything was okay now, that she was safe. The night before, it had taken every ounce of strength and common sense not to do that. If only she could forgive him at the end of all of this. "I know, Cameron, and I'm sorry."

Cameron shook her head. "That was her sister talking. As your lawyer—you did the right thing. Telling Heather the truth would have put everything we've worked so hard for at risk." She shuddered. "And I didn't get a chance yesterday to say thank you for saving our lives...even though you nearly jeopardized everything by doing something so dangerous." She slapped his arm, but her expression was pure gratitude. "Now, sit tight. We have several others to call before you, but your testimony is the one that will matter most, so just relax and tell your story up there."

When he nodded, she left him alone. He filled a coffee cup and sat in a chair near the window. On the street below, businesspeople rushed along the crowded sidewalks getting to offices to finish up the last of their pre-holiday workload. He couldn't get his mind off Heather. She was here in the city, so close... all he wanted to do was get out of there and go see her. Tell her he loved her and that he was starting to reevaluate what was truly important. Seeing her in the back of the van last night had nearly broken him.

But what if she didn't forgive him for lying and for hurting her? Putting her life at risk? Suddenly, his testimony on the stand was the easier of the two speeches he knew he had to make today.

The door opened. "Ready for me?" he asked, setting the cup on the table and turning.

His heart stopped as Maria Gonzales entered. Immediately, his hand went to his hip, but there was no gun, no taser, just the edge of his suit jacket. He was completely unarmed and coming face-to-face with...a ghost. He paled. Maria Gonzales was supposed to be dead.

"Hi, Jacob."

Jacob? She knew his real name? What was she doing here? She obviously wasn't dead. She also didn't seem to be there to inflict bodily harm; she stood near the door, hands hanging by her sides. What was going on? He glanced behind her as she entered the room, but she was alone. "Maria."

"Surprised to see me?"

Understatement. "You're supposed to be dead, so, yeah—little bit."

"I guess I have a lot to explain," she said, coming closer.

He stepped back until he was pressed up against the window.

"I work for the FBI," she said.

He blinked. What? She was an agent?

"I was undercover for the NYPD when we met."

"*You* were undercover?" He sounded like a moron repeating everything she said, but he was in shock. He'd yet to recover from the fact that she was still breathing, but to learn that the whole time he'd known her, she'd been on his side?

"Yes. And when you appeared and started asking me questions about the business and trying to persuade me to get out, I knew you were, too."

"Why didn't you tell me?" He felt like an idiot. He'd never guessed that Maria had already gotten out, that she was fighting on the good side the entire time.

"You know why. We both had a job to do. And at first, I really didn't know if my instincts about you were right. I thought you were just another one of my brother's goons, but then as we got closer and you tried to convince me to get away from the family business, I started to have my suspicions." She shrugged.

"That's why you left."

She nodded. "Once I knew for sure, I requested a transfer that wouldn't blow my cover or ruin the progress I'd made…so they moved me to the source. Convincing Leo to let me do the next pickup was easy—he saw me as a disposable commodity." Her voice hardened.

"You got caught at the border on purpose?'

She nodded. "You learn a lot in jail."

Wow, she was even braver and crazier than he'd ever imagined. "You took a huge risk."

"So did you," she said, touching his arm.

"I'm just glad I was able to locate Mario as quickly as I did."

"You did that?" She was responsible for locating Mario and bringing him in? She was responsible for getting this court case two days before Christmas? Getting him back to the city?

She nodded. "I'm sorry I lied to you, Jacob."

He shook his head. "You were undercover. It was your job. Your safety…"

"Not everything was a lie," she said, inching toward him.

His pulse raced. He realized now that it hadn't been love, but a sense of protection he'd felt for her in those extreme circumstances. He'd wanted to get her away from a bad situation, but he'd never truly loved her. Not like he loved Heather. "Maria…"

The door opened and Cameron entered. "Maria, we're ready for your testimony," she said, glancing between the two of them.

Maria nodded. "Okay," she said, and Cameron left them alone once more. "Jacob, I…"

"Maria, you are the bravest woman I know. Testifying against your own brother…" He knew what it was like to put family behind bars. It wasn't easy, and he admired her strength and her character, but he wasn't in love with her. He knew now that he never was.

She leaned forward and kissed his cheek. "Don't say it," she said. "It was a different time, a different place."

He nodded.

She let out a deep breath. "Well, this is it."

"You can do this."

She nodded as she turned and walked toward the door.

"Maria…"

"Yeah?"

"Thank you."

"Merry Christmas, Jacob."

"UNCLE JACOB!" KYLE'S excitement brought tears to his eyes as the little boy rushed toward him two hours later on the steps of the courthouse.

Bending, Jacob scooped him up for a hug. "Hi, buddy," he said in disbelief. He'd assumed they would have needed a few days to get his sister and nephew back home. He'd been hoping for New Year's…this was so wonderfully unexpected.

"Did we surprise you?" Kyle asked when he set him on the ground.

"Yes," he said, as his sister came forward. "Hi, Amber."

Her expression was unreadable for the briefest of moments before she wrapped him in a hug. "Thank you," she whispered.

He held her tight, wishing he could take credit for getting them home before the holidays. But it had been Cameron's insistence that they go to trial before Christmas that had made it all happen. "I'm so glad this is over," he said, releasing her. His testimony had been in question because of his blackout, but the previous night's bust and Maria's testimony had helped convince the jury. And the defense asked for a plea deal, knowing that they would be facing an even longer sentence if they didn't.

Jacob still had to face the department officials the next day about whether or not he would be allowed to return to his position on the force, but for now, it was over.

"Uncle Jacob, now that we're here, can we go Christmas shopping?" Kyle asked, his hopeful expression making it impossible to say no.

"As long as it's okay with your mom." He didn't want to put off seeing Heather, but he found himself unable to disappoint his nephew.

"It's fine. I have to get to the gallery and see what needs to be done to reopen it." Amber looked happier than he ever remembered seeing her, and he studied her carefully.

"The gallery, huh?" No doubt his sister was impatient to get back to the normalcy of everyday life, but there was definitely something else she was eager to rush off for.

She sighed, then smiled. "And… I have to pick up Michael from the airport."

"Oh, Uncle Jacob, you're going to love Michael. He's so awesome, and he wasn't even mad when we told him we were pretending all along." His nephew was beaming, matching his mother's expression, and Jacob was overwhelmed with joy. Things had worked out… perhaps better than he could have expected.

"He really is great, and he's looking forward to meeting you," Amber said, checking her watch as they descended the courthouse stairs.

"Okay. Well, I'll take this little stinker shopping, then we'll meet you both at the gallery?"

She nodded.

"Then can we get pizza and go bowling?" Kyle asked.

Jacob ruffled his hair. "Whatever you want, buddy." For tonight, it was all about family.

"COME ON IN, Jacob, the committee is ready to see you now."

Jacob wiped his damp palms on his thighs, and followed Mary, the secretary, into the boardroom.

The thrill of having his NYPD uniform on again was overshadowed by his apprehension. The future of his career with the force was about to be decided, and despite the uncertainty that had plagued him for months in Brookhollow, being this close to an answer was torture.

He took the one lonely chair that awaited him on the left side of the table. Four of his superiors and one of his peers sat on the right. "Hi, everyone," he said as he sat.

"Detective Marx—welcome back," Detective Cable said.

The others smiled and nodded, but the atmosphere in the room was stuffy and uncomfortable.

His career was over. He was too much of a liability; he knew it. He took a deep breath and reached for the jug of water in front of him.

"Sorry, I'm a little nervous," he said, shakily pouring the water and taking a sip.

The liquid stuck in his throat.

"Well, we won't drag this out. It's the holidays, and we all have places to be. I'm sure, after being away so long, you are eager to get to your family, as well," Detective Cable said.

He was. But he was also eager to see Heather. He was desperate to talk to her, make sure she was okay and put things right...or at least try to. But first, he had to focus on the other passion in his life. "Before you continue, sir, can I just say again how sorry I am that this happened and that I appreciate this opportunity." He clamped his lips shut. That was it. Now it was up to them.

"Well, after reviewing your reports on the case and reading your statement and testimony, we, unfortunately, have to conclude that it was your illness that caused you to black out, therefore jeopardizing the case, as well as putting yourself and other officers in mortal danger."

He swallowed hard. That was the toughest thing to hear. They'd gotten lucky that day, with only one officer suffering minor injuries from the shoot-out. It could have been so much worse.

"As well, your unauthorized involvement in last night's events at the Newark dock was unregulated and unreported…and just plain stupid."

"Yes, sir."

"Having said that, your detailed reports and your undercover service for two years are what brought these criminals to justice, and that is not something we are prepared to overlook or disregard. You sacrificed a lot, you kept your cover, and you did good, Detective Marx. Also, after reviewing the statement from DA Cameron Ashley, it is evident that you saved her life as well as another civilian's last night."

Heather. What would he have done if he hadn't been there, and he'd lost her? As much as he knew his actions went against protocol, he couldn't regret the decision that had ultimately saved her life. Even if it did cost him his job.

He let out a slow, deep breath. He couldn't read the situation. Was his performance prior to the incident enough to save his job?

"We have decided that you will be suspended for six months—"

Suspension? Not fired?

"—during which time you will be reevaluated by the doctors and insurance regulators. If they sign your clearance forms, you will return to your regular position."

He couldn't believe it. He wasn't off the hook completely, and the road ahead might not be smooth, but he was prepared to show the force that he could return to his job.

"As per protocol, undercover assignments will be delayed."

He barely heard the man as his heart echoed in his ears.

The committee stood, and so did he.

One by one, they shook his hand and welcomed him back, and he nodded in a daze of disbelief and gratitude. "Thank you, Detective Cable."

The older man nodded. "It's not going to be easy, Jacob, but we're rooting for you."

He was okay with that. His past mistakes would cost him, and he had to man up and make things right. In his professional life, but almost more important, in his personal life.

"You look incredible," Cameron said, zipping the back of Heather's tight-fitting, knee-length red dress an hour before Highstone Acquisitions' Christmas party.

She sure didn't feel incredible. "Really? Or are you lying to me like you did about Jake?" Heather turned to study her reflection in the mirror in her room at her sister's house.

Cameron sighed. "I told you—I didn't lie, I just couldn't tell you the truth." She took her shoulders and spun her around to face her. "And neither could he," she said.

Heather understood, but it still hadn't softened the blow. "Well, it doesn't make me feel better. I wouldn't have said a word to anyone." How could her sister not have trusted her? "Maybe if I'd known you were working on such a high-profile, dangerous case, I would have been prepared to be kidnapped." She shuddered again at the memory of the long, torturous eight hours they'd spent in the back of the van, leaning against one another and telling stories about their childhood in an attempt to ease their anxiety. She'd honestly believed they wouldn't be going home.

"I couldn't take the chance. I wouldn't have even known where he was had you not dragged him to New York. Jacob took a big risk coming here for you that day. And an even bigger one the other night. But if he hadn't..."

"Shhh—don't say it." Her stomach was in knots. She didn't even want to go to the party. She was pretty sure being abducted gave her an excuse to stay locked inside for at least a few weeks, while she recovered from the trauma. She looked at her sister. "How are you not still shaking?" she asked, sitting on the edge of the bed, where her shoes sat waiting for her to slide her feet into them. Unlike her, Cameron seemed to have come out of their ordeal as though it had just been another day at the office.

Cameron picked up one of the black pumps and knelt on the floor in front of her. "Give me your foot."

Heather complied, feeling the same way she had the day of her mother's funeral. Numb, yet able to feel every nerve dancing on her skin at the same time. Cameron had been the strong one then, too.

"I know the risks I take when I do my job. And I was just as terrified as you were yesterday, but we're okay now, and I refuse to let fear win."

"Spoken like a true lawyer."

"The thing is," Cameron said, sliding the second shoe on and pulling Heather to her feet, "what I do is important. Keeping people safe is important."

"But what about your family? Doing your job almost got me killed yesterday," she said with a sigh.

"But doing my job may have saved your life a dozen times before. Doing my job means one less bad guy that could hurt Dylan or Rob or you." She touched her cheek. "The same way Jacob does his job."

She nodded miserably. She'd spent four days missing him now, and her realization about his need to avoid relationships had left her heart aching. He hadn't called or texted or come to see her. Part of her had clung to the hope that he would, only to be let down even more when he hadn't. "Well, whatever it was with Jacob is behind me now." She reached for her coat.

"It doesn't have to be. He asked about you."

Heather paused, not wanting to hear the words but desperately praying they were true.

"Even with everything going on—the court case, his own future with the force on the line—he asked me how you were," Cameron said, standing. Her sister took her coat from her and held it open.

Heather sighed as she slid her arms in and lifted her hair over the collar. "Cam, I don't even know the guy," she said sadly.

Her sister hugged her tight. "Okay, the choice is yours. All I'm going to say is that I want you to be happy. And I'm really glad to have you home this Christmas."

Heather squeezed her sister back. "Me, too." As for what would make her happy…that remained a mystery.

"HEY, I HEARD about your adventure yesterday," Mike Jr. said, coming up behind her at the bar an hour later.

Heather jumped, rattling the ice cubes in her highball glass. Adventure? Wa3s that what they were calling it? The vodka on ice wasn't doing anything to calm her nerves. The noise around her and all the people in the small space were making her feel claustrophobic. "It's a story for the grandkids," she mumbled, hoping to sound nonchalant about the experience.

"Well, we're certainly glad you're okay.

We're excited to have you join us at Highstone," he said.

Good. Yes. Talking about the position might help to take her mind off other things. Forcing a smile, she nodded. "I'm excited, as well. I've been away from the corporate world far too long."

Mike Jr. placed an arm around her shoulder, and she tensed. "You know, my father is retiring next year, and I'll be taking over... I'd really love to take you under my wing, help you reach a higher level in the company."

She suppressed a shudder. Was he hitting on her, or was he being genuine? Man, two years away from the city was making her soft. Two years ago, she'd have twisted his arm behind his back the moment he'd touched her and told him what he could do with his offer. Two years ago, she might have had the same reaction and fought harder when the thug had attacked her. Being away from the city, living in a quiet, peaceful, small town, she'd really let her guard down.

She moved away from him and took a sip of her drink. "I appreciate that—thank you, Mike, but I really think I should work my way into promotions just like everyone else."

He frowned. "Did I say something wrong?"

Had she misread the entire situation? Could he have actually just been offering to help her advance her career? She couldn't rely on her gut instincts anymore, apparently. "No, not at all." *Great start to a new career with a new company, Heather.* "Sorry, I'm just a little off today." Understatement.

"You thought I was implying…"

Her cheeks flushed. "No. Okay, maybe. I'm sorry."

Mike, Jr. laughed. "Don't worry about it. I understand—don't want to repeat past mistakes."

She smiled, still kicking herself for having told them about Mel and why she'd gotten fired. Still kicking herself for having wasted so much of her life and career on that path. "Exactly," she said.

"Well, you don't have to worry. I'm married."

*Floor, just open up now.* "I'm sorry…" She glanced at his hand. Yep, wedding ring. God, she should have just stayed at home, hiding out the way she wanted to. After this, she wasn't leaving the house until New Year's.

"I just see potential in you," he said with a

shrug, checking his watch. "Hey, did you want to go somewhere a little quieter? Talk about the plans for your position?"

"Uh…" She looked around at the party, which was in full swing. She wasn't feeling the holiday cheer, and everywhere she looked, she saw reminders of Jake… Jacob…whoever. "Are you sure? I mean, shouldn't you stick around?"

Mike Jr. shook his head, then nodded in the direction of Mike Sr., who was dancing to "Rockin' Around the Christmas Tree" with the office admin staff. "I think he's got things pretty under control. Let's go." He drained the contents of his glass and set it down on the bar.

They retrieved their coats, and he helped her into hers.

Cameron shot her a quizzical look from where she sat with Rob and several other agents, but Heather just shook her head. "Thank you," she said to Mike, following him outside.

He stepped to the curb and hailed an oncoming taxi.

To both of their surprise, the taxi stopped. "Wow, you'll have to teach me how to do that. Two years in a small town and I think my ability to—" Heather stopped as the back door of the taxi opened…

…And Jake got out. "Heather?" He looked happy, surprised, then curious as he glanced between her and Mike Jr.

"What are you doing here?" she asked, wrapping her arms around her waist, as the wind blew strands of hair around her face.

"I…uh…" He looked at Mike Jr. "I wanted to see you. Are you leaving?"

She nodded.

"With him?"

What a mess. All she wanted was to push Jake back into the taxi, slide in next to him and kiss him—at least part of her did. The other part—the broken-hearted, betrayed, confused part—wanted him to believe that what he thought he was seeing was what he was actually seeing. She was fine. She was moving on with her life. But after a long, awkward pause, she settled for somewhere in the middle. "This is my new boss, Mike Ainsley Jr. Mike, this is…" She paused. She had no idea who this man was, and that was what tore her apart the most.

Mike Jr. extended a hand, but Jacob ignored it. "Your new *boss*?" he said to her. "I thought he was eighty." The jealousy in his voice was unmistakable.

Heather glared at him and pulled Jacob aside. "Just a sec, Mike," she said over her shoulder.

"Everything okay?" Mike hesitated, looking worried.

"Everything's fine. I'm a cop." Jacob flashed his badge quickly.

Heather scoffed. "And that means I'm safe with you?"

"Yes."

"Really? 'Cause if you've forgotten, I was kidnapped the other day…because of you." Technically because of Cameron, but it was also Jacob's fault.

"Heather, are you sure?" Mike still seemed uncertain whether or not to give them privacy.

"Yes, I'm fine. I'll be with you in a minute." She would be. There was no way Jacob could stop her, nothing he could say to convince her to go with him instead.

Mike nodded, sliding into the back of the taxi.

"Why are you here?" she asked him.

"I wanted to see you. Needed to see you.

Make sure you were okay," he said, reaching out to touch her.

She moved away. "I'm fine."

"I'm so sorry about what happened and about…everything else," he said softly.

The taxi driver beeped his horn and waved at her from behind the steering wheel.

"I have to go," she said. She couldn't do this with him right now. Her new boss was waiting on her to go discuss her future. One without the complications of the man standing in front of her.

"Heather…just give me a chance. You know what we had was real," he said, the pleading in his voice making her hesitate.

"I'm not sure what was real and what wasn't," she said with a shrug. "I understand why you couldn't tell me the truth, and I forgive you for that. I'm just not sure I can be with a man whose life will always revolve around lies and danger." In fact, she knew she couldn't.

He shoved his hands into his pockets and nodded. "Okay. I understand. Sorry to have interrupted your evening."

She sighed as she nodded. "Bye J… Bye."

"Merry Christmas, Heather," he said softly as she walked away.

She got into the taxi before her heart could change her mind. A merry Christmas—probably not.

WATCHING THE TAXI pull away from the curb and not throwing himself onto the hood of the car took strength he didn't know he possessed. Jacob's heart ached. He'd messed up, but he'd believed in her, believed in their connection enough to think that she would understand and forgive him.

And he was ready to make sure he was never again in a position that put his own family at risk, even if it meant giving up the undercover assignments. He'd always known the personal risks he was taking by going undercover with his illness. But he'd convinced himself he could do the job...and he could, but who would get hurt if he messed up again? Things had worked out this time, but next time he might not be so lucky.

Snow drifted from the awning of the bar, and he lowered his head, raising the collar of his jacket against the cold wind.

Something glittering in the reflection of the Christmas lights on the street pole caught his eye. Bending, he picked up a silver necklace with a scripted *h* on it. The metal was still warm, and he'd recognize the pendant anywhere.

Heather must have lost it as she'd turned to get into the taxi.

He held it tight in his hand before tucking it into his pocket.

At least he had a reason to contact her again. Christmas miracle or coincidence— didn't matter one bit. He'd take it.

# CHAPTER FIFTEEN

"YOU REALLY THINK you're going to find her in this crowd?" Amber asked, shivering in her down coat, clutching Kyle's hand on one side and Michael's on the other as they made their way through the crush of people in Rockefeller Center the following evening. It was Christmas Eve, and the place was so packed, it was hard for them to even stay together as they headed toward the magnificent tree.

Jacob never thought he'd miss Brookhollow, but the town's small size would have been helpful right now when he was shuffling along looking for Heather and her family among ten thousand New Yorkers.

"I have to," he said, peering over the tops of heads to catch a glimpse of the ice rink. She'd said her family skated there every Christmas Eve and then made holiday wishes on the tree. They had to be here.

"Why don't you just call her?" Michael said.

And say what? *Hi. It's me again. The guy you fell in love with and who broke your heart and who now plans to stalk you?* No. This conversation couldn't happen by phone or text. Though a text would help locate her more quickly. For that matter, he wished he knew Cameron's cell number.

"Jacob?" Cameron's voice behind him made him stop.

His heart sped up as he turned. She stood there with her husband and a little boy—Dylan, he assumed—but no Heather. "Hi. Um... Cameron, this is my sister, Amber, and nephew, Kyle...and Amber's boyfriend, Michael."

Cameron smiled. "Nice to—"

Her words were cut short as Amber swept her up in a hug. "Thank you so much for getting us all home in time for the holidays," she said tearfully.

Cameron returned the awkward hug. "My pleasure..." She looked to Jacob for help when Kyle joined in on the hug.

"Okay, guys, let her breathe," he said, pulling his sister back.

"Sorry," Amber said, shaking Cameron's hand. "Nice to meet you."

Michael smiled and waved.

"This must be Dylan?" Jacob said, bending slightly to talk to the kid. "Hi, buddy. This is my nephew, Kyle. I think you two are about the same age."

"Mom, can we go get hot chocolate now?" Dylan asked.

"We'll take both of them," Amber offered.

"I'll go with them," Rob added quickly. They soon disappeared in the crowd.

"So this is a coincidence?" Cameron asked when they were alone, a knowing expression on her face.

"Not at all." He didn't care if he looked like a lovesick idiot or stalker. He wanted to see Heather, and he didn't care who knew. "Is she here?"

"No."

His heart fell. "But she said this was a family tradition."

"Yeah, she hasn't been feeling very festive lately." Cameron shot him a look.

"I know she's still upset with me. I tried to talk to her last night…"

"No, she's not upset with you. She's in love with you. Anger would never cause my sister miss out on this…only wallowing in self-pity could do that."

She was in love with him. He knew that. There was no denying that she felt the same way he did, and he needed to see her. "So she's at home?"

Cameron nodded. "Fifty-four South Maple Avenue."

He frowned. "Brooklyn?"

"Yep."

Okay, Brooklyn it was. "Can you tell my sister—"

"We'll take care of them. Go, make my sister's holiday wish come true."

MAYBE SHE SHOULD have gone skating with Cameron and her family, Heather thought as she stared into the fridge for the millionth time. She wasn't hungry, and nothing appealed to her, and despite having eaten an entire bag of sugar cookies, she felt empty and alone.

Christmas Eve. Alone.

She should have gone skating. At least with her family around her, she could pretend to be okay. Pretend she believed she'd done the right thing by pushing Jake—or Jacob—away. Pretend she didn't desperately want to be spending the holidays in his tiny little apartment in Brookhollow, completely oblivious to who he really was.

She groaned and closed the fridge. Food wouldn't help. She returned to the living room, diving for the remote as she heard the first few lines of *It's a Wonderful Life*. As she switched off the TV, the doorbell rang.

Probably carolers again.

Different ones, of course. The first group had learned there was nothing but an Ebenezer Scrooge in this house tonight. She felt bad about throwing her sugar cookie at that kid, but she'd lost it for a second. Admittedly, not her proudest moment.

The doorbell rang again. And again.

"Just sing, already!" she called loudly.

*Ding dong!*

"Fine...fine..." she said, wrapping her sweater around her waist as she made her way to the front door. It was just one night. She would embrace it, be miserable, cry herself to sleep, open presents tomorrow morning, eat turkey, then sleep the days away until January 4.

Swinging the door open, her heart stopped.

"Hi," Jake said, standing on the other side.

She slammed it closed. What was he doing here? She glanced down at her oversize sweater and leggings—not her best look. She looked at her reflection in the mirror on the wall—dark mascara streaks lined her bottom lashes, and her dark hair, in a loose braid over her shoulder, had pieces sticking every which way. Oh, God—he'd seen her like this.

"You look beautiful—open the door!" he called through the glass.

Crap—he could still see her? She took a deep breath and opened the door. "What do you want?"

"Just you."

She tried to shut the door again, but this time he stopped it from closing. "That…and I also wanted to return this." He held her necklace up.

Her hand went to her neck. She hadn't even realized she'd lost it. She sighed, opening the door a little wider and taking it from him. "Thank you. If that's all…"

"It's not. I also wanted a chance to introduce myself." He pushed the door open and stepped inside, taking her hands in his.

She tried to pull hers away, but the attempt was weak.

"My name is Jacob Marx. I hate being called Jake, and I've only ever been in love once…with you. My birthday is actually February twelfth, so I am an Aquarius—which means we are compatible. I checked."

She swallowed hard, looking away. "But you're still an undercover cop, and that makes us incompatible." She loved him. Too much to be with him, knowing he could disappear for weeks or months or years, putting his life in danger…and hers.

"Heather, my future with the force is uncertain. During my suspension, I'll have to jump through a lot of hoops to regain credibility and the confidence of my peers. I may never go back to active duty. And undercover assignments are not in my future anymore. The truth is, I'm not sure I want them to be."

She held her breath. "I would never ask you to give up what you love."

"You're not. I may not have a choice, and I have no idea what I'll do if the department decides I'm too much of a liability. But what I do know is that I love you, and I want to be with you, and I'll do whatever it takes to regain your trust."

She stared at him, weighing the words. "I'm scared, Jacob," she whispered.

He pulled her toward him and held her against his chest.

She snuggled closer, breathing in the scent of him.

"Cop or not, I promise to always keep you safe, Heather." He kissed her forehead and tilted her chin up to look at him. "I mean that."

"What about my heart—will you keep that safe, too?" she asked, happiness and love threatening to choke her as they bubbled up inside her.

"Always," he whispered, lowering his lips toward hers. "Will you spend Christmas with me?"

She hesitated, the emotional roller coaster of the past few days preventing her from thinking clearly. Fortunately, her heart took over. "Only if I can spend every Christmas with you," she whispered back, rising onto her tiptoes and still falling just short of his lips. "See, this is why I wear heels."

"Let me help you," he said, lifting her off her feet. "You know I can't believe we lived in the same city our whole lives and it too hiding out in a small town to find each other.'

Heather smiled. "New York may be home for us," she whispered against his lips, "but Brookhollow was the perfect place to fall in love."

\* \* \* \* \*

# LARGER-PRINT BOOKS!

## GET 2 FREE
## LARGER-PRINT NOVELS
## PLUS 2 FREE
## MYSTERY GIFTS

*Love Inspired*®

### Larger-print novels are now available...

LILP15

# LARGER-PRINT BOOKS!

## GET 2 FREE
## LARGER-PRINT NOVELS
## PLUS 2 FREE
## MYSTERY GIFTS

*Love Inspired®*
## SUSPENSE
RIVETING INSPIRATIONAL ROMANCE

### Larger-print novels are now available...

**YES!** Please send me 2 FREE LARGER-PRINT Love Inspired® Suspense novels and my 2 FREE mystery gifts (gifts are worth about $10). After receiving them, if I don't wish to receive any more books, I can return the shipping statement marked "cancel." If I don't cancel, I will receive 4 brand-new novels every month and be billed just $5.49 per book in the U.S. or $5.99 per book in Canada. That's a savings of at least 19% off the cover price. It's quite a bargain! Shipping and handling is just 50¢ per book in the U.S. and 75¢ per book in Canada.* I understand that accepting the 2 free books and gifts places me under no obligation to buy anything. I can always return a shipment and cancel at any time. Even if I never buy another book, the two free books and gifts are mine to keep forever.

110/310 IDN GH6P

Name _____ (PLEASE PRINT) _____

Address _____ Apt. #

City _____ State/Prov. _____ Zip/Postal Code

Signature (if under 18, a parent or guardian must sign) _____

### Mail to the **Reader Service:**
**IN U.S.A.:** P.O. Box 1867, Buffalo, NY 14240-1867
**IN CANADA:** P.O. Box 609, Fort Erie, Ontario L2A 5X3

**Are you a current subscriber to Love Inspired® Suspense books
and want to receive the larger-print edition?
Call 1-800-873-8635 or visit www.ReaderService.com.**

\* Terms and prices subject to change without notice. Prices do not include applicable taxes. Sales tax applicable in N.Y. Canadian residents will be charged applicable taxes. Offer not valid in Quebec. This offer is limited to one order per household. Not valid for current subscribers to Love Inspired Suspense larger-print books. All orders subject to credit approval. Credit or debit balances in a customer's account(s) may be offset by any other outstanding balance owed by or to the customer. Please allow 4 to 6 weeks for delivery. Offer available while quantities last.

**Your Privacy**—The Reader Service is committed to protecting your privacy. Our Privacy Policy is available online at www.ReaderService.com or upon request from the Reader Service.

We make a portion of our mailing list available to reputable third parties that offer products we believe may interest you. If you prefer that we not exchange your name with third parties, or if you wish to clarify or modify your communication preferences, please visit us at www.ReaderService.com/consumerchoice or write to us at Reader Service Preference Service, P.O. Box 9062, Buffalo, NY 14240-9062. Include your complete name and address.

**YES!** Please send me **The Montana Mavericks Collection** in Larger Print. This collection begins with 3 FREE books and 2 FREE gifts (gifts valued at approx. $20.00 retail) in the first shipment, along with the other first 4 books from the collection! If I do not cancel, I will receive 8 monthly shipments until I have the entire 51-book Montana Mavericks collection. I will receive 2 or 3 FREE books in each shipment and I will pay just $4.99 US/ $5.89 CDN for each of the other four books in each shipment, plus $2.99 for shipping and handling per shipment.*If I decide to keep the entire collection, I'll have paid for only 32 books, because 19 books are FREE! I understand that accepting the 3 free books and gifts places me under no obligation to buy anything. I can always return a shipment and cancel at any time. My free books and gifts are mine to keep no matter what I decide.

263 HCN 2404  463 HCN 2404

| Name | (PLEASE PRINT) | |
|------|----------------|---|
| Address | | Apt. # |
| City | State/Prov. | Zip/Postal Code |

Signature (if under 18, a parent or guardian must sign)

### Mail to the **Reader Service**:
**IN U.S.A.:** P.O. Box 1867, Buffalo, NY 14240-1867
**IN CANADA:** P.O. Box 609, Fort Erie, Ontario L2A 5X3

# LARGER-PRINT BOOKS!
## GET 2 FREE LARGER-PRINT NOVELS PLUS
## 2 FREE GIFTS!

**⊕ HARLEQUIN®**

*super romance®*

## More Story...More Romance

# READERSERVICE.COM

## Manage your account online!

- Review your order history
- Manage your payments
- Update your address

> *We've designed the Reader Service website just for you.*

## Enjoy all the features!

- Discover new series available to you, and read excerpts from any series.
- Respond to mailings and special monthly offers.
- Connect with favorite authors at the blog.
- Browse the Bonus Bucks catalog and online-only exculsives.
- Share your feedback.

*Visit us at:*

**ReaderService.com**